Dogs of War
at
Wounded Arrow

Book Two
of the
Havelock Emerald series

© Copyright 2017
by
Tom Frye

Although this is a work of fiction, many of the places and the events in this story are real. However, names and characters are the product of the author's imagination. Any resemblance to actual persons, living or dead is entirely coincidental.

In memory of David Woodrum,
Sargent in the US Army,
and a thank-you to his daughter,
Syd, for her report on PTSD

In memory of the pit bulls
who have not been saved.
Inspired by the ones
now successfully serving
in Law Enforcement
and the US Military.

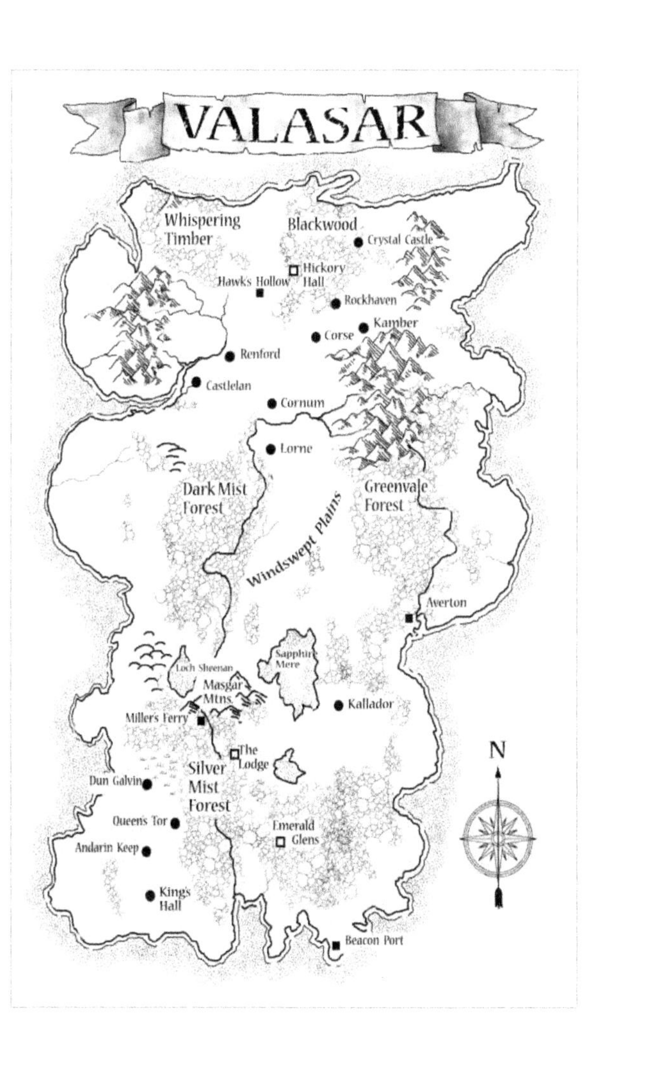

VALASAR
Whispering Timber
Blackwood
Crystal Castle
Hickory Hall
Hawks Hollow
Rockhaven
Kamber
Corse
Renford
Castlelan
Cornum
Lorne
Dark Mist Forest
Windswept Plains
Greenvale Forest
Awerton
Loch Sheenan
Sapphire Mere
Masgar Mtns.
Kallador
Miller's Ferry
The Lodge
Silver Mist Forest
Dun Galvin
Queens Tor
Emerald Glens
Andarin Keep
King's Hall
Beacon Port
N

Chapter One

Ben had been strangely silent on the drive to Lucas's school. He'd insisted the dogs ride along with them. It appeared he did not want to leave them back at the ranch, for fear the Den might nab Grunge.

Ben turned into the school's driveway and spoke. "Sorry the way that turned out. Your caseworker would file a complaint with the judge if she found out your dad simply showed up out here."

Lucas said, "Mom swears I'm as mule-headed as he is. It's why I get into so much trouble at school."

Ben said, "He has chosen a difficult path. Biker clubs are turning their comradery into a good thing, riding for charities, raising money for good causes. Others are devoted to: Defiance. It goes with the biker culture. You have a choice: Remain mule-headed, emulating your dad, or become someone you invent."

So far, living with Ben had been better than living the Yardley family. The Lakota had not tried to micro-manage his life. His only lectures had been about the dogs. This was the first time he'd offered him advice. Lucas knew Ben was only trying to be helpful.

Ben said, "Crazy Horse was a Shirt Wearer. In 1868, the Oglala council determined there was a rift among the tribes over the white man's broken treaties. The Big Bellies chose four men to serve as councilors. Made of two bighorn sheepskins each shirt had images on them. Each for a deed done in war: horses captured, a wound received, a prisoner taken, the life of a friend saved. There were 241 on Crazy Horse's shirt. Rules were: *'Be big-hearted, always helping others. Look out for widows and orphans. Think no ill of others, nor see the ill they would do to you. Many dogs come to lift the leg at your lodge Look the other way, do not let your heart remember. Do not give way to anger. Do all these duties gladly. Be generous and brave. You will lead the warriors in camp. See that all among the people has his rights respected. You must be wise, kind, and firm in all things. Never take up arms against your own without thought and council. Man living alone can do as he pleases, if he lives among others he must bow his head to the good of all. Without strong leaders, the people will break up into defenseless bands.'*

"Crazy Horse was also a Thunder Dreamer. His father was named Crazy Horse, as well. On the day young Crazy Horse had his vision of riding through a hail of bullets, his own father took the name Worm so that his son could live up to the name without competition.

Can you imagine what it took to accept such a humble name in order to move over for his son? As a Thunder Dreamer, Crazy Horse chose humility over boldness, never bragged about his great deeds, nor even shared them around council fires as many of my people had a habit of doing. He did the opposite of what people expected of him. He was his own person, without allowing others to influence him."

They shared a long silence. Lucas sat there, absorbing his words. They both looked up at the school as a bell began to ring. Soon, students and teachers came pouring out of the building, all of them looking confused when the fire bell sounded. As Lucas approached the kids milling around across the street from BEST Education, a blue Ford truck pulled up a block down the street. Nate was at the wheel. His dad sat in the passenger's seat. Both gestured at him to join them. There was a mad scramble as the entire mob of students headed back to the building. Lucas waited until the last ten kids started across the street, he then ran to the truck. As soon as Stone pulled him into the truck, Nate sped off down the street. He said, "No security at your school, Little Luke. I yanked on that fire alarm, and just waltzed out of there. Covert ops successful!"

Lucas asked, "What are you guys up to, anyhow?"

Stone said, "You wait. You'll see."

Moments later, Nate pulled his truck into a grungy-looking junk-yard. He parked before a run-down office building and shut the truck off. Stone exited the truck, holding the door open long enough for Lucas to climb out. Lucas did not like the way he nudged him firmly in the back to get him to follow Nate inside the office.

The Boar was behind a desk, his right leg in a cast. Behind him, leaning against the wall were a pair of crutches. It was obvious he had suffered a broken leg from his run-in with the buffalo. Lucas said, "As big as you are, you sure did catch some major air when that bison rammed you. But your leg? I thought he broke your butt."

Stone smacked Lucas on the back of his head. "This can go one of two ways. Run your big mouth. Or cooperate and leave here a happy little man. Your choice, son."

The Boar reached down and picked up a brand new Play station. He placed it on the desk. "All yours, Tiger," Nate said, cheerfully. "Knowing how well you like to play Call of Duty, Bro."

Lucas remained silent as Stone said, "Son, we got a lot of money invested in that monster dog your Indian friend is holding. We need you to return to that ranch and get him for us. Slip a leash on him, lead him to the road, we'll take him from there. Heck of a deal, don't you think, Little Luke?"

Lucas only had to look into the Boar's dark eyes to remind himself how cruel these dog men were. His dad and uncle were just as bad. Red-hot rage settled over him as he returned Stone's gaze. "No," Lucas said, his voice a whisper Stone swatted him hard on the back of his head. "You don't tell us no," Nate said, latching onto his shoulders, his steely fingers grinding into the tender flesh beneath Lucas's coat and shirt. "Come on, Luke. Gypsy and I bet that once you saw this Play station you would be happy to oblige. You don't want to disappoint us, do you, Bro?"

After all these long months of being forced into foster care, all he ever wanted was to go back home. He knew his dad and mom got a divorce over his last attack on her out at the lake, but he figured he would switch off, living with both, changing houses every week. All he really wanted was to be back with his family. But what if Yardley had been right about his dad's wiring? Bad? Twisted? Lucas saw his dad once in court when the judge was still trying to decide what to do with him. He was all smiles, seated before the judge, saying, "Yes, sir. No, I understand, sir."

But the moment Lucas's therapist expressed her opinion as to whether he would be safe in his dad's custody, she hit a nerve. Stone lost it. One second, he had been pleasant; the next, he glared at the therapist and said, "As if a woman knows anything about what makes me tick!"

The judge stopped the hearing to get on Stone about losing it. His dad gave the judge a look that left no doubt he was about to strangle him. Stone had that same look now. Lucas lowered his gaze, not daring to challenge him.

He said, "I don't have the heart to put Grunge in a fight. If you and the club want to do that, then, you have no heart at all."

That earned him another pop to the back of his head.

Chapter Two

Goblin looked up from napping in front of the fireplace. Lucas had just come through the door. He was carrying a leash attached to a chain in his hands. The pup knew something was terribly wrong.

Grunge? he said, moving over to nudge him awake. *Come on, Big Guy, wake up!*

Sprawled there beside him, basking in the warmth of the fireplace, Grunge lazily raised one eyebrow. *Yes,* he said. *He is home. But so what? Go back to snoozing. This fire sure feels nice.*

Lucas walked over and kneeled down, keeping a good two-foot distance between himself and Grunge. He peered down at the length of chain he held, fiddling with the leather collar attached to one end of it. "I'm supposed to take you out to my dad, Grunge," he said, tears in his eyes. "I'm supposed to betray you and get you out to the van on the road. Dad and Uncle Nate put money on you for that fight tomorrow night. They want you to go with them."

Grunge looked up at Lucas with an uncertain look in his brown eyes. *See?* he said to Goblin. *Told you not to trust this kid.*

Goblin walked over, nudging Lucas with his small head. The boy began to softly cry. *Grunge,* Goblin said, *you saw how mean his dad at visits with Ben. He's scared to death of the guy. If he was just going to give you up, why would he be crying like this? The kid has way more heart than you are giving him credit for.*

Knowing that his Dad and Nate sat out there on the road waiting for him to bring them Grunge, Lucas was desperate enough to pull out all the stops. With Grunge and Goblin watching him, he walked over to Ben's phone on the wall. "Stop looking at me like that," he said. "Never in a million years would I set you up for a dog fight."

He then hastily dialed the number to the barn. Beef picked up on the third ring. "Wounded Arrow Dog rescue—"

"Beef," Lucas said. "I'm down here at the house. How many vets you got out there in the barn with you?"

Beef rumbled, "Aren't you supposed to be in school, dude? Does Ben know you're home? What are you doing? Ditching school?"

Lucas said, "School wasn't an option for me today, Beef. My dad picked me. Could you do me a favor, without hurting him? He's parked in a van out on the road."

He then disconnected. Lucas wasted no time then. He removed his shoes and put on the snow boots sitting by the stairs leading up to the back door. He hurriedly slipped on his stocking hat, zipped up his coat, and snatched up his gloves.

As an afterthought, Lucas returned to the fireplace and removed the eagle feather from where it hung suspended from the rack of antlers above the mantle. He slipped the leather cord around his neck and settled the feather down under his shirt against his bare chest.

Lucas led the two dogs to the top of the stairs. At the door, he opened it to peek out. Straight ahead of him, Beef and five vets were out on the road. Lucas saw the surprised look on his dad's face. He was not going to be happy with him for setting up this encounter. With six unpredictable vets standing him down, he would hopefully be sensible and drive away without incident.

Lucas slipped out through the door, scooting Goblin and Grunge before him with one foot. They ran around to the back of the house, darted across the open field, and made their way to the top of the ridge. Lucas said, "We're headed over to Kooper's Steading."

With that he started off through the trees. Grunge plowed through the snow like a dog-bulldozer. They approached the ruins of the barn on Kooper Steading. Goblin loped along behind Grunge and Lucas, looking at the small beings lurking behind the surrounding trees. Spooky imps, lingering like shadows, peeking out from the cover of the trees. Grunge offered the mob of fiendish imps a warning growl. Terrified, the imps shrieked and fled, vanishing like wisps of smoke. Goblin looked up to see if Lucas had seen them, too. But he seemed to be focused on the trap door in the middle of the barn floor.

Lucas kneeled down opening the door to the cellar below. "It will be warm down there," he said. "We'll just hide in here for an hour, then get back to the ranch. Dad will be long gone by then I expect."

Suddenly, the eagle feather he wore around his neck flared with a bright light, and enabled Lucas to see a stirring of the shadows in the cellar below. A small form launched himself out of the confines of the once underground fort of the little Kooper kid.

"Kipper?" Lucas gasped. "There's someone looking for you!"

The ghostly dog stopped, and circled around, staring cautiously at the three of them. He lowered his ears, wagged his stubby tail, and let out a soft whine. Grunge spoke to the ghost dog, saying, *Kipper, we mean you no harm. Stay put, pup. Your master is coming.*

Out of the trees to their right, Danny Kooper appeared. He left scorch marks in the snow as he crossed the clearing. His eyes filled with tears as he raced toward his puppy. "Kipper!" he cried.

The burning shoes he wore were extinguished by the snow. The fire engulfing each one went out with an airy *poof!* Danny dropped to his knees, his arms extended toward his dog.

Lucas said, "I don't think he knew that was you he was running from. Lots of spooky things in the Otherworld. I think Kipper had a run-in with one and he has been fleeing from it ever since. Once he knows it is you, he will come to you."

Danny remained kneeling there, his hands outstretched toward the cowering ghost puppy. "Kipper? It is me. Danny. Remember? You were my pup. We were camping here the night the fire started."

Giving out a tiny whimper, Kipper bolted happily into Danny's embrace. The little kid scooped the ghost pup up into his arms. "Thank-you," Danny said, looking at Lucas. "My rescue mission is over. Now Kipper and I can pass on to the beyond."

"Will you be joining the dogs?" Lucas asked. "The dogs waiting for the ship on the shoreline? I saw those 58,000 dogs waiting. A ship awaits them. But I need the key to send them on their journey.'"

Danny reached beneath his shirt, withdrawing a gold key attached to a slender chain. He slipped the chain over his head and handed the key to Lucas. As Danny and Kipper began to fade, Danny said, "Tell Grandpa Koops it was not his fault. He had no idea Kipper and I were asleep in the cellar beneath the barn. It was not his fault."

The ghost boy and his ghost dog were then gone.

A loud barking came from the driveway of the Kooper Steading. Seated there in an old Dodge van was Koops. And he wasn't alone. He exited the van, pulling open the side door of the van, releasing the two vicious pit bulls from the back end of the vehicle. Both dogs set their sights on Grunge standing beside the open cellar door.

Lucas snatched up Goblin, preparing to get the three of them down into the cellar. "Come on, Grunge! Get down into the fort!"

Grunge snarled as the two pits closed with him. One dog circled to his left while the other veered to his right. But Grunge wheeled around with a speed Lucas had never seen before, snapping at the dogs. A savage fight seemed inevitable.

And that's when Lucas saw out of the corner of his eye:

A huge bear of an Indian stepped out of the woods beyond the Steading. He was thickly built and his gray hair hung in two braids past his broad shoulders. Colton Lone Wolf said, "Shush, dogs. Be still! Kid, you wear American Horse's eagle feather around your neck. Use it now to calm these savage beasts."

Lucas reached inside his coat and shirt to draw the eagle feather out. It glowed golden. Wolf made swishing motions with his hands, scattering shimmering particles down between Grunge and the two pit bulls. The Native said, "Use the feather to dispel their rage!"

Lucas waved the eagle feather, sending glittering particles down onto the dogs' bulky shoulders and their heads. Wolf looked each dog in the eye and said, "There will be no fighting here today." The two pits rolled over, exposing their throats to Grunge. Goblin let out a shrill yip as Koops appeared there in his wide-brimmed hat and long, black duster, a shotgun gripped in his hands.

"What kind of drugs," he snarled, "did you give my dogs?"

Chapter Three

Lucas held up the eagle feather. "Indian voodoo?" Koops laughed. "Won't work on me! I should blow this beast to kingdom come!"

Lucas drew the feather back to his left shoulder, then shoved it forward as if wielding a knife. A cloud of sizzling specks flew out of the eagle feather, and with a rumble of thunder, the pulsating cloud struck Koops full in the face. The old man cried out as the barrage of sizzling particles swept him off his feet. He flew backward, his hat ripped from his head, his black duster flapping. The angry wind tore his shotgun from his grasp.

Koops scrambled up to his knees, offering Lucas a terrified look.

Lucas was surprised that the magic of American Horse's eagle feather had a devastating effect. He just acted, and Native magic came to life, blasting the cranky old man off his feet. Lucas was tempted to blast him again, but he needed to get the dogs out of there. Draping the chain attached to the eagle feather over his head, Lucas glanced back at the bearish figure of Koops. "Your grandson, Danny, told me to tell you it wasn't your fault. The fire. He and his pup were camping down in the cellar. Evidently, you didn't know."

Koops bowed his head. His two dogs sidled up to him to give him comfort. Koops draped his arms around the shoulders of either dog. Lucas looked with pity at the sad old man. "All these years," Koops said, "I blamed myself for that fire. The dog men planned to burn Ben's place to the ground. I assumed Danny was safe inside the house. A man got careless with a torch and the barn caught fire. Afterward, my son blamed me for punishing Danny by locking him in the cellar. My son came to believe that lie. He's not spoken to me since. I loved the kid. I lost my heart that night."

Lucas said, "Maybe now that you know Danny never blamed you, maybe you can find your heart again."

Supported by his two dogs, Koops stared at him with this lost look in his red-rimmed eyes. Lucas turned then, sucking air through his teeth as he fought back the urge to cry. Grunge, Goblin, and Wolf fell in beside him, and as they exited the Steading, Koops bawled long and loud. It was a sound Lucas would never forget.

When Ben arrived home, he found Wolf seated in the den before a roaring blaze in the bear-faced fireplace. The Native looked up as he entered the den, stomping snow off his boots.

"The little rogue," he said, "had a difficult day. Go easy on him."

"Difficult?" Ben asked. "Could you be a little more specific?"

"Family issues," Wolf said. "His dad and Beef had words. Beef ended up with one beauty of a shiner. The biker president left here with a bloody nose. He and his brother came here to get Grunge. The biker boys were just leaving when I showed up. Did I ever tell you I did recon over in Viet Nam?"

Growing a little impatient with how calm Wolf appeared to be, Ben said, "Thanks for your service. But are you coming to a point? I need to find Lucas and the dogs."

Wolf said, "A sniper in enemy territory, I became a master at spying. Skills I never thought I'd use again until today. The boy and the dogs snuck back over to the Steading."

Ben said, "Do you always talk in circles?"

Wolf chuckled. "All old Lakota men talk in circles. We old ones get bored so easily. We have to find ways to make life intriguing. Don't worry about your boy. He wielded American Horse's eagle feather, like a true Thunder Dreamer."

Ben asked, "How can that be? Lucas is a white boy."

Wolf laughed and offered Ben a look of admonishment.

"Racist!" he said, then cackled like a old hen.

Several moments later, Lucas opened the door to Ben's home, and followed the dogs down the stairs. "Am I in trouble?" he asked. "Dad nabbed me from school and carted me out here to get Grunge. My dad wanted to throw Grunge into that fight tomorrow night."

Ben said, "I know. What happened between you and Koops?"

Lucas opened his mouth, yet before he could say a word, Grunge yipped like a little puppy, then lowered his head and walked over to Wolf seated in Ben's recliner. The big pit whined as the old man placed a hand on his head, spreading his fingers. *I was just a pup,* Grunge told Goblin, *when this man was caretaker over me. He was kind to me. Good for my soul. Spoke doggy-talk to me. Scolded me when I got too near the river. Coddled me when he settled me into bed. Those truly were the only good times in my life.*

Wolf offered Grunge a warm smile. "The Pup is what I called you when you were just a puppy. The Thunder Beings were active on the night you were born. Thunder. Lightning. You were destined to do something special in your lifetime. But the fights? You poor, poor puppy. You pretty much had the love beaten out of you. No dog should be subjected to the wrongs forced upon you."

Grunge remained stone still as Wolf kept his hand connected to him. Goblin scooted closer to Grunge, nuzzling him with his nose. "Lucas?" Wolf said, gesturing for him to join them at the couch. "Are you committed to walking the path on this dog's journey? If so, touch him that you might know where he's been to reach this point."

Lucas crossed the room to the couch. Grunge cringed as he reached out, his fingers within inches of his left shoulder. The moment he touched Grunge's shoulder, Lucas gasped out loud. The images that came to him were so clear, he wanted to break the connection to the big dog, when but he saw: *Nate Holland snatching Grunge up when he was just a puppy. He shoved him into a metal kennel, placed it in a van, and drove Grunge away from the reservation. After that, Nate used cattle prods on Grunge, forcing him to train against bait dogs. He then used a whip, forcing him to enter the fight ring where he was forced to kill or be killed. It was a slow-motion view of terrible images, all suffered by Grunge as he rose through the ranks to be King of the Ring. There was blood, blood, and more blood.*

Grunge turned his head and looked directly into Lucas's eyes, and the dog saw: *Lucas's dad standing before him, cursing, shouting at him, chewing him out. He cuffed him. He drew him nose-to-nose, growling words. He made him feel smaller than an ant, as he dealt a thump to his chest, a whap to the back of his head.*

Grunge witnessed all that Lucas had been through growing up in such a hostile environment. He empathized with him, pressing his face against his chest, rubbing his head beneath his chin. They each knew at that moment just what the other had suffered in the past.

Wolf said, "Angry spirits that should have never been aware of you were attracted to you when you disturbed the thin fabric of the Otherworld with your bitter outbursts or your savage attacks. You were infected by these wrathful beings who fed off your own rage and lent more power to your tantrums and beastly tirades. You must both overcome the influence of these spirits, kick them out, send them packing, or they will torment you the rest of your lives."

Chapter Four

Ben escorted Lucas to the boy's bedroom. Lucas lifted Goblin onto his bed, surprised when Grunge leaped up beside him, leaving him two feet of space to crawl under the covers beside him.

Ben pointed to the dreamcatcher hanging above the bed. "Dream catchers are made of willow hoops, on which is woven a net. A dreamcatcher includes sacred items, feathers, or beads. Traditionally they are known as the 'Spider web' charm. In old times, this netting was made of nettle fiber. Two spider webs were usually hung on the hoop, and it was said that they caught any harm in the air as a web catches whatever comes in contact with it. Dream catchers catch any bad thoughts, bad spirits, or bad dreams in their web, then when the sun comes up, the sunlight evaporates all the things snared during the night."

Ben exited the room and soon Lucas drifted off to sleep. He had another dream: *He ran over a grassy hill and approached Cora on a beach. Behind her, in one massive group stood the 58,000 dogs of Iraq. Cora said, "Do you carry the key that will open the gateway to the Beyond?"*

"I do," Lucas said, slipping it out of his jeans pocket.

Cora said, "All this time, Danny has been chasing after his lost pup. It was you that stopped Kipper to explain that Danny had been searching through the Unseen realm to find him. You are special kid. No matter how many people declare you are a troubled little boy. You have been chosen for this task. Because of your efforts, 58,000 dog souls may now pass on to the Beyond. That is a very great deed on your journey to be a Keeper of Hounds. It is a title for the gift you have. Dog Whisperer, Dog Handler. Dog Trainer. Keeper of Hounds. In truth, you have been chosen to work with dogs the rest of your days. It is a serious undertaking and one that will transform your life. He who has known troubles can relate to those struggling with troubles of their own. Each dog who passes through your life, will have its own challenge for you to deal with."

She took the key from him. Waving it around in the air before the thousands of dogs, she said, "We can pass through the gateway, you Dogs of Iraq. It is time to go home now."

The dogs all raised their heads and let out one long, joyous howl. One by one, they all watched the large ocean liner cruise into the bay. A long boarding ramp was lowered to the beach by several white-cloaked men on the ship. As soon as the ramp touched down on the beach, each dog ran up the ramp and onto the ship. There were so many of them that they looked like a long, furry caterpillar slowly proceeding up the ramp, their tails wagging as they poured onto the deck. Cora said, "Thank you for making this all possible. Kipper was terrified of the things in the Unseen realm, but you were a calm in his storm."

She then reached out and touched Lucas on his forehead, saying: "A dog is a man's best friend.

"Dogs leave paw prints on your heart forever.

"Dogs love you unconditionally, no strings attached.

"Dogs live only in the moment.

"Dogs are instruments of God.

"Remember the old Cherokee Proverb. There is a battle of two wolves inside of us. One is evil. Anger, jealousy, greed, resentment, lies, and ego. The other is good. Joy, peace, love, hope, kindness, and truth. The wolf who wins? Is the one you feed."

Lucas stood there on that beach watching the ship of dogs sail away across calm waters. Only after the ship became a speck on the distant horizon did he start up the hill toward home.

***

Lucas woke up that next morning to hear Grunge softly snoring. He had his head resting on his chest. Totally surprised, Lucas lay there, his hand hovering inches from Grunge's head. He could not believe that the big dog had sidled up next to him without putting up a fuss like he usually did. *Grunge?* Goblin said, quietly. *What are you doing, Big Guy?*

Slowly opening his eyes, Grunge said, *Bonding. Connecting.*

Cora Red Cloud greeted the dogs and Lucas when they entered the kitchen. She had a stack of pancakes on a plate in the center of the table. "Morning," she said with a warm smile.

Lucas smiled back at her, not daring to say anything for he felt like a floodgate would open inside of him. Not because of any sadness he felt, but because as she joined him at the table, she reminded him of his mom. Lucas missed his mom, but Cora made him feel at home in Ben's home that morning.

She said, "Ben is speaking on *Smoke Signals*, Wolf's radio show, trying to raise money for the dogs of Pine Ridge. Ben asked me to keep an eye on you until he gets back. *Canine Light Shine* cannot operate without Wolf's help there on the rez. When you're done with breakfast, I have a cantankerous guest of the furry sort locked inside my Animal Control van out front. We're going to return him to the wild where he belongs."

Grunge eyed the pancakes greedily and walked over to the table, placing his chin in Lucas's lap. He whined. Goblin leaped up, planting his front paws on Lucas's leg. Cora looked at Grunge. "Since when has the dog gotten so comfortable with you? Did something change between you two?"

Lucas's hand came to rest on Grunge's head resting in his lap. "I think Grunge took several paw steps forward when he reconnected with Wolf, his former owner. He is slowly beginning to bond with me, too. Do you remember my dream about those 58,000 dogs?"

Cora froze, a fork full of pancakes halfway to her mouth. "Yes, I had this same dream. I am pleased that all those dogs completed their journey. I've often wondered about them."

After Lucas had finished his breakfast, Cora whipped up another batch of pancakes for the dogs. Grunge and Goblin ate like kings when she scraped them into their dishes next to the stove. Lucas said, "There is a battle of two wolves inside of us. Grunge and I have come to a crossroads. We need to starve this bad wolf out."

Several minutes later, Nate Holland descended into the den, a rifle in his hands. He reached the bottom of the stairs, smirking at Cora. "Fight night," he said. "I'm taking Grunge to the fight of his life. Put a leash on him. Get him out to my truck, kid, or I will shoot him with this tranq gun. We're wasting time here. Get cracking!"

Grunge moved up to stand beside Cora. He did not growl. He simply stood there, facing down the dog man with the gun. Lucas stood up from the couch. "You and Dad are heartless, Uncle Nate!"

"Suck it up," Nate said. "Your dad thinks you're a wimp! You had better get some meanness in your bones if you want to become a member of the Elder's Den, Buttercup!"

That hit Lucas right between the eyes. To be wimpy by his dad was a low blow. He knew Nate was trying to manipulate him, but he was also sure his dad had said that about him. At a sound behind him, Nate wheeled around to find himself standing in the shadow of Colton Lone Wolf. Wolf launched himself down the stairs, latching onto the rifle, wrenching it out of Nate's hands. Wolf turned the gun around and pulled the trigger, sending a dart into Nate's chin. He fell to his knees. He then drifted into unconsciousness.

Cora placed a hand on Lucas's shoulder. "Uncle Colton? What are you going to do with him? Is it Lucas should see?"

Wolf chuckled, "Fear not, dear niece. There will be no blood."

Grunge and Goblin followed Lucas outside to the snowy yard. The three of them watched Beef, summoned from the barn, carry Nate out of Ben's home. Another vet came up the walk and helped Beef cart the unconscious biker over to the barn. "What," Lucas asked, "are you going to do with him, Wolf?"

Wolf said, "Sometimes, bad men need to be dealt with badly."

A sudden growl erupted from Cora's van ten in the driveway. It was such a horrific sound that Lucas actually moved away from the van so fast he bumped into Cora. "What in the world was that?" he asked, staring at the Animal Control van.

Cora said, "That was my furry guest I caught this morning."

The furry guest let out growls as if warning the humans outside the van to keep their distance. Wolf walked back toward Cora, his eyes on her van. "If I'm not mistaken, that was a badger."

Wolf reached out, opened the door of the van, and looked inside. The badger let out another fierce growl, then charged the wires of the cage to try to attack Wolf standing there, a big grin on his face.

Lucas followed him inside the barn, being careful not to get too close to the snarling badger in the cage. His markings of black and white fur were beautiful. He reminded Lucas of a miniature bear. He was fierce, too, angrily hissing at all of them.

Goblin whined, cowering at the looks of challenge from the ten Pits, two Dobies, and three Rotts staring at Grunge walking boldly into their domain.

A strange silence fell there inside the barn as Beef scooted a chair with Nate in it into the room. Beef had blindfolded an unconscious Nate, then bound him to the chair with rope.

He sat slumped in the wooden chair, snoring.

Chapter Five

Wolf positioned the annoyed beast's cage about two feet away from the slumped figure of Nate, tied and blindfolded in the chair. He picked up a broom from a nearby corner. He filled a plastic bucket with cold water. With the broom, he tapped the top of the cage. The badger let out a fierce growl. Wolf said, "With your help, Little Brother, we are going to have a good time!"

He tossed the bucket of water on Nate. At once, he sat up in the chair, straining at the ropes that bound him, turning his head, trying to see through the blindfold. "Where am I?" he croaked.

Wolf whispered, "Pine Ridge! Home of the Oglala Lakota!"

Tap! Tap! Wolf tapped the top of the badger case gently. The badger let out a low growl. "What was that?" Nate asked.

Tap! Wolf struck the cage again. The badger let out a guttural growl, a sound that promised a severe mauling.

"You have crossed a line," Wolf said. "You are now a guest of the Dog Soldier. I am soon going to release you. You will then flee."

Nate sat up straighter in his chair. "Flee?"

Wolf said, "Run. You will be soon racing across the rez in terror."

Tap! Tap! The broom came down on top of the cage, igniting another fierce growling fit from the annoyed badger.

Nate cried, "What is that thing?"

Wolf whispered, harshly, "Wanagi, Demon of Darkness."

Wolf poked Nate in the chest with the handle of the broom. He said, "In the year 1895, in northern Nebraska near Pine Ridge, there were brutal attacks on herds of cattle and the cowboys who tended them. Animals were slaughtered. These vicious attacks were done by what many swore was a . . . VAMPIRE. The attacker would using only his bare hands to wrestle the beast to the ground and tear the creature apart with supernatural strength. He lapped the blood of his victim the way a dog laps water. Many tried to capture him. All failed. Jack Lewis, a cowboy, had an encounter with the vampire. One evening, Jack wandered away from his companions to check on the cows. When from out of the shadows sprang the vampire. The beast clawed at his neck. Jack fired his gun. The gunfire attracted his companions. The savage attacker fled. Jack was badly torn about the neck by the man's teeth for he had bitten his throat."

Tap! Tap! Wolf thumped the top of the cage, causing the badger to erupt with more agitated growling. Nate squirmed and wrenched at the ropes binding him to chair. "Is that the thing?" he asked. "You drug me all the way up to Pine Ridge? What for?"

Wolf said, "I am going to set you free so that you can race against the Vampire Beast, who will bring you to a red bloody end!"

He scooted the caged badger across the floor and directly toward the kenneled dogs. At once, the badger saw the threat of so many dogs and let out a battle roar. The dogs, in turn, let out fierce growls of their own. The sounds of all of those creatures was terrible to hear, especially inside the confines of the barn. *Snap!* Wolf snapped his fingers. The dogs fell silent at once. "Oh, Gawd!" Nate wailed. "What do you want from me!"

"Oh," Wolf said "Leave Grunge out of this fight tonight. Never bother this dog again."

Nate cocked his head to one side. "Is that what this is about? No more fights for Grunge?"

Wolf turned and made walking motions with two fingers, urging Cora to exit the barn. Lucas fell in behind Cora, and as Grunge and Goblin followed him, Beef closed the door behind him, stepping out into bright afternoon sunlight. The ex-Ranger offered Cora a grin. "Your Uncle Colton is one strange cat. Remind me to never get on his bad side. I almost felt sorry for Nate."

Moments later, Wolf exited the barn, carrying the caged badger, who was not in the best mood after his experience in the barn. Wolf smiled at Cora. "Sweet niece," he said. "Don't be concerned with how I handled that. Nate will never report it to anyone. Besides, I honestly think he's retired from being a dog man. In ten minutes, Beef will let him loose, sending him on his way."

Cora led Lucas and the dogs over to her van. Wolf placed the cage inside the van. As he climbed into the passenger seat, he said, "Cora Red Cloud who has witnessed the hurt and misery inflicted on these poor dogs by these heartless dog men, you need to toughen up some, girl, if you're going to continue dealing with this criminal element. Only the rez way will work with these low-lives."

When Cora finally parked the van in a forested grove at the end of a country road, Wolf removed the cage from the back of the van.

He gently settled the caged badger on the ground and opened the cage door. "Thank you so much for your help, Little Brother," he told the sullen badger as he slowly exited the cage.

The beast snarled once at Wolf, then scurried off into the trees.

Chapter Six

Ben arrived back at Wounded Arrow as the sun was setting. Snow started to fall in blusters. He smiled when he saw Cora's Animal Control van parked in the drive. She met him at the doorway, offering him a cup of coffee. "I know it's not Thanksgiving, but I've smoked us a turkey. Tonight is a night to celebrate!"

As she joined Ben at the table, she said, "Kooper had a change of heart due to his encounter with Lucas over on the Steading. He turned state's witness against a dozen dog men across the state. He gave the county attorney information about the Barn, where Grunge was to fight tonight. As dog men converged on the Barn, dozens of arrests were made. Dozens of rescued dogs."

Ben was surprised. "Why the change of heart?"

Sheepishly, Lucas said, "Kooper's son blamed him for punishing Danny by locking him in the cellar. Koops never did that. But his son believed that lie. He has not spoken to the old man since. Koops loved that kid. He would have never harmed him. He lost his heart that night. He found it again on account of me telling him about what happened to Danny."

Ben, Cora, and Lucas ate their dinner and, afterward, gave a plate of leftovers to Grunge and Goblin. While the dogs pigged out in the kitchen, Cora presented the movies she'd rented. Old Yeller. Savage Sam. Rez Dog. While the three watched them in the living room, the dogs sprawled out before the crackling blaze in the fireplace.

Grunge said, *We are both lucky to be cared for in this home. Ben loves us. Lucas loves us. We never have to worry about being mistreated. No more cruel owners for us. And to think, I could have faced a death match in the ring! I trust Ben. He has a good heart, and is determined to see that I tamp down my anger. He also gives me space, respecting me. But Lucas is still volatile, losing his temper at a moment's notice. Some disturbance in him keeps me at bay.*

Goblin said. *Look at me, I am the easy one. Lucas wrestles with me, throws a ball to me, snuggles up beside me at night. I'm easy to love. Can you imagine the way it would make Lucas feel if he changed you into a teddy bear?*

The movie ended. Lucas lay wrapped in an old Indian blanket on the couch. Ben sat in a recliner. Cora sat in a chair, a blanket wrapped around her shoulders, her feet drawn up beneath her.

"*Estar roto*," she said. "In Spanish that means 'to be broken.' As I spoke the other night about the dogs I was ordered to destroy in Iraq, I stirred feelings I thought I had put aside. Like me, many vets carry hurts due to cruelties they saw in service to this country. It is a mental condition triggered by a traumatic event. Symptoms are anxiety, depression, mood swings, and flashbacks. In the Civil War, it was known as Soldier's Heart. The earliest case of PTSD was in 490 B.C. An Athenian warrior went blind after seeing the man beside him brutally slain. In the 17th century, doctors noted soldiers with the same symptoms, calling it homesickness. In World War I, doctors determined it was caused by shock waves causing trauma to the brain, known as Shell Shocked. In 1915, the Committee for Mental Hygiene decided something had to be done to combat it."

Cora stared at the embers popping and whizzing through the air in the fireplace. She continued. "In World War II, severe cases were treated with electroshock. The Vietnam War brought new issues. To deaden the pain of atrocities committed, drug use became common. The military called it Battle Fatigue. But, in 1980, it was named Post Traumatic Stress Disorder. 200 hundred years ago during the Indian wars, there was no record of warriors coming back to the tribe suffering from the same symptoms. They left as a band and returned as a band. They dealt with the effects of the battle together. Long ago, humans were programmed to stay together as a group to keep from being eaten by predators. Soldiers who say they miss the war, miss the comradery. And yet today, what does America do to combat this condition? We overmedicate, taking us further away from the belief that comrades who experienced the same trauma are the best thing to help with the condition."

She glanced over at Lucas supposedly asleep on the couch. She said, "The kid shows symptoms of the trauma he's been through. Who knows the violence he's seen? Something in his past triggers his blow-ups. Just like me, only instead of rage, I experience sorrow. All these men and women who pass through Wounded Arrow, partner with a damaged dog, so that both sides of the dog/man partnership becomes whole again. Dog, man's best friend, says it all for what you accomplish out here. Telling you my story triggered off my own suppressed feelings of trauma. I, too, suffer from PTSD."

As Lucas lay there, faking sleep, Cora's words hit him hard. He was just a kid, so he knew little about cause and effect. He had no idea if he acted up because of growing up around his dad. He thought it was normal to get a beat-down when he did wrong. His dad dealt out discipline, even if it did border on abuse. He lay there, wondering if all those times he'd blown-up, was on account of the beatings he took from his dad. His mom's punishment was grounding or taking away his gaming privileges. Lucas thought if she had ever slapped him, he would have died of shock.

But Stone justified fists to his arms and chest, claiming it would make him biker-tough. Usually before a beating, he had to endure angry cuss words that rang in his head for days afterward.

He opened his eyes to mere slits, to look over at Cora, then at Ben. He wanted to ask if maybe they thought he had this PTSD, too. But he didn't want them to think he was being snoopy.

Chapter Seven

The winter months passed. Spring came to Nebraska. Greens, reds, and burnt-toast brown dotted the landscape. During this transition, Lucas still had problems with most teachers, failing to do as he was directed a good deal of the time, but his rage-fests subsided, and there was talk that because of his corrected behavior he might be returning to a regular school setting.

Ben thought perhaps Lucas's bonding with Grunge had made quite a difference in the behavior of both kid and dog. He could only hope the change was permanent. But then, the visitation required by juvenile court began. The judge ordered Ben to supervise monthly visits with Lucas's mom and dad. Each visit was to be separate, with the two parents meeting once a week at Wounded Arrow. Since the weather was pleasant, Ben set up a picnic table beneath an oak tree before his underground home. It afforded a nice view of the forested hills to the north, and a view of Steven's Creek beyond to the west.

Upon meeting Lucas's mom, Ben was surprised. Maggie Holland was a slender woman in her late 40's, and while she wasn't movie-star beautiful, she was good-looking in a rugged way. She had long, raven hair and amazingly brown eyes that reminded Ben of a fawn.

Maggie joined Ben and Lucas and the dogs beneath the oak tree there in his yard. She smiled and said, "Thank you for taking care of my son. He tells me you're a dog whisperer." Offering Lucas a hug and a kiss on his forehead, Maggie went on to say, "Lucas tells me you're Lakota. Have you ever heard of the Morning Star?"

"Dull Knife," Ben said. "Morning Star was the name my Lakota people called him. A great leader among the Cheyenne. Born in 1810. Died in 1883. Buried in Lame Deer. Due to his courage the Northern Cheyenne still own a home in Montana. He was known as Dull Knife, but his Cheyenne name is translated as Morning Star. After Custer's Last Stand, during the Great Sioux War of 1876, he rode with the Lakota against the US—"

"The Cheyenne," Maggie said, "were sent to reservations with the Lakota. They suffered from starvation. In 1878, Morning Star led the tribe and outfoxed US troops across the Nebraska Sand Hills. He ended up living with Red Cloud on Pine Ridge. In 1879, after the Fort Robinson massacre, he settled on a rez in Montana."

Lucas stared at her curiously. "How come you know so much about him, Mom?"

"I'm one of his descendants," she said, "on my mother's side."

Lucas asked, "Does this mean I could be a Thunder Dreamer?"

Maggie said, "What have you been filling my son's head with?"

She was smiling and Lucas said, "Not Ben's idea, Mom. I've been having dreams—"

"Dreams?" Maggie said. "You best pay close attention to them, Luke. Visions and dreams are not to be taken lightly."

***

Those first couple of visits with Maggie went well. Ben liked her. He wasn't judging her like Lucas's foster parents did. Although he had to be present whenever Maggie visited, Ben sometimes drifted off to take care of chores while she and Lucas remained at the picnic table talking about plans of moving back home. In a way, Lucas looked forward to it, but one part of him sure would miss the dogs. Maggie tried at every court hearing to convince the judge that there was no longer any risk to Lucas if he moved back in with her. But the judge demanded that she take parenting classes, and he set goals for Maggie before he allowed Lucas to move back home.

Stone met with them, too, once each week at Wounded Arrow. Ben never left him alone with Lucas. Stone had not forgiven Lucas for betraying him to save Grunge from the dog fight. He still carried a grudge. Every time he thought Ben wasn't looking during his visits, he would shoot glares at Lucas. He never once spoke about it, for fear that Ben would end the visitation, but Lucas could tell he was still one unhappy camper. What set Lucas back in his treatment of anger management was the day Stone showed up at the same time Maggie did.

The roar of his bike came from the driveway. The president of the Elder's Den parked his Harley, climbed off the bike, and ambled over to the picnic table. "Mags?" he said. "Fancy meeting you here."

Maggie looked uncomfortable. "Your visit isn't until tomorrow, Stone. Besides, you're violating the restraining order."

Stone glared at Ben. "Look, Chief, those court orders don't mean anything. Just because some judge orders me to keep away from my ex, doesn't mean you need to stick your nose in my business."

Grrrrr! came from Grunge. He remained seated beside Ben, but he stared directly at Stone. *Grunge?* Goblin warned.

Grunge said, *They list us as vicious dogs if we cross a line, but this one needs to be put in his place.*

Yes, Goblin said, *but it would just get you in trouble. He would make sure of it.*

Ben stood up from the table, placing himself between Grunge and Stone, and the two men stood there staring at each other. Stone said, "I know about that dog's violent history. I should have my lawyer petition the court to have Lucas removed from here. Hard telling when that pitty might attack my son. Any judge would know I had a legitimate concern. Look at the lawsuit I could bring against the state for placing my boy in such a dangerous environment."

Ben said, "Stone, I give you two choices."

It was Lucas who tried his best to diffuse the predicament. "Did you get your days mixed up? I do that sometimes. I get all mixed up. Today is Mom's visit. Tomorrow is yours. Ben even bought a Chess set so you can teach me how to play better. No one like you when it comes to Chess, right, Dad?"

Stone's gaze flickered over to Lucas seated at the table. "Your foster imposter's playing a game of Chess. Aren't you, Benjy Boy?"

Ben said, "Two choices. One, you can leave right now without any consequences and return tomorrow. Or two, I can involve the police to enforce that restraining order. First violation is 90 days in county. Of course, as intelligent as you are, you already know that."

The *Screeee!* of a hawk caused Stone to peer up. The raptor glided over the ranch, then spiraled as he passed over the hills to the north. "Checkmate," Stone said. "We'll have to see how things go tomorrow over a real game, right, Luke?"

Not realizing he'd been holding his breath, Lucas sighed, "Yes, Dad. Tomorrow. See you then."

The thunderous roar of his Harley heading off down the road a few minutes later, caused Ben and Maggie to sigh in great relief.

Chapter Eight

The next day in school, Lucas had his first blow up in a long time. His thoughts whirling, he could not handle getting chewed out by one of his teachers and he let loose with a major flare-up. The scene of Ben and Stone having a standoff at the ranch kept playing in his head. He kept seeing the cold look in his dad's eyes compared to the calm look in Ben's. Several scenarios played out inside his head. In one, Stone leveled Ben with a barrage of punches. In another, Ben met Stone's attack, using martial arts moves that left him sprawled on the ground. In yet another mini-movie in his head, Grunge defended Ben and tore into Stone, mauling him.

Lucas was in the middle of this last scenario when Mr. Wendle, his Math teacher, asked him to stop fiddling with his comb. Lucas didn't hear him when he told him to put it away. But when he reached out in exasperation and yanked his comb from his hand, he was right in the middle of running it through his wild blond strands. It snagged in his hair and set him off. Lucas came out of his seat as if he had a spring beneath his butt. Wendle took his head in his gut. It took two techs to cart Lucas off to the Quiet Room. Which was anything but quiet as Lucas let everyone in the school know the madman was back.

Two weeks went by, and every day for Lucas turned into a nightmare. He left Ben each morning with the promise that he would control his rages, but later during the day Lucas had a meltdown. Ben met with Lucas's anger management counselor. She could not come up with a solution. There was an adjustment to his meds, but that had a paradoxical effect, and instead of calming him down, it ramped him up. His therapist suggested Lucas be institutionalized. Ben appealed to the juvenile judge to lift his order for family visits and call a halt to the weekly meetings until Lucas got himself under control. Despite his recommendation, the judge would not relent.

Grunge and Goblin could both tell there was something terribly wrong with Lucas. He still took them on walks around the ranch, and allowed them into his bed each night, but Grunge said, *He's blocked up with bad memories that hurt him. It's like he can't get over them. Every time he turns around, one more memory surfaces and sends him into a tizzy fit. It only takes a little prodding to ignite the hellfire that follows.*

***

Lucas's big blow-up came just before summer started. Ben, Cora, the dogs, his teachers, and Maggie had been walking on eggshells, trying not to set him off. But the one thing none of them understood about his rage-fests is he could go for long periods without a meltdown, but if something ticked him off, his anger blew like a tornado.

It happened at school. Shawn Bailey, a Goth kid, had just bent down to get a drink, when Lucas slid up beside him, stuck his finger in the nozzle, and squirted cold water all down the front of his jeans. Shawn madly scanned the crowded hall to see who had pulled such a prank on him. Lucas pointed at Shawn's wet jeans and said, "Look, everyone, Shawn needs Depends!"

Soon loud laughter erupted, and so, too, did Shawn.

Lucas met his attack, waiting until he came within three feet of him. He performed a spin-kick, his heel catching Shawn on his left jaw. Soon applause broke out, which caused Shawn to launch himself up off the floor and come right back at Lucas.

Three techs broke up the severe clobbering Shawn was dealing out to Lucas. They carted him to the quiet room. Next thing Lucas knew, he was escorted to the juvenile detention center. Two days later, he was transferred to the Child and Adolescent Psychiatric center. There, he remained in a locked cell for three days under evaluation. After a good deal of poking and prodding, the doctors released him back into Ben's care.

Goblin and Grunge remained glued to his side on the ride back to Wounded Arrow. They acted like he had been gone for many years. To make sure he did not vanish before their eyes, both stuck close to him. It made Lucas feel good to know he was loved by them.

Ben hadn't given up on him. He was willing to put up with his mood swings and temper tantrums, which said a lot to Lucas. He wanted to be known as a kid who had changed, a kid who had been repaired. The key to his own success was the work Ben allowed him to do with Goblin and Grunge. Grunge was a challenge, but even with all the damages he'd suffered in his fighting days, Lucas knew he had touched his heart. This was a great boost to his self-esteem.

When they arrived at Wounded Arrow, Old Man Kooper was there to greet them. He wore the same wide-brimmed hat and long, black leather duster, but he had a warm look in his eyes.

Kooper said, "Ben Black Bull, I have a rescue operation to offer you. Want to save some dogs?"

Koops led them back to the Kooper Steading. As Ben joined him at the trap door inside his burned down barn, the old man handed him a paper. "The deed to my land. I've had my lawyer sign it over to you, Ben. The kid did a good thing by giving me peace in regards to my grandson. It caused me to reflect on the cruelty I've been involved in all these years. I'm done with the fights. I want to donate the entire Steading to the Wounded Arrow rescue service. But first, I need you to clean out my underground den."

Lucas, Grunge, and Goblin followed Koops and Ben down into the cellar. The old man said, "This place has been operating for the past twenty years. It was started by my daddy back in the day. Been in operation even after the fire in which I lost my grandson. Ironic, that it is right next door to Wounded Arrow, one place brought so much pain and suffering into the lives of the pit bulls who passed through it, while the other place is rescuing this noble breed."

Koops led them down a long, dark hallway. They emerged into an amphitheater with rings of seating around a fighting arena. Koops said, "Stone Holland? What are you doing down here?"

Lucas sucked in a sharp breath as his dad and his three of his club members stepped out of the shadows to one side of the arena. Behind them stood two rows of metal cages with several dogs inside of them. Nate gestured at the pits in the cages. "We've come to dispose of the dregs from the last fight. These dogs are worthless since they all lost. Time they be on their way."

Lucas could see that the five dogs were all injured in some way or another. It appeared they had been in brutal fights and no one had treated them for the injuries they had sustained. His heart twisted inside of him to think that his dad and his uncle were going to dispose of the creatures. Lucas moved in front of the cages to face Stone. "Dad, Ben and I will take them to Wounded Arrow. All of them need to be treated."

Nate moved to confront his nephew, but Grunge gave a growl, and Nate froze. Ben said, "My advice is, admire your son for having a heart. These dogs need treatment."

Nate lunged toward Ben. He was stopped by Koops. "Knock it off, Nate! All of you, boys, stand down! The Indian is right. Your nephew has sand in him. He doesn't stand a chance against the Den, but look at him standing there making his pitch."

Nate and Stone looked to the pistol the old man had pointed at them. Koops said, "Lucas speaks for the dogs, because they can't speak for themselves. He wants to rescue them. That's his purpose."

A long silence followed. Ben and Lucas faced off the four bikers. Goblin sidled up to Lucas. Grunge peered at the men with menace in his eyes. Finally, Stone said, "We're done here, boys. Time to leave. Lucas has earned this."

To save face, Stone chuckled. "See you next visit, Little Luke."

Chapter Nine

Ben spent the next two hours supervising Beef and four of the vets from Wounded Arrow as they carefully removed the five injured dogs from beneath the barn of the Kooper Steading. The dogs seemed to know that Ben and his crew were there to help them, and while they had to be handled gently because of the wounds they suffered from, each accepted the help offered in a friendly manner. Once Ben had a veterinarian tend to them and the dogs healed, they would make fine pets for someone willing to work with them.

Koops left the Steading with Ben's words ringing in his ears. He, of course, thanked him for his generous gesture of deeding his land over to Wounded Arrow, but Ben was plenty angry that he'd left the poor injured dogs underground and that he had been running the fights there for so many years. He mentioned turning him in to Cora, and only backed off when Koops broke down and started weeping, swearing he was done with the fights for good. In the end, Ben had shaken his hand, saying something about redemption despite all his past cruelties. Koops drove away a humbled man.

As evening shadows fell there at Wounded Arrow, Cora pulled up in her Animal Control van. She and Ben carried on with chit-chat for several minutes as they stood beside her van. Bored with their talk, Lucas joined the dogs as they snooped around the nearby entrance to the dog cemetery. Suddenly, Lucas stared in alarm at the sleek, dark forms emerging from the wooded hilltop to the north. "Devil dogs?" Ben said as he and Cora joined them there in the cemetery.

The mad pack of huge, wolf-like dogs charged directly at them. There were hundreds of them. Sleek black fur, large broad chests, and faces that appeared to be part badger. They spread out as they came on. A second later, the pack of black, wolfish dogs reached the arbor at the entrance to the cemetery. And Grunge sprang forward to meet the oncoming dogs with a vicious growl. The big pit skidded to a sudden stop just inches before the entire mass of canines, serving as a shield to protect and defend Lucas.

Lucas clawed at the eagle feather dangling from the cord around his neck. He raised the feather above his head, and golden sparkles of light flickered from the feather. The scattering sparkles drifted down and sizzled and hissed as they connected with the Devil Dogs. Each one they touched swirled away in black vapors, vanishing as they were sent back to the Otherworld.

Stepping before the mass of ghost dogs, Ben held up his stone arrowhead that glowed with a mystical blue aura, sending forth a cloud that evolved into ethereal warriors on multicolored horses. Luminous tomahawks rose and fell as these ghost warriors rode through the pack of ghost dogs, turning them into wisps of black smoke that evaporated with eerie whispers. Crazy Horse. Sitting Bull. Red Cloud. American Horse. He Dog. Standing Bear. Little Hawk. White Bull. Kills Crow. Warriors of great renown amongst the seven tribes of the Lakota. Soft thunder echoed as they hurtled back into the Unseen Realm, taking the Devil Dogs with them.

Grunge and Goblin barked at the retreating shadows. Ben walked over to Lucas, handing him a medicine wheel attached to a leather cord. "In the battles ahead, may this help you to stay focused and help you to defeat the demons of rage that afflict you. This medicine wheel will help you to stay on the Red Road. The Medicine Wheel used by my people for thousands of years has spiritual purposes. It is shaped like a cross, but the pattern is older than the Christian symbol. One of the first Medicine Wheels was created 2,000 years before Jesus died on the cross. A Medicine Wheel heals illness that comes from spiritual imbalance. The focus of healing is to treat the source of the problem, not the symptoms. In Native American spirituality it creates a roadmap to a sacred space."

Lucas held the medicine wheel out to Cora. "Would you attach this to a cord so that I can wear this around my neck?"

"Yes," she said, taking the wheel from him. "What do you think? The eagle feather and the medicine wheel? Do you think these will bring harmony to your spirit?"

Ben said, "With kids in my past it's been a 50/50 chance that they would heal properly after suffering so much trauma in their lives. 50 percent of the kids became better. The other 50 percent never left the juvenile justice system. It all depends on Lucas."

It wasn't until an hour later, when Goblin snuggled up next to Lucas sound asleep in his bed. Grunge lay sprawled on the other side of him. Peering up at the dream catcher above the bed, then over at the medicine wheel hanging down from the bed rails at the foot of the bed, Goblin said, *Grunge, you still awake?*

Grunge grumbled, *I am now. Something troubling you?*

Goblin said, *Do you think Lucas even has a chance?*

Grunge raised his head, looking over Lucas's sleeping form. *As Ben said, he's got a 50/50 chance. And it's all up to him.*

Lucas made it home safe as summer arrived. No more tantrums. No more take-downs. Aware that if he had a blow-up, he might attract an evil entity drawn by a magnet because of his red-hot rages, he still had bad days. He still did not play nice with others. He still gave teachers headaches. But he was getting better. No one could expect him to suddenly have a miraculous change. It just didn't happen that way. His change came slowly, but Ben constantly assured him that he was making progress.

The judge was allowing Lucas to return home in the next few weeks. He was to live with Maggie and have weekly visits with Stone. No one in the juvenile division was comfortable with Lucas living with Stone Holland. He was to go live with his mom.

It was a warm summer wind that buffeted Lucas as he stood there in Ben's dog cemetery. Grunge and Goblin romped through deep patches of grass, while Ben spoke solemn words to him. They both peered up as a red-tailed hawk glided through the blue summer sky. He was an aerial acrobat, winging his way over Wounded Arrow, spiraling in tight loops on the wind currents without a wing beat.

Ben said, "I would do you a disservice if I allowed you to adopt these dogs without giving you fair warning. Some dogs live to the ripe old age of 15, maybe 16. Some pass much earlier than that. But once they've formed a bond with you, one of the most difficult things in the world is letting go of them. It is one of the most heartbreaking things you will ever do in this life. To have a dog grow close to you through all its phases is a thing to cherish. But when it comes time for that dog to leave your life, it will crush you. It will hurt deeply, and though you think you will never get over it, it is all part of having a good, loyal, faithful, loving, playful dog. You will cry like a baby. You will fondly remember all the days and nights you spent with your dog. You will wish you'd walked him more. You will wish you'd thrown one more ball for him to fetch. Given him more leftovers. Given him a treat more often. Just looking at his bed, you will break down and cry. Seeing his favorite chew toy will cause more tears to fall. It will be the saddest day of your life."

The hawk came soaring back toward them, its wings spread wide, head tucked in tight as it passed over Grunge and Goblin. The hawk flew over cedars on the nearby hilltop and was then gone once more into the summer skies.

"I wanted," Ben said, "to prepare you for this, but nothing can fully prepare you for the day you lose the love of your life that has been a constant, but know it will be a life-changing event. One that you will slowly recover from until the next dog. And believe me, it never gets easier. But that is all part of loving a dog. Loving one is easy, it is the losing of one that will tear you up inside."

Ben left him standing before Rambo's headstone there in the dog cemetery. He made his way up toward the dog barn, seeing to his duties for the day. Grunge and Goblin watched him go, and for a few seconds they looked like they were going to follow him, but then they both looked at Lucas. He did not pat his leg. Nor did he whistle at them. He wanted them to make the choice and was pleased when they did. Goblin came first, hopping his way through thick green grass. Lucas kneeled to pet him. Grunge was at his side a second later, head-butting him gently.

***

Two weeks later, Lucas's life was shattered. Maggie was in a fatal car accident. At this turn of events, Judge Sully ruled in court that Lucas was to return home to Stone Holland's place.

Two days after Maggie's funeral, Lucas ended up back at his dad's house, the sadness of losing his mother now ripping through his heart.

Chapter Ten
One Year Later

Lucas raced down the hallway toward the Boy's rest room at Havelock Elementary School. 12-years-old and in 6th grade, the slender reed of a kid was late for class. Having made a mad dash from home, his shaggy blond hair looked like he'd taken an egg beater to his wild tangles. In the space of four blocks, he inhaled a strawberry Pop-tart and swigged down a carton of orange juice even as he ran.

He belched suddenly, tasting a remnant of the juice he'd guzzled. "Whew! That OJ backwash tasted like monkey butt!"

Upon entering the room, Lucas saw a small boy shoved to the ground by three bigger boys surrounding him. The boy peered up at his three tormenters, tears in his eyes. "My father," he said, "claims we are guests here. There is an honor when a host takes in a guest. Are we to repay that guest by doing him great harm, Jabar?"

Jabar kicked him then, his tennis shoe connecting with his chest, sending him back against the wall behind him. The small dark-haired boy struck his head, leaving a red spot on the white wall. "Hakeem? Aaban?" Jabar snapped. The two other boys yanked him to his feet. Jabar said, "Fulfill your vows as Moloch commands!"

It was then that Lucas intervened.

He reached out, grabbing Jabar by the long curls of his hair. He turned the kid's head to land a solid punch on his left cheek. Jabar sailed back against the wall. As the tall, lanky boy struck the wall, something small and black fell out of the waistband of his pants and clattered on the bathroom floor. Lucas scooped up the .22 Ruger pistol. Jabar scrambled to his feet. "Give me my gun!" he hissed. "It is mine! It belongs to me!"

Jabar was furious. Lucas had not only interfered in his recruitment activity, he had taken away his advantage. His plan had been ruined by a boy who had absolutely no give in him. "If you don't give me my gun," he hissed, "we will come to your house and kill every-one! Mother! Sisters! Brothers! Your father!"

Lucas said, "Don't got no mother, but my dad would love to meet you. He is Elder's Den! If I you see you even sneer at me in the halls, you will meet Den justice. Now, get out of here!"

The three boys offered him an enraged glare yet were gone within seconds. The small boy said, "My name is Ali." He gingerly touched the wound on his head.

When he brought his hand back in front of his face, he grimaced at the blood on his fingertips.

Lucas said, "That might need a butterfly to close it."

Ali stared at him in puzzlement. "A butterfly?"

"Butterfly Band-aid," Lucas said.

The two studied the pistol for several moments. It was formed of black metal with scorpions on its pearl-handled grips. The engraving of a dragon on its barrel ended at the end of the muzzle creating its open mouth. Tucking the gun into the waistband of his jeans, Lucas met the kid's tear-filled gaze.

"Thank you," Ali said, his hand held out to him.

Lucas glanced down at the outstretched hand. "Don't mention it."

Without shaking the hand Ali offered him, Lucas latched onto his shoulder and guided him toward the door. He could feel those black, sorrowful eyes boring into him even as Ali exited the bathroom.

Minutes later, Lucas headed past the office. The three Middle Eastern boys were talking to Mr. Headlee, the principal. Jabar wildly gestured at him, then pointed to the red welt on his left cheek where Lucas had punched him. Lucas cringed when Headlee looked out past the office window. The man beckoned for Lucas to join them. "Holy Dogs!" he whispered as he bolted down the hallway, defying the school principal.

He skidded to a stop, plowing into his metal locker when he reached it. He hastily spun through the numbers on his combination lock, pulling it open. Lifting his shirt, he clawed at the butt of the pistol and snatched it from the waistband of his jeans. He placed the gun inside his backpack at the rear of the locker. Slamming the locker door shut, he locked it.

"Lucas Holland?" came blaring out of the speaker above his locker. "Report to the office this instant!"

Peering up at the speaker as if it were a drone hovering there in the hallway, ready to blast him out of his Keds, Lucas resigned himself to deal with the trouble. Now that the gun was out of the way, he was confident he could put on his usual charm and worm his way out of the bad situation ahead of him. In seconds, Lucas passed by the three boys seated in the principal's office. He smiled at Headlee. He said, "Saracens. That's what my dad, an Army Ranger, said about them. In the fifth century, Saracens descended from Abraham's son Ishmael, come from Abraham's wife Sarah, instead of his slave Hagar. Saracens."

Headlee said, "These three boys belong to a rigid assimilation program, and as such, Lucas, a little tolerance and acceptance would go a long ways. You and I need to sympathize with these poor refugees exiled from their war-torn country."

Jabar said, "This wild-haired maniac viciously attacked me! The gold-haired demon maliciously yelled racial epithets at me. Then struck me directly in the face. Didn't he, Hakeem and Aaban?"

By the time the three boys had told their side of the story, Lucas was made to look like a racist bigot, determined to make life hell for anyone who only wanted to assimilate into this country. He was after all, the kid that no one messed with. He'd grown up with violence as an ever-present influence in his life. He'd seen too many of his dad's club issues settled by fists to ever allow himself to back down. If his dad, president of the Elder's Den, heard he'd pussied out of a violent situation, there would be hell to pay at the Holland house. He knew his dad would not be pleased that he'd helped Ali, but he would at least respect the fact that it was three against one, and not something Lucas could easily ignore.

Lucas often charmed his way out of consequences for confrontations he'd had in the past. From 2nd grade on, he had been sent to the office for each slug fest he'd started. Three times during 2nd grade. Five during 3rd. Seven times in 4th and 5th, and now in 6th grade, only once, which is why he still remained in a normal school setting as opposed to the school for behaviorally challenged students. When his violent outbursts had escalated during 5th grade, Lucas had been court-ordered to attend the school for kids who could not function in an ordinary school setting. And Lucas had hated it so bad, he put every effort into controlling his red-hot temper.

He had been in 6th grade for three months with no fists used to deal with situations. Lucas knew there was a line he dare not cross. He wouldn't like being separated from his dad, as he'd already lost his mom this past year in the car accident. He'd spent time in foster care with Lakota dog handler, Ben Black Bull, helping the Native deal with troubled dogs at Wounded Arrow. During his stay with Ben, Lucas had learned about anger management. All he had to do is abide by a few stupid rules to put another day behind him.

By the time the meeting ended that day, the whining weasel Jabar made himself out to be the victim of the incident, and when Lucas refused to apologize for striking him, Headlee threatened to send him back to the alternative school setting.

Chapter Eleven

When school ended, Lucas was in a real huff. As he walked down the sidewalk toward home, he muttered, "All because I was helping that little kid!"

"Hey, Lucas!" came an excited voice behind him. "I have Skittles to share for your earlier kindness you showed me!"

Lucas turned, rolling his eyes as Ali came running down the sidewalk toward him, a big smile on his face. "Save your Skittles. Those morons were out of line for triple-teaming someone as wimpy as you."

Ali studied the backpack slung over Lucas's right shoulder. "Do you have the gun?" he asked, his brown eyes looking like two shiny marbles. "Jabar wants me to shoot kids in our class. He believes in the god Moloch, who demands obedience from his followers."

Lucas snorted, "To hell with any god who commands you to kill! If a god is so powerful, let him kill people who offend him himself! Sounds like Bones Bridger, an OG of the Elder's Den. Bones is a chief manipulator with all the trickery of a Mafia don. He speaks. Others listen. He orders something done. It gets done. Anyone who disobeys his command gets punished. Been sixteen knifings in the past year out at the State Pen, and not even the guards dare point a finger at Bones. He is that all-powerful. My dad says Bridger rules behind the scenes like a vengeful, wrathful god. If I was a god, and that powerful, I'd do my killing myself, not command wimpy men to do it for me!"

Ali said, "My father says—"

"You say that a lot," Lucas said, cutting him off. "Who cares what you father says? My dad says a lot of things and yet I don't blab about it to others. I suppose you try winning arguments by bring up what your mother says, too, right?"

A stillness came over Ali, a deep sadness filled his dark eyes. "My mother is gone from us. She died in a car crash."

Lucas offered him a look of sympathy. "Yeah, mine, too. She got run off the road by someone my dad is still trying to find."

Ali trailed behind him for the next four blocks. Lucas would have to ditch the kid, for they would be approaching the Holland house soon, which also served as club house for the Den. No telling who might see Lucas walking with Ali, and there would be hell to pay when Stone Holland heard of it later. Or his dad might be out working on a bike in the driveway, and he would freak when he saw his son walking with an Arab boy. The two of them had just crossed the sidewalk on Logan Avenue four blocks from the school, when suddenly Lucas's eyes went wide with alarm. He latched onto Ali's left shoulder and pushed him to the ground behind a row of shrubbery, looking at the two burly men exiting the Ford van a block down the street. Lucas said, "That's Uncle Nate! He sees me with you and I am dead! You have no idea how badly the Den despises your people. Dad and Nate claim you're all a bunch of spies, infiltrating for a takeover. Dad would tell the club I was a traitor!"

Ali said, "We would not want that now, would we? I suppose he considers all refugees as whacked out terrorists. It would break my father's heart to even bring harm to any living creature, let alone blow you and your father and his gang to pieces."

"Club," Lucas corrected him. "It is called a club, not a gang. Big difference between bikers who just want to ride and enjoy the road compared to gangsters who do drive-byes, sell drugs, and kill each other. Bikers are cool. Gangbangers are the scum of the earth."

Scooting forward and pushing their faces into the bushes to see down the street, Lucas and Ali lay shoulder-to-shoulder looking like turtles straining their necks in order to feed. They both watched the scene unfolding before them. Nate Holland, a huge bear of a man, the tattoo of a dragon dominating the left side of his bald skull, wore a cut-off jean, revealing tattoos inked up and down his forearms. He turned his gaze on his companion. "Mange," he said in a gravelly voice, "how much dope did you put in the tranq gun? Hell, you shot him over an hour ago!"

Mange, a biker even larger than Nate, growled, "I put in enough to keep him from coming to. There would be hell to pay if he did before we got him to the Barn!"

The two men walked up the driveway and headed toward the house's backyard. The moment they vanished from sight, Lucas slung his backpack over his shoulder and ran toward the van. Ali hesitantly followed behind him as he sprinted down the sidewalk. "These are very bad men. Who do you think they shot?"

Ignoring his annoying babble, Lucas approached the back door of the van. "Crazy loons!" he gasped, breathlessly.

Creeping across the grassy lawn between the sidewalk and the street, Ali tip-toed his way over to the Ford van, his wide eyes fixed on Lucas. "And you say, my people are bad," he said.

Lucas reached out and latched onto the door handle. He pulled both doors open. "What in the holy hells is that?" came from Ali, who stood there peering into the van, his brown eyes grown large.

Lucas climbed into the van, moving directly up beside the large Pit bull sprawled on the carpeted floor. It was a beautiful dog, with black fur masking his face, and the same black fur trailing down his back, blending with his broad white chest. All four of his paws were black, as well. The dog was out cold, due to the tranquilizing drug injected into his system by way of the gun Mange had used on him.

Running his hands through the dog's thick fur, Lucas tried to rouse the sleeping dog. He glanced back at Ali. "Uncle Nate goes all over town stealing pets! He uses them as bait dogs to stir pits up inside the fighting rings! If I had a gun, I would—"

He stopped mid-sentence, his thoughts and his words frozen.

I do have a gun! he suddenly realized. *It's in my backpack.*

Slinging the pack off of his right shoulder, Lucas unzipped the pack and reached inside for the gun. "We're gonna save this dog!" he cried, looking outside the van to Ali.

"Why?" Ali asked. "Dogs are prohibited animals. It is traditional among Muslims all over the world to regard the dog as a dirty animal that when touched would infect the one who touched it with dirty impurity! The Prophet, Mohammad ordered the killing of dogs and gave numerous hadith that prohibit the keeping of dogs! Hadith tell us that angels won't enter a room where there is a dog. Hadith tell us that if we touch a dog we become impure that we have to wash seven times. Some hadith say that we must kill all black dogs, because they are devils. There are five animals that can be killed at any time; a snake, a vicious dog, a crow, a rat and a scorpion. I cannot touch that dog. Allah forbids it."

Chapter Twelve

The dog slowly raised his head, his green eyes fixed on Ali. Still looking at the dog in open disgust, Ali quietly said, "I am obligated to help you because of the help you gave me this morning, but do not make me touch this dog."

Lucas said, "I want you to run two blocks down the street. You'll see a chopper mailbox sitting to your left."

Looking confused, Ali asked, "Chopper?"

Lucas said, "A Harley, with chopped forks. We have a mailbox with chopped forks with a wheel at the bottom. That's my house. Check the garage, my dad might be working."

Ali looked uncomfortable. "Your father is not going to like me."

"True," Lucas said. "You tell him I'm getting jumped by a bunch of Outlaws. Start crying if you must. Just get him down the street!"

Picking up the pistol with one hand, Lucas said, "If you run fast enough, Uncle Nate won't end up with a bullet in his butt."

Tears sprang to Lucas's eyes. Patting the dog affectionately, he sobbed. He loved dogs. He would never throw one into a fight. Nor could he understand how his father and his uncle could ever do such a thing. Growing up around the Den, he knew Stone and Nate were deeply involved with the fights. In fact, they had ended up with a notorious pit bull who had won over fifty fights in his career.

Two weeks after Lucas's mom had been killed, the courts had returned him to his dad's house there in Havelock. Ben had insisted that Lucas take Grunge and Goblin with him. The dog therapy he had included Lucas in had done wonders for the rage-plagued kid, and his time at Wounded Arrow would have a lasting impact on the troubled boy. Lucas's dad had taken in Goblin, but Stone knew that Grunge had been legendary in the dog fighting circuit. Lucas had begged his dad to let Grunge retire, but Stone told him to quit being such a pansy. Failing to save Grunge from any more heart-breaking, bone-crunching, brutal bloody battles, Lucas resorted to dropping a dime, calling Crime Stoppers to report plans to involve Grunge in a fight. As a result, Officer Beef Tory had confronted the Elder's Den at church, the term for biker council. He made it clear that blowback would be headed their way by law enforcement who knew the Den was involved in the outlawed sport. Months went by and Nate stay-ed beneath the radar, but not without Lucas finding out about his covert dog thefts.

Thump! Thump! came from directly beside him. Lucas actually fell back against the wheel well, trembling in alarm. *Thump! Thump!* The sound filled the entire van. Lucas grinned, wiping tears from his eyes as the pit bull wagged his tail. "Good boy," he soothed quietly, running his free hand through the fur behind the dog's head.

The dog let out a whine. Lucas said, "You've been doped up by two loons who don't have good plans. I'm going to save you."

The pit bull tried to rise, but it could barely open its eyes let alone lift its head. At a sudden noise from outside the van, Lucas took the pistol in a two-handed grip. Outside the van, Mange appeared, a small gray pit pup in his hands. Lucas gasped, "Goblin?"

The big, burly man nearly dropped the pup when he spotted Lucas seated there not six feet away from him, aiming a gun at his face. "Lucas?" he grunted, placing Goblin down on the floor next to the larger pit bull. "Goblin ran away. Nate and I just rescued him from this house. Get that gun out of my face!"

"Gun?" said Nate, stepping off the curb to reach the van. "Little Luke has a gun? Holy Jesus! Put that down!"

Using his free hand to fend of Goblin's excited greeting, Lucas said, "Uncle Nate, you're not taking this dog! I will shoot you!"

Nate nailed him with an intense gaze, his rage boiling just beneath the surface. "You stick a gun in my face and threaten me?"

"No threat," Lucas said, settling Goblin at his side. "A promise. Push me. Go ahead. I'll send you the way of Trailer, Ox, and Mighty Mike Morgan! All three of them can welcome you to the gates of hell, Uncle Nate! I swear!"

Mange and Nate exchanged uneasy looks. The bikers had died in a shoot-out outside of Omaha last summer. Nate had ridden up there, with the three men as backup to settle a score against a rival club. Nate was the only one who rode away, leaving behind three dead bikers of the Den. An investigation followed. No arrests were made. Nate had not only dodged a bullet with the Dodge Street Apaches he had avoided a prison sentence due to the fact that nothing connected him to the murders.

Stone, though, had shared his thoughts on the matter one night at the fire pit in the Holland backyard. Unaware that Lucas was above him silently listening in his tree house directly above the fire, Stone had told his warlord, Gypsy, "Find out what you can about a deal Nate made with the Apaches after the shooting took place out there on the Platte. Instead of settling a score with Crow Harper, president of the Apaches, rumor is, Nate shot Trailer, Ox, and Mike, and six members of Crow's club to make a two-way split over a million-dollar cartel deal."

Recalling that conversation that he had no business being privy to, Lucas boldly said, "Uncle Nate, I need to ask you something."

Trying his best not to flinch, Lucas asked, "Did you betray the club out there on the Platte River?"

Lucas could see by the look in Nate's eyes that he'd hit him hard with the question. Nate said, "Stop with the crazy talk, Little Luke."

Mange growled, "Enough, you little Moonbat!"

The big, brawny biker started to climb into the van, determined to retrieve the pistol, but Nate latched onto the collar of his jean jacket. "No, Mange. He's got issues, been that way since his mom died. He may shoot you. How about a new Playstation, Little Luke?"

"Damn!" Lucas cursed. "You can't bribe me, Uncle Nate. How about I go get Dad? Let's see what he has to say about this."

Nate stiffened at this. Mange looked down the street beyond the front of the van. "Oh, hell!" he said. "Stone's coming, Nate!"

Nate said, "If you cost me the loss of this dog, Luke, I will put you in the ground!"

The two bikers walked around the van, and Lucas scooted himself out onto the street. If his dad caught him with the gun, he would not be able to sit down for a week. Going into panic mode, he peered down at the drain sewer beside the van. He hastily tossed the pistol down into its open mouth, hearing a slight clunking sound as the gun landed down in those dark depths.

Lucas looked past the two bikers to Stone Holland striding down the street, trailed by Ali. They made a strange pair, small, shaggy-haired Ali trying to match the big man's strides. Stone moved with catlike grace as he came toward the van, his collar-length black hair trailing back from his bearded face, twin Celtic hoops glinting in the lobes of his ears. He wore faded jeans, scuffed boots, and a black T-shirt. His beard was trimmed, his hair neatly combed. But there was a ruggedness to his face that reminded Lucas of a mountain man.

Chapter Thirteen

"The Golden Boy," Nate said to Stone, "pulled a gun on me! You had better rein him in, Brother! He's out of control!"

Stone stood there peering into the van. "Damn you, Nate! Do you know who this dog belongs to? Award-winning dog of Reason Nelson. The biker who became a K9 handler. Reason was the former VP of the Outlaws. You looking to start a war? Anything happens to this dog, Outlaws will be gunning for us."

Nate responded, "I'm selling this dog to Crow for ten grand."

"Crow Harper?" Stone asked. "You've gone very dark, Brother."

Mange said, "It's on account of a six-million dollar shipment that the Juarez cartel was sending to the Apaches up in the Big O. Lobo alerted to the drugs and now the Juarez cartel want to see this pitty torn to pieces this Saturday night at the Barn."

Stone strode purposely over to Nate standing on the curb. Raising one hand, he coldly said, "Hand me your keys."

Muttering angrily, Nate dug into the pocket of his grubby jeans and retrieved the keys to his van. Tossing them to Stone, he said, "What about the gun? It ain't right that your behaviorally disordered son threatened to shoot his uncle."

Stone started toward the driver's side door of the van. "Lucas? Hop in the van. We'll be taking the dogs to our house."

Gesturing at Ali beside him, Lucas said, "What about him, Dad?"

Pulling open the driver's door, Stone gave a heavy sigh. "He can go his own way. He is not your friend, son."

Stone slipped into the driver's seat, saying, "Nate? You can pick up your van after we get these dogs settled at the house."

Stone started the van, glancing back once to make sure Lucas was inside with the dogs. He drove away, without looking in the rearview mirror to see his brother standing there focusing on Ali striding away as fast as his small legs would carry him.

***

Khalid Karim was waiting for his son when he returned that day from school. He smiled warmly at Ali as he came through the front door of their residence five blocks from Ali's school.

A man of average height with broad shoulders, a narrow waist, and thick, muscular arms, Khalid was not your typical Muslim. He kept his beard trimmed short, yet he wore his silky raven hair past his ears and to his collar. Iraqi by birth, he was a handsome man, with brown penetrating eyes. His late wife jokingly called him her, *Arab Antonio Banderas.* Khalid's wife, Alisha, had been killed two years earlier in a car accident. Ali still talked about her, but he no longer wept when he did so. For many months after her death, he was afraid that Ali, being the fragile boy that he was, had suffered permanent damage due to his mother's unexpected death.

Ali graciously accepted the steaming mint tea his father poured for him from a carafe situated on the edge of his oak desk. Beyond the desk, taking up the entire back wall of the living room were six computer monitors, essential tools to Khalid's trade.

Khalid smiled, tiredly. "Ah, the Hound is spent for the day. I'm afraid the jackals have all gone to ground in their dens, Little Ali."

Ali asked, "Why are you known in intelligence circles as the Hound? Aren't all dogs cursed?"

Khalid said, "The Prophet said, '*A Muslim man was walking in the desert dying of thirst when he found a well. He went down to drink and upon coming out he notices a dog dying of thirst. So he climbed back in and filled his shoe with water. He gave the dog to drink and God forgave his sins.*' The Prophet then said, '*Helping any living thing has a reward!*' All animals are a part of Allah's creation and belong to Allah. Muslims are custodians of this beautiful planet. We are accountable to Allah."

Ali proceeded to tell him about his encounter with the bikers. He mentioned Lucas several times, swearing that he'd never touched either dog during their rescue. He called Lucas his friend, but he ad-mitted to himself that Lucas really didn't want anything to do with him. Ali told him about the incident with the three boys. Khalid gestured at the monitors situated on the wall before him. "You think their selection of you was random? This had to do with locating a terror cell. Wouldn't it be just like Waziri to make a countermove?"

Ali then told his father about the gun, telling him about the engraving of the dragon on the barrel. "Come, Ali," Khalid said. "I must speak with this Lucas."

***

Lucas sat in a lawn chair in the Holland backyard. The large pit bull was walking unsteadily on wobbly legs, recovering from being shot by the tranquilizer gun. Stone coaxed him to follow him around the yard. He was a friendly dog, showing no signs of aggression.

"Lobo," Stone said. "This dog is famous as a K9 sniffer. He's alerted to millions of dollars of drugs. No wonder the Mexicans want to see him in a dogfight. He's cost them many pesos. Once this big boy is fully recuperated, we have to get him home without getting caught at it. That K9 handler would ask all kinds of questions. We wouldn't want that dog handler to think that the president of the Den was a nice guy. This is a covert ops mission: You sneaking him back into his yard without him knowing you were there."

Lucas was just assuring Stone he could get Lobo home when a knock came from the front door. Stone silently ushered both dogs inside. Curious as to who had come calling, Lucas stepped onto the front porch to be greeted by a big, blond man in a three-piece suit. A smile creased his gold beard. "Lucas?" the large man said.

Stone came outside. He met the cop's gaze with a cold look, and said, "Detective Tory, ex-warlord of the Outlaws, known as the Viking. What brings you to my door?"

Beef Tory kept his smile in place and said, "We received a report that two men were seen carrying a dog out to a van over on Kearney. The dog happens to be that sniffer that put a dent in some cartel's business up in the Big O. Why don't we get him safely back home?"

Stone said, "Sorry, we can't help you. Good-day, Tory."

With that, Stone ushered Lucas inside the house, and without a backward glance, he joined him, closing the door behind them.

Once Lobo was walking around, recovered from the tranquilizer, Lucas walked him two blocks over to the dog handler's house, a stone house among several ranch-style houses. Lobo had remained by his side the entire walk, not once even paying attention to the squirrels nattering at them from overhead branches.

"Welcome home, Lobo," he said, ushering the dog into the yard. Suddenly, Lobo bolted and ran toward the back door of the house. He nosed the door open and darted inside. "Hello," Lucas said when he reached the open backdoor.

He crept forward, listening to Lobo's nails clicking on the floor of the den. He glanced at the display of awards taking up the greater portion of one wall. Next to them were photos of Reason Nelson, showing a steady transformation, starting when he was a shaggy-haired biker. In that first picture, he was holding up a leather jacket with the words "Outlaws, Nebraska Chapter," displayed on the patch across the top the jacket, while below was a patch displaying the words "President," in red letters.

In the next picture, Reason wore his cut with no shirt beneath it. His arms and his chest were rippled with muscle. The tatt of a fire-breathing dragon covered his right shoulder, while a leaping panther tatt took up most of his left shoulder. In a third photo, Reason wore jeans and a blue sweatshirt, displaying the words, *K9 Handler* on the front. His raven hair was tied back in a ponytail, while his goatee was trimmed so he looked like a rakish pirate, and someone had labeled this picture, *"The Celt."*

A second set of pictures showed Reason seated at a table, a dozen of his books on display before him. Next to this photo was a newspaper clipping with a heading in bold print: **Author for at-risk kids becomes Truancy Tracker to state-wards**. Directly across from this was an article about his work as a private investigator, and it detailed how Reason had tracked a runaway kid up to the Big O, where he led police to a drug network involving a street gang. His badge was held in one hand, while a flashy-looking pistol was held in the other.

Lucas said, "How many roles does this guy play? President of the Outlaws? K9 handler? Truancy Tracker? Author? Private eye?"

Lobo nosed at a small wooden chest situated on the floor before them. Lucas flipped the lid of the chest open, revealing three gold rings resting in black velvet. He gasped when he heard words inside his head: *When my master wields the rings, wonders never cease.*

Lucas stared for long, uncertain moments at Lobo peering up at him. "What the hell?" he whispered. "Did you just speak to me?"

Lobo sent a message inside of Lucas's head: *Everything he puts his mind to, he can do ten times better while wearing a ring.*

Blinking in amazement, Lucas scooped up all three rings. He had never been a thief, but he wanted these rings. As he slipped them into his front pocket, he heard the front door opening. He headed for the back door, his gaze fixed on the far corner of the yard, when a voice said, "Hold on there!"

Chapter Fourteen

Lucas turned to face Reason Nelson. He had dark, shoulder-length hair, a beard, broad shoulders, a narrow waist, and he wore jeans and a black T-shirt. Lucas thought, *He reminds me of Cullen Bohannon from Hell on Wheels.*

Lobo nosed his way out through the house's screen door. Barking a friendly greeting, he darted over to his master, dropping down at his feet. "You beautiful hound!" said Reason.

Lucas lied, "I saw him running loose down at the ball diamond. Someone told me he belonged to the dog trainer guy."

Reason said, "You rescued an award-winning Narco dog. You did a good job. Certainly, you've heard about me from your sister. It was my report that got Celeste sent to treatment."

Lucas gasped, "The Park Narc? The Snitch Bitch? Patron Saint of Havelock's Stoners? You're *that* Reason Nelson? Celeste hates you with a passion, dude!"

Celeste had been sentenced by Judge Sully to treatment in Omaha due to Reason failing to get through to her. Lucas said, "Celeste hated you for getting her to school, but she's read every one of your books while she's been in treatment in the Big O."

"Here," Reason said, handing him two bills. "For rescuing my dog, how does two-hundred sound to you?"

Two-hundred dollars? Lucas thought. *The insult alone would kill Uncle Nate with his ten-thousand dollar deal!*

Lucas took the bills. Reason said, "Sniffer dogs detect explosives, drugs, or blood. Some search for human remains. Some are trained to search for firearms. Nose-work mimics professional detection tasks. One dog and one handler form a team. The dogs must find a hidden target odor and alert the handler. After the dog finds it they are rewarded. When I picked him up from Pine Ridge rez, I trained Lobo to be a multitasker."

Lucas said, "This past year, I lived at Wounded Arrow. Ben Black Bull was teaching me how to train dogs."

Reason said, "I have CDs put out by my friend Jim Osorio, owner of Canine Encounters. He trains cops how to deal with aggressive dogs. You can take them home with you. Once you think you learned something, come back and we can try it on Lobo. Deal?"

Lucas nodded. "Deal. My sister said you wrote 15 books for kids. If you're rich, why do you still live in smalltown Havelock? She said you're an investigative journalist for an online magazine. She said thousands of kids read it with 2 million subscriptions."

Reason said, "*Storm Haven* is where I post stories each month, dealing with kid issues. Anything that will help kids deal with life. Recently, I wrote about dog fighting that pissed off your uncle Nate. Did she tell you about the journal left on my porch by an anonymous source that was my source of information for the story?"

As he stood there, Lucas knew how much Celeste had gotten by with before she was hammered by the courts. She had been wild and unruly. Until Reason had been assigned to her case by Judge Sully. And now, she was locked away in treatment.

Lucas said, "Before Celeste got sent to treatment, she read the words some kid spray-painted down in the tunnels. It said, *'Reason Nelson was right!'* It was her way of telling me she wished she'd listened to you. Lots of kids consider you a legend, with all the books you've written."

Reason laughed. "Just trying to make a difference in my little part of this world. God only knows why some kids go down in Kamikaze mode. At my last book signing, dozens of my readers came to get copies. Bikers, Natives, probation officers, cops, teachers, parents, and even the Red Hat Society. Diverse group. My books are demographically sound, ten-year-olds through eighty-year-olds read them. When I was a kid bored to death in school, I vowed to never write a book that bored kids or put them to sleep. I accomplished that goal, too. *Eight Ball* is the most stolen, lost, missing book in the public libraries. Kids like it, so they steal it."

When a knock came from the front door, Lucas stayed out of sight behind Reason and Lobo as they answered the door. A slender man and Ali, the boy he'd saved from taking a beating at school, stood there on the porch. The man said, "My name is Khalid Karim. You are a social worker, correct?"

"Tracker," Reason said. "Truancy tracker."

Khalid said, "You do investigative journalism. You write for *Storm Haven*, a youth-oriented site where thousands of kids log on each week to read about drug use, running away from home, being suspended from school, being placed on probation, and teen suicide. I've read the *Storm*. I researched you. Your books are nationwide. Your target audience is alternative schools, treatment and detention centers. I have a story for you that may stir up a hornet's nest. You could reach thousands of youth being recruited into killing in the name of the Canaanite god, Moloch. Have you heard of the Red Vipers? I am known in my country as the Hound. I came searching for a very bad man. If we were in our homeland, I would deal with the leader of the Vipers differently, but this is America, where the laws about such things would bring bad consequences."

Khalid extended his hand. "I know who you are, Storm Writer. I have been reading your posts on *Storm Haven*. You pull no punches when you write about the radicalization of kids. Your words are read by hundreds of youth."

Khalid handed him a business card. Reason accepted his card, quietly reading the contact information. Khalid said, "We have a lot to discuss, my new friend. Do you like coffee? Strong, black coffee sweetened with sugar cubes?"

Reason grinned. "The sweeter the better. Is this your son?"

He gestured at Ali standing there, staring at his dog, a look of disgust on his face. Reason said. "Would you like to pet him?"

"Oh, no sir!" Ali said, a look of horror on his face.

Khalid said, "Call me. For now, I must see to an urgent matter."

***

A block away from the Holland house, Ali raised his father's cell phone, focusing on the chopped forks attached to the mailbox ahead of them. "That is the home of Lucas," he said, impersonating a narrator shooting a docudrama. "In moments, we walk fifty steps to the Holland front door. What you are witnessing is the Death Walk of young Ali Karim, whose stern father insists I join him."

Turning to zero in on his father's face with the cell phone camera, Ali asked, "Could I just go home now?"

With a twirl of his cane he carried, Khalid said, "I will need you to be a witness. Your friend may lie to me when I confront him."

"He is not," Ali said, "my friend. Just an acquaintance."

Ali started to follow him. Khalid stopped. Ali bumped into him. Father and son stood in the shadows cast by an oak tree as a man pulled up in front of the Holland house in an old Buick down the street. Raising the cell phone to focus it on the beat-up car, Ali continued to film as a white man with dark dreadlocks exited the car. In his hand, he carried a fist-sized bag of white powder. He crept up beside a red pickup and opened the door. Looking in all directions, he shoved the bag beneath the driver's seat of the truck. He closed the door and turned back toward the Buick. The phone held out before him, Ali recorded the man climbing back inside the Buick. He filmed the car as it sped off down the street. Ali stood there, silently studying what he had recorded. He stopped the images flashing past him on the screen, freezing one image. He said, "That word on the man's jacket is Apaches."

Ali cringed each time his father's cane struck the front door of the Holland house. He knew Lucas would never forgive him for telling on him in regards to the gun. At the fifth solid knock on the front door, it opened. Stone Holland said, "Whatever you're selling, I am not buying."

He closed the door.

Khalid spoke directly to the closed door, saying, "Aren't you concerned about the gun your son has brought home from school?"

The door swung back open. Stone's large frame took up the space beyond the threshold of the porch. "This is the second time today that I've heard about this gun. What's up with that?"

Khalid told Stone the story of how Lucas intervened, preventing Jabar from recruiting Ali for a attack on his fellow classmates.

Khalid slipped one hand beneath his black suit jacket, removing a leather billfold. He flipped it open, holding it out so that Stone could see the badge it contained. "Have you heard of the Phantoms?" he asked as Stone started intently at the badge.

Stone said, "I served two tours in Iraq, special forces with Delta. Phantoms are counter-terrorist agents who hunt down terrorists. But I heard a story on your Shadow agents. You and I both know there is no cure for these radicals. You find them, you kill them, right?"

Khalid said, "I've carried out dozens of missions. Perpetrators of horrendous acts of terrorism have been arrested. It is unlawful to assassinate a terrorist. Perhaps, too many spy novels in your past has led you to believe otherwise? My plan is to track down a terror cell. This cell is here in the States posing as a film crew producing a docudrama. Terrorists known as Red Vipers. Waziri, the leader, has come to Havelock to claim a special-made pistol. His son took it to school with him this morning. Your son now has it."

Stone said, "During my tours to your god-forsaken country, the News reports the conflict between Jews and Palestinians, while missing the bigger picture of the wars in the Middle East."

Stone was just preparing to close the door again, when a black Suburban pulled up in the street, followed by a Sheriff's cruiser.

Chapter Fifteen

Lucas slipped down the hallway, the gym bag in hand. He'd nearly made it to the back door when he heard a voice toward the front the house, "Narcotics would like to give Lobo a final send off!"

"My dog is retired, Beef," Reason said. "That new opiate out there has caused the deaths of several sniffer dogs. My plan is to have him die a ripe old age. He served faithfully, he deserves that."

Detective Tory said, "One more job, live and televised! Backed by the warrant I obtained, all we need is a legitimate cause, and Lobo could provide it. It would certainly even out that run-in you had with Nate back in your Outlaw days. Remember when Nathan brought a shipment of meth into Havelock, and you burned it?"

"Yes," Reason said. "Stone can't control his brother, but I've never known him to deal in drugs."

Beef said, "These drugs are inside of Stone's truck. It will be a slam dunk, with Lobo alerting to narcotics and being filmed while doing so. What do you say? Lobo's registration as a sniffer runs out in two months. He's still registered for active duty, Reason!

Inside the den, Lucas so badly wanted to defend his dad. *Drugs?* he thought. *Dad doesn't deal drugs! He's blocked Uncle Nate every time he's tried dealing drugs! The Den does not deal in drugs of any kind! I best get home and warn Dad.*

The door bell rang a second time. Lucas paused, curious about this new arrival. Against his better judgment, he crept down the hallway to peek at the African-American lady entering the house. Dressed in a tailored suit of dark green, she was tall and slender with short-cropped hair. She said. "Agent Gloria Raynes from Homeland. Homeland has granted a film crew visas to produce a docudrama here in the states. A terrorist cell, the Red Vipers, are posing as the producers of this film, led by a man named Waziri. He was given a pistol by another operative. A thumb-drive was inserted into the gun with directives on. His son took it to school with him. The pistol was stolen during an altercation. I wish to use your dog to deal with a matter of national security."

***

By the time Lucas ran the four blocks back home, the Holland residence was surrounded by a small army of cops. Several cops formed a perimeter around Stone's truck, while others stood some distance away, regarding the truck as if it was about to blow up at any second. Taking cover behind a nearby tree, Lucas took a sneak-peek at his dad walking through a group of officers in the front yard. Detective Tory detached himself from a circle of cops gathered next to the driveway entrance. He walked directly up to Stone, offering him a smirk. Lucas ran down the alley to the Holland back gate. He ran to his bedroom window. The moment he wormed through the window, Goblin leaped up on his bed, licking his face repeatedly.

"All right!" Lucas chuckled. "Glad to see you too, Cornball!"

Goblin nuzzled him beneath the chin, then rolled over, wanting his belly rubbed. Lucas complied for several seconds. He told Goblin, "All those cops outside! Come on, let's go take a look!"

Lucas darted to the front window, Goblin scampering along behind him. Boy and pup poked their heads in between the curtains to peek outside. They watched as Tory and Raynes began a debate, the word "Jurisdiction" echoing down the street. While the white detective and black agent continued their red-hot exchange, Reason walked up the sidewalk across the street, Lobo at his side.

Detective Tory shouted, "Put that dog to work, Reason!"

Raynes snapped, "That is not how this is going to play out!"

Reason gave a gentle tug on Lobo's leash. Before the two were even halfway across the street, Agent Raynes interposed herself between Lobo and Stone's truck, saying, "Proceed to the house. Do not bother with the truck, Nelson!"

Detective Tory opened the truck's door and pulled out the bag he found beneath the seat. He cried, "Holland, you are under arrest!"

Tears sprang to Lucas's eyes, trickling down his cheeks as he watched his dad being placed inside a police cruiser. Sensing his anguish, Goblin nuzzled his leg. Lucas kneeled down to embrace the affectionate dog. Goblin whined, and Lucas wept. A voice from the front yard alerted him to a new danger. "We're covered by the warrant! Let's go check inside the house!"

Scrambling to his feet, Lucas was nearly to his bedroom when the front door flew open and crashed against the wall. Goblin gave a soft growl. Lucas scooped up the pup and scurried down the hall and into his bedroom. Placing Goblin on his bed, Lucas closed the door. He heard Reason say, "Raynes, put that gun away!"

Raynes snapped shot, "These Hollands own a killer pit! I heard a dog growl when we stepped inside!"

Reason said, "Wrong residence. Nate's the one who owns the pit, not Stone. Just put the gun away, Agent Raynes!"

Lucas and Goblin settled on the bed in the far corner of the room. "What are you doing?" Reason's voice came from the front room: "Stand down, Gloria."

Raynes pounded on the bedroom door. The agent shoved the door open. Goblin sprang off the bed and took a protective stance in front of Lucas, growling fiercely. Raynes raised her gun.

Lucas sprang off of his bed, screaming, "No! Don't shoot!"

Raynes snapped, "Stay back, kid!"

She took careful aim and began to squeeze the trigger. Reason, coming up the hallway behind Lobo, reached down, grabbing onto the outstretched wrist of her gun hand. He said, "The kid and the dog are not posing a threat. What? You going to shoot the pup?"

Raynes stepped past Reason. "Why don't you use that mouth to tell me where that gun is you carried home from school."

Lucas said, "Like I have a clue what you're talking about."

Raynes stood there, shaking her head. "And I thought you would work with me, Lucas. Dad goes to jail on drug charges. Sister is in treatment. You can't stay here alone. What options do I have? Youth services? Emergency foster care? Now, about this gun?"

Sniffling, Lucas bowed his head and muttered, "Still not a clue."

Chapter Sixteen

Reason and Lobo conducted a thorough search of the house. When they were finished, Lobo located two hunting rifles and two drugs, one for high blood pressure, the other for allergies. During Lobo's search, Agent Raynes remained in Lucas's room grilling him relentlessly about the pistol. Lucas had perfected playing dumb over the years with every counselor his problem behavior put him in touch with. His dumb act had infuriated the best of them.

During the thirty-minute interrogation, Raynes was nearly at her boiling point, when Reason came back into the room, Lobo trailing him. He said, "The search turned up nothing. No pistol found."

Ruff! Ruff! burst from Lobo's mouth. Reason produced a treat from a pouch at his belt, handing it to Lobo.

Raynes nailed Lucas with a hard stare. "This is what happened this morning at your school. You walked in on a boy brandishing a gun with scorpions engraved in its hand grips. Jabar threatened you with it. So you hit him. Before he could recover, you snatched the gun out of his hands and put it in your pack."

Lucas said, "Who is Jabar?"

"The boy who first had the gun."

"What gun?"

"Lucas! We are so far past that at this point!"

"Point? Is there even a point to any of this?"

"Gawd, kid! How in the hell do your teachers deal with you?"

"Why? Getting annoyed? Maybe you need anger management, Cop Lady. Lots of anger is bad for your blood pressure."

"Enough of this, Lucas! You think this is some kind of game?"

"Game? I don't know, is it?"

"Stop it!"

She shot Reason an enraged glare and muttered, "Watch him for me, I'll be right back!"

Once Raynes left the room, Lobo planted his head in Lucas's lap, fixing him in his sad-eyed gaze. "He's empathizing with you," Reason said. "He knows you are distressed about your dad."

Lucas lowered his head, so that Reason could not see his tears. "There's been some kind of mistake. My dad hates drugs."

Reason kneeled down behind Lobo, politely keeping his face turned from Lucas so as not to humiliate him. "That was a lot of powder, Lucas. How do you explain it being in your dad's truck?"

Goblin placed one paw on Lucas's back while Lobo burrowed his head into his lap. Both dogs picked up on his sad vibes. Lucas was tempted to tell him that Nate had stolen Lobo and that he had rescued him, foiling Nate's deal, but he did not want to be a snitch. He knew the biker code, the one that said you never snitched. He asked, "How come you didn't want Lobo involved in any more searches, Reason?"

Reason let out an exasperated sigh. "A new danger has been introduced into the drug war: Opiates mixed with fentanyl, so lethal that sniffer dogs have died after inhaling a small amount. Departments carry Narcan. It counters the effects of the opiates. Dogs are vulnerable. They're not decked out in protective gear. Fentanyl is so toxic that even a tiny amount is all that's needed to kill. It poses a problem to officers, too. One cop doing a field test on what he thought to be heroin went into opiate intoxication. The high potency due to man-made procedures has made it a heroin substitute. You heard of Deep 9? An airborne toxin. It has a chemical compound that tells the brain to shut down, demanding its user stop breathing."

***

Khalid and Ali were preparing to leave the Holland place. Ali looked up. "Father, what about the pictures I took on your phone?"

It was then that Detective Tory came storming out of the house. The detective rushed over to two uniformed officers standing outside their cruiser. "Where's that damned packet I gave you?"

An officer retrieved the packet of white powder from inside the cruiser. Beef took the bag from the officer and plunged his pocket knife into its center. The moment his knife penetrated the plastic bag, a fine white mist drifted up into the detective's face.

Detective Tory suddenly dropped where he stood.

Minutes later, paramedics loaded Beef Tory inside an ambulance and rushed him to the nearest hospital.

***

Inside the house, Reason looked up as Raynes placed her laptop down beside Lucas on the bed. She told him about the situation out front. Reason listened in deep concern, his eyes straying over to Lobo. "This is exactly why I didn't want my dog involved, Raynes!"

Raynes picked up her laptop from the bed. While her back was turned, Lucas bounded up onto the bed, placed his fingers before

56

him, and dove out through his open bedroom window. He tucked and rolled to the lawn below. Goblin landed on his back there in the yard. Both then raced across the backyard. Lucas knew Raynes wanted that gun so badly it now made Lucas curious as to how important it was. He decided he was going back to reclaim the pistol he'd tossed down through the drain sewer.

Ali and Lucas collided just as he and Goblin exited the alley at the end of the block. Lucas peered up into the amused-looking face of Khalid. Placing his cane before him, leaning on it with both hands planted on its dragon-headed hand grip, Khalid smiled warmly. "I am Khalid," he said. "Ali's father. Come home with us."

"Home?" Lucas said. "To your house? Why would I do that?"

Keeping the smile on his bearded face, Khalid said, "Why not? Do you have other pressing matters to attend to, son?"

Refusing to shake the man's hand, Lucas stuffed his hands in his pockets in a defiant gesture. "I'm not your son, good sir!"

Khalid's look of disappointment caught Lucas off guard. "Why the hostilities, young Lucas?"

Lucas began to say, "My dad says—" then stopped himself when the loud thunder of a Harley came rolling down the street from the opposite direction of the Holland house. Nate Holland, his bald head gleaming in the sunlight, pulled his Harley to the curb, killed the engine, put his kickstand down, and dismounted. The thunder of a second bike filled the air, and a hulk with dreadlocks pulled up to park his Harley beside Nate's. "Crow Harper," Lucas said at the sight of the president of the Apaches.

Nate said, "We ain't done with this. And you're gonna help me."

"No," Lucas said. "I'm not. You are dirty and evil, Uncle Nate. Far as I am concerned, your compass is broken."

Crow Harper shook back his dreadlocks as he walked up beside Nate. Khalid said. "A ten-thousand dollar deal with an MC out of Omaha, involving an award-winning dog? Surely, I thought this had to be a farfetched tale. But then . . ."

Khalid shifted his cane to his other hand so that he could reach inside his suit jacket to remove his cell phone. The Muslim man held the phone up so that Lucas, Nate, and Crow could see the screen, which showed Harper planting the bag in Stone's truck. Nate said, "Give me that phone, Arab!"

Khalid struck Crow in the forehead with his cane, sending him down to the curb. Khalid moved swiftly, delivering a series of well-aimed blows with his cane. *Snick! Snack! Crack!* The man moved like a fencer, his cane landing blows on Nate. Khalid jabbed him in the forehead, sending him down to the street beside Crow.

Crow sat there, trying to figure out where he was, Nate was out cold. Khalid said, "I would advise that we move away from here."

Lucas and Ali fell in behind Khalid as he moved off down the alley. Goblin stayed close on Lucas's heels. "Nate did this to Dad," Lucas said, fighting hard not to sob. "Why didn't you turn it into one of those cops swarming my place? I need to show that to Gypsy."

Khalid said, "It is imperative that I get that gun you took from Jabar. His father is on a terrorist watch list, posing as a filmmaker. It is my duty to stop him. This needs to be seen by the county attorney who is in a position to help your dad. You will retrieve the gun."

"Maybe," Lucas said. "But you still should have showed this to Beef or Raynes to clear my dad of any charges."

With that, he took off running, leaving Khalid and Ali standing there looking puzzled and perplexed.

Ten minutes later, Lucas stood before Reason Nelson's house, but when he got there, the heavy metal lid leading to the sewer would not budge. Goblin gave an excited, "*Whuff! Whuff!*"

He then bolted up the driveway toward Reason coming through the gate. He kneeled down to catch the pup as he leaped up into his arms. "Goblin!" he said. "Where did you find this rogue, Lucas?"

Lucas lied, "Uh, my dad found him. He's actually my dog."

Reason said, "Agent Raynes is looking for you. She wants you placed in emergency care. Too bad she didn't consult with me. I take in emergency stays all the time."

Lucas asked, "You would take me in?"

"Yes," Reason said, handing Goblin off to Lucas before stepping up onto his wrap-around front porch. "I'll call and make the arrangements. Come on inside."

Reason slipped inside his house. Lucas turned to find Ali running up to the porch. "Did you retrieve the gun?" the little kid asked.

Lucas walked over to the manhole in Reason's front yard. "This thing weighs a ton! We're just gonna have to go down to the tunnels by Ballard pool. I hate walking the sewers at night, but it's the only way to get the gun."

He added, "But we're gonna need a flashlight."

Chapter Seventeen

Lucas decided to get a flashlight by car-shopping. As he tip-toed up to a car parked along the street, Ali asked, "What are you doing? You could get arrested for such a risky prank. Have you no honor?"

A quick search of the car and Lucas found a Maglite. He flicked it on and shone the light in Ali's eyes. "Honor? What do you think I am doing? I am going to get that gun like your dad wanted me to. You coming?"

Five minutes later, they stood before the opening of the Havelock storm tunnels. The ceiling was nine feet above them with a ten-foot passage between the cold walls. Ali stood gaping at the large black opening as if it were the entrance to hell. Goblin let out a weak, *woof!* and backed away to take a stance behind Lucas.

By the light of the Maglite, Lucas, Ali, and Goblin trudged along in the dark depths of the tunnels. The first three blocks, Lucas had entertained the young Muslim kid by shining the light on the spray paintings taking up the walls on either side of them. The artwork was very graphic, and left Ali blinking like an owl in bright sunlight. He could not believe his eyes, that American kids had so crudely left such dirty images on the walls. His face burned with shame to even see such vulgar images. Lucas said, "This tunnel runs four blocks to the railroad yards. Once, Mike Truax went butt-surfing in the culvert leading to these tunnels. It had been raining. The culvert was slick with moss, so he could slide down it on his butt. A flash flood came. Mike got swept into these tunnels. He was in nine feet of water, with only his nose between the water and the ceiling. He should have drowned, because there at the last three blocks it turns to three-by-four-foot around. He was moving so fast that he got caught in an air pocket. He went sailing along at about 60 miles per hour and got shot out of the tunnels into the pond at the railroad yards!"

"Wow," Ali said. "I wonder was he thankful to God afterwards?"

Lucas said, "I just know he never went butt-surfing ever again."

"I would thank Allah daily," Ali said, "if he brought me safely through such an ordeal."

"Daily?" Lucas said. "Wouldn't once be enough?"

***

Reason sat at his desk, Lobo snoozing on the floor behind him. He reviewed his tapes recorded from his front porch security cameras.

He watched as Nate Holland entered his yard. Mange scooped up Goblin from the yard. Both bikers headed to the van parked in the street. A second later, the big biker placed Goblin inside of the van. The moment Lucas appeared on screen, waving a pistol at his uncle, Reason sat up in his chair. Seconds before Stone appeared on the screen, Lucas tossed the pistol into the mouth of the sewer.

A knock came from his front door. When Reason opened the door he found Khalid standing on his porch. Khalid removed a device from the pocket of his jacket. "Up until fifteen minutes ago, I was keeping track of my son. Little did Ali know, my wristwatch he carries has a GPS device inserted into it."

Reason said, "Does this have anything to do with a gun? I think they are in the Havelock tunnels."

Khalid said, "Do you know these tunnels well?"

Reason laughed. "Been playing in those tunnels since I was a kid. That GPS? I've got a dog who is far more reliable than that."

***

Ali froze when a sudden sound came from the tunnel behind them. Startled by the sound of footsteps echoing off the cold cement walls, Lucas swung the Maglite up, shining its weak yellow beam down the corridor. Goblin growled. The footfalls ceased at once. Only silence came back. "Hello?" Lucas said. "Someone back there?"

They traveled ten more feet when Ali said, "You seem surprised I would thank Allah so profoundly. Islam is a religion that professes there is only one God, Allah. Mohammad is his messenger. With over 1.8 billion followers, Islam teaches that God has guided mankind through prophets and the Quran, and the teachings called the sunnah composed of accounts called hadith of Mohammad. Muslims believe that Islam is the universal faith. The Quran is the unaltered word of God. Islam originated in the early 7th century in Mecca. The Islamic Golden Age was from the 8th century to the 13th. Muslims have two denominations: Sunni or Shia. Muslim, the word for a believer, is one who submits. It was once Mohammadanism, but that was offensive because it suggests that a human rather than God is central to our religion. I prefer Saracen. We are descended from Sarah the wife of Abraham."

They walked another two blocks, their tennis shoes slapping on the cement floor, Goblin's paws creating a soft tapping. Lucas could see a shaft of moonlight slanting down from a drain sewer ahead of them. "That is the drain I dropped the gun in."

Ali asked, "Is it loaded? Does it even have bullets in it?"

"Don't know," Lucas said, even as he used the beam of the light to study the iron rungs embedded in the wall just beneath the manhole cover nine feet above them. Off to one side of these steps was the recessed section that was situated two feet below the drain sewer opening. By the sounds of the gun clunking earlier when he'd tossed it down into the sewer opening, he figured it landed on the ledge above. Whipping the Maglite up, Lucas used its beam to search the darkness behind them.

"Here," he said, passing the Maglite to Ali. "Shine its light on me so I can see where I'm climbing. Goblin? Stay put. I'll be okay."

Ali raised the light beam so that it illuminated the nine iron rungs embedded in the wall leading up to the manhole cover far above them and very near the recessed ledge where Lucas figured the gun to be. Springing up from the floor, Lucas latched onto the rung a foot above his head, and planting his feet on the rung below, he clambered up the wall. He reached into the recess, searching for the pistol. His hand closed on cold metal. He took a hold of the gun. Clinging to the one rung with one hand, he aimed the pistol down the corridor behind them and pulled the trigger. *Click! Click! Click!* The cylinder turned three times, the hammer falling on empty chambers inside the gun.

Click! Click! Lucas continued to pull the trigger, hoping to at least hear a thunderous roar. But the gun held no bullets. Even if Jabar had forced Ali to take the gun from him in the bathroom, Ali would have pulled out an unloaded gun on his fellow students.

"Jabar is a terrorist wanna-be!" Lucas said. "He took his dad's gun to school, without even checking it for bullets!"

A low snicker drifted up the corridor. Achmed Waziri pressed the trigger on the taser he held as he stepped out of the darkness. Sparks of blue light illuminated the narrow features of his face. His gray-streaked hair and his ratty V-shaped beard gave him a goat-like appearance. He growled, "Give me the gun!"

Clambering down the rungs to the floor of the sewer beside Ali, Lucas shoved the pistol into the waistband of his ragged jeans. Goblin fiercely growled at Waziri as he closed in on the two boys. He raised the taser and blue sparks sizzled within its metal prongs. "Hand it over, or I zap you with this!"

Ali stood there, terrified. Lucas's defiance disorder was kicking in big time. This man may have been terrifying Ali, but his crude tactics were setting off a rebellious rage inside of Lucas.

Waziri lunged at him. Lucas dodged a strike from the crackling prongs of the taser. Waziri crashed into the cement wall in the place Lucas had just vacated. Lucas ripped the Maglite out of Ali's grasp. Ali and Goblin yelped in alarm and wheeled around, fleeing down the corridor they had traveled to get there.

Pup and kid came face to face with Lobo silently slinking up the center of the tunnel. The big pit ignored the two as they cowered on the floor before him, totally focused on the dark-clad man attacking Lucas. Lucas's eyes widened in surprise when he saw Lobo. *Attack him!* his thoughts screamed. *Bite him!*

And though he knew it wasn't possible, he imagined he heard the pit bull say inside his head, *I find things. I find drugs. I find guns. I find things that blow up. My handler has never asked me to attack. He instructed me to find you. I have done so. My task is over here. If I injure this man, there will be consequences. I will be listed as a vicious dog. I will be quarantined, maybe even put to sleep. There are some things even my handler can't protect me from.*

Chapter Eighteen

Waziri launched an attack. Lucas whacked him hard in the face with the Maglite. The taser flew out of his hand and he fell to the floor of the tunnel. Ali peered down the corridor. "Someone is coming!"

Reason's voice came some distance down the passage: "Lobo? You up there, boy? Where did you get to?"

Lobo gave a soft whine. Lucas whispered, "Go, boy. Go meet up with your master. Sounds like he's worried about you."

Lobo took off down the tunnel, barking a greeting even as he ran.

Lucas, Ali, and Goblin whirled around, racing in the opposite direction. Three blocks ahead of them, a circle of white light marked the exit of the tunnels. If they ran in silence, perhaps they could enter into the railroad yards and slip away into the night.

As they ran, Lucas crammed the pistol into the waistband of his jeans. When they came to the end of the tunnels, the little pup would have plunged into the pond before them. As it was, he tottered on the rim of the tunnel, the scummy waters of the pond before him. "Skirt the pond," Lucas instructed Ali as he scooped up the pup and leaped down to the bank to the right of the exit point. He landed solidly on the grassy bank. A second later, Ali came down beside him.

Lucas tossed down the Maglite as the moon was bright overhead. "Stick to this path. It leads past sets of railroad tracks and over to a hole in the fence. Been in and out of there hundreds of times."

Ali screeched in terror when Waziri suddenly shoved him out of his way to get to Lucas. The Muslim man punched Lucas in the center of his back, sending him down to perform a face plant on the hard ground. Goblin flew from his hands, the gun slipped out of his waistband, and for moments, Lucas struggled to breathe. Blackness swirled at the edge of his mind, and he nearly passed out.

Waziri scooped up the gun, then headed for the opening in the fence forty feet ahead of him. "He has the gun!" Ali cried.

"Jesus!" Lucas snapped, clambering slowly to his knees. "To hell with that damned gun! Did you see how hard he hit me?"

Waziri was just approaching the hole in the fence when Ali made a running leap, wrapping his arms around his legs. Waziri raised the gun, preparing to send it down into Ali's upturned face.

Poof!

The sound caused Lucas to stare up at Waziri in bewilderment, his eyes fixed on the red-feathered dart stuck in the center of the man's forehead. And then, Khalid was there, the bottom end of his cane emitting a cloud of smoke from the opening the dart had came from. Waziri fell to one knee. Khalid reached down and took the pistol from him. Waziri struggled to his feet, and staggered back into the tunnel, vanishing into the dark depths.

A little surprised to see Reason there with Khalid, Lucas picked up Goblin and headed toward the fence. Scrambling through the hole, Ali and Lucas reached the sidewalk running adjacent to the train yards. Reason and Khalid followed the boys.

It wasn't until they were three blocks away from the yards that Lucas gestured at Khalid's cane and said, "What are you? A Muslim James Bond?"

Khalid said, "During the Kennedy assassination in 1963, there were rumors that a fleshette fired the fatal bullet. I dismissed this because a high-caliber firing device installed in the unstable casing of an umbrella defied logic. The bullet that blew through Kennedy's head had not been a mere .22. Based on the designs of a fleshette, I paid a gunsmith in Iraq to fashion a similar device inside my cane. He installed a CO2 powered device to send a dart down its barrel. Many assassins use lethal potions on their darts. I use tranquilizers."

By the time, they reached the Karim house, Lucas was dead on his feet. Ali led him into his bedroom, where he graciously offered him his bed, saying he would take a place on the floor since Lucas was a guest of honor. Lucas did not argue. He slipped into the bed. Ali grabbed an extra pillow and blanket from his closet. Just before spreading the blanket on the carpeted floor beside the bed, Ali picked up Goblin, placing him beside Lucas. Lucas was asleep within seconds of his head hitting the pillow.

In the kitchen, Khalid studied the pistol with the engravings of the dragon on the butt and barrel. Retrieving a screwdriver from a kitchen drawer, he removed the ivory piece, exposing the thumb-drive resting inside the butt. Placing the gun back on the counter, Khalid held the drive up. "Let's find out what's on this."

As he slipped the drive into his laptop, Khalid said, "Waziri is the high priest of a sect that follows a Canaanite god, Moloch. As an anti-terrorist agent I was sent here to hunt him down. I'm known as the Hound due to my *dogged* persistence tracking down terrorists."

He narrowed his eyes as he read from the screen, "It is an article, *Havelock, Home to Dogs of War.* Years ago, service dogs were discarded in foreign countries. Too expensive to ship them back. The military did not have the resources to care for them. Now, all US dogs are sent back here and adopted or used by law enforcement. This article is about Thunder Dogs, a litter of pups born on Pine Ridge on a night the Thunder Beings were active. A Lakota holy man gifted these pups to a company of Cheyenne K9 handlers, the Ghost Company. They led dozens of bomb-finding raids in Iraq, surviving many missions as they brushed up against the Otherworld.

"In Mosul in 2014, a deadly weapon was left behind: A cache of cobalt-60 inside a therapy machine, ingredients of a dirty bomb. The Ghosts were sent to find it. They played a game of cat and mouse with the Vipers led by Waziri. The Ghosts found the machine. Rather than alert the Vipers, the Ghosts led them on a chase and ended up trapped at a dead end in the city. They were rescued by my Phantom agents and I. The followers of Moloch never did find the cobalt-60. When they discovered it was a unit of K9 handlers who humiliated them, causing them to be the laughing stock of the world, the Vipers put out contracts on the dogs, shipped out of the war zone and placed at a rescue ranch. The Ghosts now work at the compound, helping service dogs transition from other war zones. There are two-hundred dogs at Wounded Arrow, owned by Lakota dog handler, Ben Black Bull. The directives on this drive instruct Waziri to use the Deep Nine dust in the ventilation system where the dogs are kept."

Looking up from his laptop, Khalid said, "As an honored guest here, if I can prevent Waziri from causing harm on your soil, I will."

Chapter Nineteen

The next morning, after waking Lucas up, Reason walked him over to the Holland house to gather extra clothes for the kid. On the walk over, Reason said, "Agent Raynes put an ABP out on you, I asked Judge Sully if I could provide emergency foster care for you. Sully agreed, and so here I am. Beef Tory is still recovering from inhaling the chemicals. Despite his own brush with the dust that nearly killed him, he showed Khalid's phone recording to the city attorney. Cops need to question Crow before they release your dad. The county attorney is keeping your dad in custody since the powder contained in that packet was laced with Deep 9. Beef called Wounded Arrow and warned Ben about Waziri's plans. I uploaded the story. Due to my story on *Storm Haven*, American Vets are guarding Wounded Arrow to prevent these Vipers from taking revenge on the Ghosts."

Lucas stared at him. "This is all good, right? So, what's wrong?"

Reason said, "Ben called and asked me to get Grunge away from Nate by any means possible. You do know Grunge, right?"

At the mention of the notorious fighter, Lucas felt really bad. Ben had entrusted the care of Goblin and Grunge into his hands when he'd returned home to live with Stone. Goblin had been accepted into Stone's house, but because of Grunge's reputation as King of the Ring, he had ended up in the kennels behind Nate's place. Tears came unbidden to his eyes because he knew Grunge was to be thrown into the fighting ring at the Barn very soon.

A sudden rumble came from the front of the Holland house. Lucas ran down the hallway. Peering out through the screen door, he watched the rider park his Harley in front of the Holland house and shut it down. Tall and rangy, his long, gray hair reminded Lucas of a wolf. He thought, *Aragorn from the Lord of the Rings.*

The man approached Reason, the ghost of a smile on his weathered face. "Why are you standing on Stone Holland's porch, son? I thought you didn't like big, bad bikers."

After a heavy sigh, Reason responded, "Hi, Dad."

Lucas stepped out onto the porch. "Rain Nelson is your dad, Reason? President of the Outlaws? Why didn't you tell me this?"

Reason said, "Dad, this is Stone's son, Lucas. He's been placed in my custody while Stone is in jail."

Lucas said, "Dad told me long ago the Angels came to Lincoln to settle a fight between the Screaming Eagles and the Association. The

Angels disbanded the Association, creating Nomads, who later became the Den. The Angels tried to shut the Den down. Dad said you had a face-to-face with the president of the Angels in Omaha, asking him to ban the Elder's Den here in Havelock."

Rain gave a rueful grin. "This is touching, the history of the Den and Outlaws, but I got a call from your dad. You are on the radar of the Apaches. Crow Harper insulted the Juarez cartel, and they are pissed at him about cancelling some dogfight you interfered in. Cops are looking for him. They won't release Stone until they hear Crow's side of the story. Stone wants the guy off the streets. I need to go to church with the Den. Let's go there, now."

The three of them walked behind the Holland house and to the red barn at the back of the property. In a parking lot adjacent to the alley were thirty Harleys, most chopped and sporting ape-hanger handle bars. Church was in session. Lucas pounded on the door. The door of the barn opened and the warlord of the Den stepped outside.

Tall, slender with shoulder-length raven hair, due to his Romani blood-line, Gypsy was Cingane with a family heritage that stretched back to Wallachia when Gypsies roamed that countryside in painted wagons. Lucas had heard tales of Vlad the Impaler so many times from Gypsy that he knew them by heart. The dark-skinned man had been his dad's right-hand man for twenty years. And yet, Gypsy also had a history with Rain of the Outlaws, having once rode with them. Gypsy's black eyes flickered over to Reason, while Rain made his case to be allowed into the Den's council meeting. "Yes," he said, "I grant you permission to attend church, Rain. And you, Writer, if you'll tell us about this plot to kill service dogs."

Despite Gypsy's objections, Lucas followed them into the barn, then stood before the large, oak council table, and due to protocol, waited in silence. At the sight of Rain, Nate lurched to his feet. "What the hell, Gypsy?"

Gypsy said, "Stone sent him here."

Nate said, "When did Stone ever allow trespassers into church?"

Rain said, "Stone called me from jail. He was worried about his son. Seems he got himself in the crosshairs of Crow Harper, Apache from the Big O. I'm here to put the Elder's Den on full alert."

Nate said, "Message received. Little Luke can stay with me until Stone gets released. The Den will place him on a 24/7 watch."

Rain said, "Stone doesn't want Lucas staying with you. Instead, he wants you to get things settled with this cartel."

Lucas scanned the faces of the Den members, expecting to see them all glaring at the Outlaw, yet finding instead, that they were all staring at Nate, unreadable expressions on their faces. Rain glanced at Nate. "The Angels have their own problem with this cartel at the moment. We don't need any sparks flying between the Outlaws and the Den. You understand?"

Giving Rain an ugly sneer, Nate slowly nodded.

Lucas said. "Do you have my dog?"

Nate replied, "Do I look like I have a dog on me?"

Gypsy said, "Lucas? Go out to the kennel. Get the dog there."

"Damn you, Gypsy!" snapped Nate.

Lucas exited the barn through the back door and immediately spotted Grunge. He opened the kennel gate, receiving a good dose of attention from him. The big Brindle pit trailed him out to the street to Reason's van. Lucas opened the side door, ushering him inside, closing the door. The moment he stepped back the barn, he looked over at Reason and said, "He's safe inside the van."

Suddenly remembering the reward that Reason had given him for returning Lobo, Lucas said, "Uncle Nate, Grunge is fighting this weekend, right? Would two-hundred dollars buy him a pardon?"

Nate said, "I've got five-hundred placed on Grunge to win against some killer wolf dog! You got five-hundred squirreled away in those pockets of yours, Little Luke?"

Lucas dug into his pocket and withdrew the hundred dollar bills. He slapped them down on the table, "There, I'll owe you three!"

Nate's asked, "Where did you get this, Little Luke?"

Rain said, "You're talking about Grunge, right? It's a shame what has become of such a noble dog." He removed his billfold from a back pocket of his jeans. He opened it, pulled out a one-hundred dollar bill, and placed it on top of the other two on the council table. Nate snorted, "Three-hundred? Don't quite cut it, dude."

There was a stir amongst the Den club members, and Gypsy, Toker, Big Charlie, and Ratchett had placed their own money on the table directly in front of Lucas. The gesture brought tears to Lucas's eyes. He quickly wiped at his cheeks before they ran down his face. Nate said, "Seven-hundred? What about the fight?"

Rain said, "Scrap this particular fight. Besides, if you and the kid were playing Chess, he put you in Check. I admire his spunk."

Gypsy looked at Reason. "Writer, tell us about this terrorist threat to destroy service dogs."

Chapter Twenty

Khalid placed a pistol on a shelf in the kitchen, when Ali stepped through the kitchen doorway. "Father," he said. "I am hungry."

"Okay, my son," Khalid said. "I shall feed you."

For several moments, Khalid busied himself placing a glass of milk and a box of graham crackers on the kitchen table. The phone rang on the kitchen counter. Ali, dipping a graham cracker in his glass of milk, noted his father's rigid stance. Khalid answered the phone, saying, "Agent Raynes, I know Waziri has obtained another of the Viper pistols. And you think the tracking device inside the gun will give you warning before Waziri makes his move? I appreciate your surveillance, but I have prepared for a possible visit by him."

Khalid eyed the pistol he had just placed on the nearby shelf. It was a Mosin Nagant, complete with a sound suppressor. The Hound was an experienced hunter. He had stalked dozens of extremist prey to their safe houses. Each time, he'd caught his targets unprepared for his deadly attack. He had succeeded on each of these missions only because the terrorists had become careless. He would not make the same mistake they had. He was armed and ready.

Hanging up the phone, he said, "You, my son, go and visit Lucas at Reason's house. Authorities have not yet released his father. The boy might enjoy your company."

Ali said, "He has unclean dogs in his home. The Quran says—"

"My son," Khalid said, "Allah looks kindly on those who care for the creatures he has created. Many great followers of Islam have owned noble hounds throughout history. Some to guard their houses. Some to hunt with. Others to just grow fat and lazy."

Khalid picked up a large envelope. "Make certain Reason gets this dossier of Waziri. If I am forced to eliminate him, this dossier should prevent me from ending up like Lucas's dad."

Ali said, "I listened last night to your phone call to Iraq. You asked about a green light. What did you mean by that?"

Khalid wanted to end their conversation on a good note. It could be the last time that they spoke to each other, and he did not want to send his son away thinking he was disappointed in him.

Forcing a slight smile, Khalid said, "Ali, you do know Waziri is a bad man, right? The threat on the service dogs is bad enough, but his cell is responsible for the bombing of a mosque in Iraq. One that killed dozens of women and children. An indiscriminate bombing not carried out on enemy insurgents, but upon innocents there that day to worship Allah. Waziri is an evil man. The worst of the worst.

"And I have been given a green light to take him out, my son."

***

For a kid with such low self-esteem, Lucas felt good about himself. Reason said, "Rules were broken to allow you in church, yet the diplomatic skills you showed maneuvering your uncle into that deal over that dog were awesome. If some ghostly scribe is keeping track of biker history somewhere beyond the clouds, I'm sure his ink was barely dry on the page when you brought Grunge's fight to the council table. Amazing, kid, simply amazing!"

Most of his life, Lucas put up with his dad's belittling, figuring that it just came with the territory of being the son of a biker president. Any time he got into trouble at school, Lucas knew he had coming whatever punishment his dad dealt out to him. Stone had no parenting skills, nor was he the nurturing type, and yet rarely did he lay a hand on him. But still, he did psychological damage addressing his son's behavior problems with angry tirades that rolled around inside his head for days afterward. Lucas often sat in school, listening to his fellow classmates complaining about a scolding they received from their parents. *Yeah,* he thought, *boo hoo! Try these words on, you crybabies! Twisted! Mental! Wrongly-wired! Retarded! Happens all the time at my house. My dad is a real motivational speaker when he wants to be!*

Lucas had never had anyone talk so positively about him like Reason did. "Thanks," he finally managed to say, turning his head so Reason couldn't see how red his face was turning at such praise.

Reason laughed. "And no dog had a better advocate for his cause, Lucas. You did good, kid."

Lobo nosed Reason's left hand, while Goblin wormed his way beneath his right one. Reason hugged each one, then turned to exit through the side door. Rain approached the van. He said, "Heading out to Wounded Arrow to make sure the boys have a welcoming party for these damned terrorists. The Den is parking an RV in your driveway. Gypsy is posting two club members inside for a watch on Lucas due to this threat by Crow. See you later, son."

Reason quietly said, "Yeah, see you, Dad."

On the drive back over to Reason's house, Lucas eye-balled him. "Do you have a gun?"

"That," Reason said, "is a long story. It all started with a murdered narc named Kelly Drake. Later, I wrote a book about her. My
dad, an Irishman to the core, claims this whole story is like a Celtic
Hoop, one strand of fate interweaves with another, and like a snake
chasing its tail, it keeps circling back to impact my life.

"You see, when I was a kid, I stumbled across the evidence to
solve her murder. I had a run-in with the man who killed her: Jack
Holland, your grandfather. Your uncle Nate vowed vengeance for his
death. And that's the reason I got a gun."

Lucas said, "I never knew my grandfather. Sounds like Grandpa
Jack was a bad man."

Reason said, "He was."

"Uncle Nate blames you for his death?" Lucas asked.

"That," Reason said, "is a story for another time."

Chapter Twenty-One

Ali sat there on the front porch, looking up to greet them as Reason pulled his van into his driveway. Lucas exited the van, setting Goblin on the ground, while Reason ushered Grunge inside the house to meet Lobo. Satisfied when the two dogs sniffed each other and gave each other head bumps, Reason stepped back outside onto the front porch.

Ali handed him the envelope. He said, "From my father, so he does not end up in jail like Lucas's father."

Reason asked, "Has something happened to your father?"

Ali sniffled. His small nose scrunched up as worry lines creased his brow. "It is not what has happened, but what is soon to happen."

Reason said, "Your father is in danger?"

"Yes," Ali said. "But not the danger you are thinking. He is the Hound, a title he earned as an Agent of Phantom. He is a dangerous man. He portrays himself as a kindly man devoted to his faith, one who is scholarly, educated, and well-refined. But he is a badger. If Waziri invades our house to assassinate the Hound, he will die."

Lucas knew that Khalid may be facing Waziri sent to kill him. He admitted that he should not care, saying, "My own dad would be ashamed of me for even wanting to defend a Muslim, but he didn't see Khalid handle himself when Nate and Crow attacked him. And that encounter with Waziri at the train yards? Hell, he shot a dart into his forehead, using only his cane! If you let me get Big Charlie and Ratchett from the RV, we could go over there and—"

"Have a shoot-out?" Reason said. "Great idea, Lucas!"

In a huff, Lucas stormed off to the backyard, Ali and Goblin trailing behind him. As a safeguard, Reason stationed himself in his den where he could keep an eye on the two boys as he read the dossier Ali had given him. Lobo and Grunge whined, knowing that Goblin had gone outside with Lucas and Ali. Reason said, "Take a nap."

The dogs turned and with grunts of displeasure, sprang up, planting their front paws on the windowsill. It only took Reason minutes to discover how dangerous Waziri was. His terror attacks took up a page in the files. He had grown up as a boy radicalized by this sect of Moloch. He had vowed to take the fight to America, but France and Spain also felt the burn. Bombings in all four countries were attributed to the sect of Moloch, carried out by Waziri.

***

Lucas sauntered over to the back gate. He shot a wary look toward the house, where he saw Reason seated at his desk in his den. When certain he wasn't looking his way, he gestured to Ali as he opened the gate and darted out into the alley.

Nearly tripping over Goblin who eagerly followed Lucas out into the alley, Ali said, "Have you no sense of honor? Reason has opened his home to you, and this is how you repay him?"

For a moment, Lucas felt bad. Ali was always one to do the right thing in any circumstance, even when a psycho killer might be headed for his house and gunning for his dad. And Lucas appreciated the fact that Reason had stepped up to the plate, intervening when Agent Raynes had wanted him locked up. He felt bad that he was breaking Reason's trust, but his defiance disorder overruled those feelings. "Do you want to save your dad?" Lucas asked.

Ali stepped into the alley, closing the gate behind him. "Have you not heard anything I have said, Lucas? I do not fear for my father. He is capable of dealing with these assassins. Besides, these men would not hesitate to kill you. In fact, they would enjoy doing so."

Lucas continued on down the alley, Goblin loping behind him. "If it was my dad, I would want to do everything I could to save him."

Spurred to anger by the remark, Ali said, "Do not question my loyalty. I love my father as much as you do yours, Lucas Holland!"

Lucas quickened his pace, his sights on the end of the alley, when suddenly, Goblin came to an abrupt halt, his gaze fixed on the last garage at the opening to the alley. Growls and barks erupting from his tiny mouth, he leaped up, planting his front paws on Lucas's knees. His claws made scraping sounds on the fabric of his jeans.

"Look," Ali whispered, "Someone is hiding beside that garage!"

Lucas said, "There's no one—"

Yes, there is! came a soft voice inside his head. *There is danger there! Do not go any farther! There is a man waiting there!*

Lucas gasped. *Goblin?* he thought. *Are you speaking inside my head? Can I hear you just like I did Lobo in the tunnels? Is this some sort of mind trick pulled by a dog?*

No trick, came the soft, child-like voice inside his head. *There is a man at the end of the alley who means you great harm!*

Lucas gasped, "Holy crap! This pup is talking to me!"

Ali kept his gaze fixed on the alley opening. "So am I, Lucas! Let's just go back inside Reason's house!"

Snorting an astonished laugh, Lucas said, "That's what Goblin just said inside my head! This happened once before with Lobo back in the tunnels. I can hear dogs? Either that or I am losing my mind!"

***

Reason hurried into his den. He removed his 9 millimeter Ruger from his gun safe. He tucked it into the back of his jeans, draping his shirt over it, for fear some neighbor would be alarmed by an armed man running down the streets of Havelock. Before closing the safe, Reason seriously thought about what he was about to do. When he'd first purchased his gun, he had checked the laws in regard to shooting a home invader. If the invader had broken into his home and was armed, then it would be justified to shoot him. The key words being: Inside the house. He had read stories of home invaders getting shot after they had entered a house. The law was specific when it came to shooting them. There was a good chance the shooter, whether he owned the property or not, would be cited for homicide if he shot and killed someone merely trespassing.

Thinking of another way to deal with Waziri, he removed the handcuffs he kept in the safe. As he turned to exit the den, he looked out the window and saw that Lucas, Ali, and Goblin had vanished.

Chapter Twenty-Two

Nooooo! came Goblin's voice inside his head.

Unnerved by the spooky way he could actually hear the pup's thoughts, Lucas glanced back in bafflement. The next thing he knew a burly biker with dreadlocks stepped out from beside the last garage at the end of the alley. Running at full bore, Lucas ran right into him, performing a painful face-plant on the big man's stomach.

"Gotcha!" Crow Harper said, grabbing at him.

Shoving himself away from the Apache president, Lucas ducked beneath his grasping hands. Before Crow could close in on him, Goblin darted boldly between them, placing himself directly in front of Lucas. The pit pup growled fiercely at the grungy biker.

"Shut up!" Crow snapped as he reached down and snatched the pup up into his grasp. Grabbing onto the scruff of his neck, he drew a gun from beneath his sleeveless jean jacket. Even as Goblin began to squirm, Crow planted the muzzle of his pistol against the pup's head. "Come with me or I will put a bullet in this flea bag's head!"

Click! echoed across the alley, causing Crow to freeze.

"I've never shot a man before," Reason said, taking a firmer grip on his pistol as he shoved the muzzle up against Crow's left temple. "But if you don't lower that pup to the ground, Harper, I swear I'll send you to see Jesus!"

Lucas stood there caught off guard by Reason appearing behind the ruthless biker. Lucas sprang forward and snatched Goblin out of Crow's grasp. Crow attempted to wheel around, but Reason struck him forcefully in the side of his head with the butt of his gun, dropping him to his knees. Crow groaned and his gun fell from his hand, even as blood spilled from the cut on his head.

"Lucas! Ali!" Reason said, removing his cuffs from his back pocket. "Take Goblin and get back inside the house! Now!"

Reason snapped one cuff on Crow's right wrist, then forced the biker over to a metal dumpster beside the garage, his eyes on the handle on the side of the metal container. Reason snapped the cuff onto the handle. Crow slumped down beside the dumpster. Goblin followed Lucas as he ran down the street. "I'm heading to your house!" Lucas said over one shoulder.

Ali said, "Next time, listen to me! You are bullheaded always! If we get to my house and Waziri is there, listen to me, or you might die from your own stupidity!"

Khalid sat in his reclining chair in the living room of his house. Beside him on the end table was his Mosin Nagant. It was a powerful weapon. Khalid was confident he would only need one shot to eliminate the threat that Waziri posed. As an agent of Phantom, he knew exactly where to place a bullet to wound or kill. In the case of Waziri, he had determined his one shot would be fatal.

As a follower of Moloch, Waziri had left a trail of blood and tears in his wake on his own personal jihad, and there was no chance of de-programming him. And Khalid thought, *I can justify taking a mad man's life, considering all the tragedies in his lame belief that causing such catastrophes is pleasing to Moloch.*

Khalid had always been conflicted when it came to his sworn duty to take another man's life. He often thought it ironic how easily some Muslims could kill in the name of Islam. He was never certain Allah condoned such killings. Having been a devoted believer in Islam, he knew there were millions of Muslims who had never taken a life. Khalid referred to this as good sense, and Islam had inspired him to be a good person. A good husband. A good father. He had never felt obligated to carry out senseless killings. And now that he had two men coming to his house to eliminate him, what choice did he have?

He heard a noise. It came from the back patio. Earlier, he had considered moving out there to await the arrival of those coming to kill him. The confrontation with Waziri was going to be bloody. Slowly picking up the pistol beside him on the end table, Khalid now wished he had taken up a defensive position outside on the patio. He was confident. As an expert marksman, he would place his bullets skillfully with head shots to avoid sending hot lead flying. He did not wish to place any of his fellow neighbors in danger. He had brought this fight to the suburb of Havelock, and the last thing he wanted to do was to create a tragedy in an American city.

The noise came again.

It sounded like someone had bumped into one of the three metal lawn chairs situated on the patio. Khalid was sure he'd heard it. He looked toward the two glass doors leading to the patio. He'd opened the shades as an open invitation to Waziri to try the unlocked door. Flicking off the safety on his pistol, he arose and swiftly moved down the hallway and into his bedroom. Holding the gun out to one side, he peeked outside through a crack in the curtains. Movement came from the back of the garage. Khalid spotted Waziri blending with the thick shrubbery at the back of the patio.

The man was an expert in hand-to-hand combat. He could move with lightning speed, using fists, feet, or knives to do damage to his victims. But today, Khalid saw that the big man was armed with a silenced pistol. Waziri was lean with a hawkish nose. He gestured at someone near the house, signaling his accomplice to stand down. Which seemed odd to Khalid.

A faint *whoosh!* of sound came from the kitchen. Khalid knew at once the sliding glass door had been opened, and someone entered the house. Khalid took his pistol in a two-fisted grip and started toward the kitchen. He said, "Achmed, if it is me who walks away from this, I assure you I will get a message to your son, letting him know your passing was swift. How odd isn't it that we both traveled here to America, and our sons end up in the same school? If us fathers had adapted here and assimilated, maybe our sons could have one day played together as most boys do."

The voice that came from the kitchen startled Khalid: "Shut up, you dog! Be prepared to eat a bullet!"

Khalid entered the kitchen, his pistol raised. He looked into the dark eyes of the assassin that had come to kill him and froze, unable to pull the trigger. He lowered his gun. "If you were my son, he would ask himself if I would really want him to do this thing. Taking a life is a serious matter. If you end my life, all you will accomplish is placing sorrow in your father's heart by being separated from him when the US courts sentence you to prison."

Jabar puffed up his chest. "I am not Waziri's son! My father was killed in Iraq! I am a Warrior! Waziri is my handler! Prepare to die!"

Khalid said, "Walk away from this, son—"

"I am not your son!" Jabar snarled. "You did not lose a father! Achmed recruited me to come here posing as his son! When I have accomplished my task, I will be a legend! Drop your gun!"

The gun clattering on the floor at his feet, Khalid offered Waziri a glare as he entered the kitchen. "It is a mistake to involve children in your terror attacks. You create time-bombs, recruiting innocent children who should have been playing kickball in some dusty field. Children should never have been infused with so much hatred and condemnation of anyone who does not accept your faith. You have nothing more than a brain-washed child who lamely believes that killing pleases Moloch. Now, how do you reel him in?"

Chapter Twenty-Three

When they reached Ali's front porch, Lucas guided Goblin through the door while Ali darted inside and ran past Khalid standing at the kitchen doorway. It took the little Muslim boy seconds to realize Jabar stood there, his gun aimed at his father.

In that instant, Jabar latched onto Ali, looped his free arm around his neck and drew him against him. Planting the muzzle of his pistol against Ali's head, he snarled, "Hound, I will kill your pup!"

"No!" Khalid cried as he stepped forward to prevent such a tragedy from taking place. Jabar placed his back against the kitchen wall, holding Ali in his grasp. "Stop! Or I will shoot this maggot!"

Khalid immediately moved back to his place at the kitchen doorway. Sliding the muzzle of the pistol up against Ali's left temple, Jabar said, "Moloch commands me to kill heretics! This is the son of the biggest heretic to our faith! It would please Moloch to kill him!"

Lucas latched onto Goblin and steered him away from the kitchen doorway. As he tugged on the pup to guide him into the living room, he noticed Khalid's cane resting against his couch. "Stay!" he said to Goblin, while he reached for the cane.

He listened to the terse words being spoken in the kitchen, his eyes on Khalid's backside in the doorway. He examined the trigger on the cane, switching off the safety to one side of the trigger. He then tried to work up the courage to bolt into the kitchen and arm Khalid with his cane.

Before he could move, Goblin ran into the kitchen. At the sight of the pup, Jabar gave a startled cry of dismay, peering down at Goblin as if he carried the Plague. The pup caused the boy to lose his composure as he sniffed at his shoes. Ali latched onto Jabar's wrist, forcing the pistol away from his head. It was then that Lucas entered the kitchen, watching as Waziri raised his gun. Khalid slapped his right wrist down against his thigh. At once, a slender knife shot from the spring-loaded device attached to his wrist and buried itself in Waziri's right shoulder, causing the pistol to fall from his hand.

Lucas raised the cane and aimed its tip at Jabar. *Hissss!* A breath of air released from the CO cartridge inside the cane sounded like the hiss of a viper. A second later, a dart appeared in Jabar's forehead. He fell back, still holding onto the gun. Lucas slammed the cane down on Jabar's right wrist, sending the pistol flying from his hand. Jabar peered up at him with glazed eyes.

He swooned, and slumped to the floor, unconscious.

Waziri wheeled around and exited through the open sliding door. Agent Raynes was just approaching Khalid's house when she had a fraction of a second to notice the blood leaking from the man's shoulder when he backhanded her. Raynes sailed backward into the bole of a tree at the center of the yard. She struggled to rise, but the blow to her head had knocked her senseless. Waziri hovered above her fallen form, a knife in his hand raised to strike. He found himself facing Khalid who appeared in front of him. Slashing at him with the knife, he latched onto the dazed Raynes, using her as a shield to get past Khalid and hastily climb into a van parked in the street. Raynes groaned as Waziri raced past them, speeding down the street.

***

Reason heard loud knocking coming from his front door. Shushing the barking of the two dogs, he went to the door and opened it. It was Nate Holland, the red lettering on his leather jacket depicting the words, *Elder's Den*. Before Nate could say anything, the rumble of Harleys came from the street behind him. Nate looked to the four bikers pulling into Reason's driveway. Reason read the patches on their leather jackets: *Apaches*.

As Lobo and Grunge stepped outside beside Reason, Nate held his hands up in surrender. The four bikers shut down their bikes. The largest member of the Apaches, a giant with red hair and a braided beard, nailed Nate with a cold stare. "Where's Crow?" he growled.

Nate said, "Well, he's not here."

The red-haired giant turned his head, his dark eyes settling on Reason. "You're him, aren't you? The Outlaw they called the Celt."

Reason eyed him back. He was six inches shorter than the giant, and the red-head outweighed him by two-hundred pounds. The giant glanced back at the three Apaches standing behind him, letting Reason know he had their backing should things go south.

"Red," said the rat-faced Apache with greasy blond hair to the left of the giant, "check the dogs? That's El Lobo and Grunge!"

All four of the Apaches looked to Lobo standing beside Reason. "Celt," Red said, "the plan is for your award winner here to be pitted against a wolf dog owned by the Juarez cartel. Surely you would want to make ten-thou if Lobo kills the Beast."

Nate said, "Red, you guys go find Crow. Let me deal with the Celt." Red offered him a frown. "Yeah, we need to find Crow."

79

The four bikers started up their bikes, and slowly rode away.

Reason kneeled beside Lobo, and the pit rolled over on his back, exposing his stomach to his master. Reaching down to stroke the dog's chest and belly, he said, "Do you know how much trust a dog places in their owner when they roll over on their back, exposing their entire belly to you? A certain honor passes between dog and owner. Before dogs descended from the Gray Wolf, they used to do this in their pack to establish trust, placing their lives in the teeth of an Alpha male who could easily tear out the submissive wolf's throat if it chose to do so. Today, when a dog rolls over on its back, he is saying, 'I trust you entirely. My life is in your hands. You will either harm me or nurture me. I have placed myself in this position, because I love the attention, but also to honor you by making a statement that I trust you.'

"The dog who does this is sharing a bonding moment with its owner, one that stretches back into time when submitting to an Alpha male built trust among the entire pack. So imagine what it is like for those dogs who are thrown into the fighting ring. They are betrayed by cruel-hearted thugs whose only purpose is to force that dog to be savagely mauled, and oftentimes killed.

"Tragically, these dogs have taken their trust to another level, all for a master who throws their lives away at a whim. I could never in a million years think about throwing my dog's trust away by forcing him into the blood-sport. It would break my heart to have my dog ripped to shreds by another dog who is only trying to please his heartless master. You Dog Men see nothing wrong with having your own dogs savagely killed in the ring. You harm the dogs of this world and Karma's going to be mad bitch in heat one day."

Nate said, "Enough of the lecture. I've got a problem you might help me deal with."

Chapter Twenty-Four

Nate said, "Being an accessory to murder tends to change one's perspective. The shoot-out between the Apaches and the Den up in Omaha this past year? Beef Tory and homicide from Omaha placed me at the scene of the crime. Me and Crow. Tory made us his informants. Either that or Crow and I could go to prison. He involved us in a matter involving real live Arab terrorists, too."

Reason could not believe what he was hearing. For any club member to turn snitch and align themself with law enforcement was the lowest of deeds. One that would result in that biker's death if anyone discovered he was working for a cop. That Nate Holland was telling him this shook him to the core.

Nate said, "I work for Raynes. She wants credit for taking down the Powder King, a chemist who developed that powder, Deep 9. Rumors from Homeland is that there is a terrorist cell wanting to buy the chemical. The chemist produced meth for the Apaches. Crow was setting him up for an arrest by Detective Tory."

Reason nodded. "Why are you trusting me?"

Nate said, "You are my Ace in the hole, Reason. The life span of an informant is short if the wrong people find out about the double life they lead. I am in deep, not only with Tory, but I have ties with the Juarez cartel that places me in a world of hurt. And now because of my little nephew, Juan Juarez has put a price on my head. Waziri paid me big bucks to retrieve these so-called magic rings from you. He claims the rings allow you to call forth powers. All I am asking is you give me one. Or you can continue to look over your shoulder for the rest of your life. Magic rings won't help you if you're dead."

Reason stared at him for long moments. He then said, "What have you been smoking, Nate? Magic rings?"

***

Shortly after the brutal attack in Khalid's kitchen, paramedics carted a sleeping Jabar out of the house. Seated beside Ali at the kitchen table, Lucas was pleased that Jabar would be charged with attempted murder on Khalid. He was also pleased to listen to Agent Raynes getting grilled by her supervisor about how far out of line she was by not informing him of her activities and failing at her plans to arrest Waziri with her rogue operation. During the dressing down her supervisor gave her, Raynes looked once in Lucas's direction, and he smirked at her. He hoped she got canned for her stupidity, and also for the threats she made to have him locked up in detention.

Reason stepped into the kitchen. He shook Khalid's hand and drew Lucas out of his chair. "Time to go home, bud. Call you later, Khalid. You can tell me what happened here."

Khalid offered Reason a sad smile and said, "Lucas can tell you on his ride back to your house. If it wasn't for Lucas and his pup causing a distraction, things might have gone terribly wrong."

Ali blurted, "Will my father be charged with any crimes?"

Raynes looked Khalid. "You acted in self-defense. Although the county attorney is going to want to talk to you, I'll be there to speak on your behalf, Mr. Karim. Your captain in Iraq appraised me of your role as an anti-terrorist agent. Perhaps, we can work together to apprehend Waziri. At this moment, he's in the wind!"

***

Reason drove Lucas away from one crime scene only to drive directly into another. "What the hell?" Lucas said, sliding out of his seat, barely keeping Goblin from doing a nose-plant on the dash. Reason peered through the windshield, amazed to see five cop cruisers blocking the street, and two more parked in the alley.

"Wow," Lucas said, "all these cops just to arrest Crow Harper?"

Reason saw his handcuffs dangling from the handle of the metal dumpster, a spattering of blood running down the side of the metal container. He followed the blood trail down to the alley and spotted what looked like a hand severed at the wrist.

"Oh," Lucas gasped. "Is that a hand?" Behind Reason, Lobo and Grunge growled as a man in a suit approached the driver's side window. "Quiet!" Reason commanded. "It's just Beef Tory."

The dogs wagged their tails. Beef said, "Someone wanted to take Crow. They left his hand behind. Dispatch got a call from a caller saying he had Crow cuffed to a dumpster. Any clue who that was?"

Making direct eye contact with the big ex-biker, Reason was reminded of the days he was still a kid and getting grilled by Beef. "He threatened the kid, so I cuffed him to the dumpster, and put in the call. And Crow had both hands at that point."

Beef looked over at Lucas seated there in the passenger's seat holding Goblin. "Your Uncle Nate and Crow are both on some kind of hit list of this cartel, Lucas. Rescuing Reason's dog, resulted in consequences for two bikers with bad intentions."

82

Resting his chin on Goblin's small head, Lucas said, "If the cartel snatched Crow off the street, then he's dead, right? How is the county attorney ever gonna talk to him?"

Lucas was close to telling Reason about Nate's scheme to sell Lobo to the cartel, building the case against him as to why he'd paid Stone back by having Crow plant the powder in his truck. Instead, he kept his mouth shut. Beef said, "Take Lucas to your house. Read him one of your stories. And put him to bed, a dog on either side."

***

Back at Reason's house, Lucas fed the dogs, then joined Reason in the kitchen where he was making dinner. He said, "You trust this cop, Beef? Both of you used to ride with the Outlaws? Is that true?"

A rush of memories washed over Reason. "It wasn't until I was 14 that I met my dad. My uncle Jessie Dalton told me that Rain was serving time at the State pen. Rain and Jessie are brothers, different mothers same dad. They were raised by their dad, president of the Outlaws. Ten years after the Vietnam war, drugs began to flow into America. Their dad, Chase Nelson, refused to allow the Outlaws to deal drugs. Chase was killed by the Nomad, sent by your great-grandfather Daws. Ten years later, Rain ended up at a rock quarry. Daws Holland planned to kill Rain, and yet Jessie showed up there at the quarry, providing the distraction Rain needed to pull a gun of his own. Daws died. Rain was sentenced to prison for the murder. Beef became a cop, and Jessie became a private eye. He thought by connecting the dots on Jack Holland's dealings, he could one day exonerate his brother for the shooting at the quarry."

Lucas shook his head, causing his blond tangles to swirl away from his eyes. "No wonder you're not a biker. I always thought I was locked into this thing with the club, you know growing up to be a biker like Dad and Uncle Nate. I love Harleys. I love riding in the wind behind my dad when he takes me out on his beast. But even with my red-hot temper that gets me into all kinds of trouble, I don't like the fights or the taste of beer. If you didn't follow in your own dad's footsteps, it means I got a choice, too."

83

Chapter Twenty-Five

Later that night, Lucas confessed that he'd stolen Reason's three rings from the chest in his den. Surprised by his calm attitude, Lucas settled next to his computer desk in a gaming chair. As small as he was, the large chair swallowed his lean frame. He sank deeper into the chair as he asked, "Do you know Gus Howard? Celeste does research for him. He's a writer like you. He collects ancient relics. Gus also dredges up stories about . . . ghosts."

Lobo sent, *He knows you took them, Lucas. I told him about you snooping through his chest. He knows you know they are rings of power. Stop playing games with my master, and he will share the magic of the rings with you.*

Lucas sighed. He drew a single ring out of his pocket. "I gave the other two to Gus Howard to check to see if they were magical. I'm sorry I broke your trust. You can kick me out if you want to."

Five minutes later, Reason, Lucas, and the two dogs stood before a house two blocks away from Reason's place. "I've tried to settle things," Reason said, "with the ghosts of two boys, but they never listen to me. Since you're a kid, maybe they will listen to you."

"Ghosts?" Lucas asked, skeptically. "You believe in ghosts?"

Reason said, "A strange activity took place in Havelock. 75-year-old Lon Dormer told me about George Dormer, the oldest son of his great-grandfather. Lon's family always referred to it as the Dormer curse. Rumor has it two boys had gone hunting and were found shot in the head in a cornfield with their guns lying by their sides. They are buried in the Havelock cemetery, Fairview, and Lon's relatives tell the story every year on Memorial Day when they visit their graves. George was killed at age 9, 1913. Lon's mother once told him there was fire on the two boys' graves, and the mother of the Reese boy wanted to pray them out of purgatory, she was Catholic, but Lon's great-grandmother, a Lutheran, refused to allow that.

"After hearing this story from Lon, I ventured to the Historical Society. I found a fact-based story in the Lincoln News: Sept. 8th, 1913. John Rhys, found dead in a pasture Saturday, fatally wounded George Dormer, his nine-year-old companion, and in remorse shot himself. Powder burns were found upon Rhys, indicating that the weapon had been held close to his breast when the shot that killed him was fired. George Dormer, 9, and John Rhys, 16, were found dead in a pasture north of Havelock. Dr. Ballard, the coroner, said he examined the small boy and found a gunshot to his abdomen made by a .22 bullet. The story made news all over the US. In one story, they were charged by angry, territorial bulls. In another, they shot one another. A third story is they were murdered. This fact-based story makes more sense. Not a murder. An accident. Lon came back to Havelock to visit the lady who lives in his grandparents' house, where George once lived. She spoke about the ghost of a boy wearing a hunting hat seen dozens of times outside the house. It's the ghost of George, trying to get back inside the house. Although I don't encourage taping into the Otherworld for fear of attracting an Unseen entity, I'm going to allow it tonight."

Reason handed the ring to Lucas. "Put it on."

Lucas slipped the ring on his ring finger, and at once, the entire world turned a brilliant shade of violet. Houses and parked cars were a dull blue. The trees and shrubbery were all pulsating with emerald light. Tiny bars of multi-colored light zipped past the van, moving too fast to resemble any shape other than six-inch bars of rainbow colored light. Lucas looked up and saw fairies trailing sparkling dust behind them, their wings fluttering madly as they performed loops and spins above the front lawn. They were tiny magical beings three inches in length. The tiny fairies gave off a violet aura as they flittered about before the house. The entire company of fairies stopped quite suddenly, their gazes fixed on a shimmering at the edge of the yard below them. There, a doorway appeared, blue mist spilling from a plane beyond this one.

When the ethereal figures of two young boys sprang out of the portal, the fairies clapped their hands in glee. One boy wore an orange hunting cap. He stood about 4 feet tall and looked to be a child of ten. The two insubstantial boys began to run across the yard. The smaller ghost sprinted away from the bigger ghost. The bigger boy had his hands outstretched toward the smaller boy as if trying to get him to stop. Even though his features were smoky, Lucas could see the anguish in the older ghost boy's eyes.

"Sweet Jesus!" Lucas said. "The shooting took place over 104 years ago! How many nights has this played out?"

A sudden movement came from the front porch, where the ghost of George Dormer appeared, his hunting hat askew. He darted up the steps to the front door and he began to bang on it. But no one inside could hear him banging from the Otherworld. The ghost of John Rhys came running from the side yard, and the chase was on again.

Lucas stepped forward. "I know what happened to you two."

George snapped, "He shot me!"

The spunky little ghost pointed down at his abdomen where John's .22 bullet had entered and taken his life. Lucas nodded at George. "But look there below his left breast, George. He felt so bad about the fatal injury he caused you, he took his own life."

George studied the hole left in John's chest where he had inflicted his own wound to end his life in remorse for what he'd done. John bowed his head, crystal tears welling up in his eyes.

"Your parents, George," Lucas said, "forgave John, for you were buried close beside each other at Fairview cemetery. With this ring, I see the realm where you've been trapped for over one hundred years. It's time to let go. Time for both of you to move on."

John said, "I'm so sorry, George. Will you please forgive me?"

Slowly, little George Dormer clasped the older boy's hand in his own. They went through a five-step handshake performed in 1913, crossing wrists, slapping palms, releasing with their thumbs pointed to the sky, both were grinning. John wrapped his big arms around George and wept, "Oh, Georgie!"

A moment later, the ghosts of the two boys vanished.

Lucas was in a daze on the walk home. Goblin nuzzled up beside him, while Lobo nudged him on the other. *Shadow companions,* Goblin whispered. *Here to lend you support, Luke.*

Lucas said, "I used magic to send them on their way. I wielded magic. Wolf was right about me being a Thunder Dreamer."

Reason said, "Don't know about this thunder dreamer, but consider this a one-time deal for now. I want my ring back to store it in a safe place. There are others who want to misuse them."

Still shaken by his encounter with the two ghosts, Lucas reached over and dropped the ring in Reason's outstretched hand.

Chapter Twenty-Six

The next morning, Reason drove Lucas, Ali, and the dogs out to the rescue ranch. Only a year ago, Lucas had been placed there with the owner of the ranch. Ben Black Bull, the Lakota dog handler, had a gift for working with damaged dogs, broken vets, and troubled kids. If anyone was a kid whisperer, it was Ben.

At Wounded Arrow, despite his own volatile nature, Lucas had bonded with Grunge. Even as Reason drove them out to the ranch a mile away from Havelock in the country, Lucas remembered that conversation they had about him working with the badly damaged older pit bull. As Reason drove up to the gateway leading to the dog compound, Lucas said, "Stop here."

Reason brought the van to a stop beneath the wooden sign that read, *Wounded Arrow*. "Ben is gonna be mad at me," Lucas said, adjusting Goblin in his lap. The pup was fidgeting with excitement. He knew where they were and he was eager to be reunited with Ben.

"Mad at you?" Ali asked from his place in the backseat.

Lucas made a sour face. "Everything happened so fast when I got returned home after living out here. Ben said I was going to remain with him at least another year, and then Mom got killed in that wreck, and the judge ruled that I be returned to Dad. Me, Grunge, and Goblin ended up back in Havelock within a week after Mom had her wreck. Dad didn't trust Grunge on account of his years in the fight ring. He let me keep Goblin, but Grunge had to live in the kennels behind Uncle Nate's place."

Lucas looked ahead to the assortment of motorcycles parked in a long line to one side of the three large barns taking up the back quarter of Ben's property. He then saw the bikers gathered on the ranch, some walking the fence line armed with guns, positioned in strategic locations. Any attempt to harm the service dogs residing at Wounded Arrow was going to be a difficult task for Waziri and his cell.

"See," Lucas continued, "Ben promised Grunge when he took him in out here that his fighting days were over. This is the reason why Grunge finally settled down and quit being so cantankerous. You should have seen him when he first got here. Because of all those fights he'd been forced into he was a spooky beast. It took a lot of magic to heal his heart. Ben's a gifted dog whisperer. He's got a special talent for bringing some of the most vicious dogs back from the brink of being outright mean and wild. He invites them into the Sacred Hoop, where spirits of hatred and anger from the Other-world cannot attach themselves to them and cause them any more damage. He did the same to me. Maybe we should go back home. Ben has enough to deal with here with all these bikers. I should have called him to let him know Nate had thrown Grunge back into the fights. Ben would have turned Uncle Nate into Cora Red Cloud. Cora's uncle, Colton Lone Wolf, calls himself the Dog Soldier, and he would be more disappointed in me if he found out I did nothing to stop Nate from involving Grunge in the fights."

Lucas focused on the tall, long-haired Lakota stepping out of the center barn. Ben Black Bull was dressed in faded jeans, jean jacket, and dusty cowboy boots. His raven hair flowed back and over his broad shoulders, and his handsome features were creased by a grin as he spoke with Beef outside the dog barn. The two men appeared to be amused by whatever they were discussing. Beef, standing there in his suit, towered over the Lakota dog handler by six inches, and yet Ben met his gaze, even though he had to look up to do so.

Reason let up on the brake and the van began to roll up the drive-way. They were halfway to the dog barns before Ben and Beef looked their way. Beef waved at Reason, and Ben waved a friendly greeting to his former foster son. Fighting hard not to tear up, Lucas placed a hand on Goblin's head and peered at the buffalo scattered across the field to the north of the ranch. "It will be okay," Reason said as he shut the engine down. Knowing that Lucas was having a meltdown, he reached over and patted him on one shoulder. "You stay here. Pull yourself together. Ali and I will go meet Ben. I'll give you some time to gather your wits, okay?"

Lucas nodded, sinking his chin on top of Goblin's head. Grunge sent his thoughts up at him: *Call it a gift, but yes, you can hear me. Listen closely. One evening, while I lay beneath the kitchen table at your dad's house, your dad was angry over Nate forcing me back into the fights. It was during their heated words that Detective Tory showed up. Beef said that in order to get the judge to place you back with your dad, Nate ran your mom off the road. Nate denied it. Beef asked him if he planted an open bottle in her car. Police reported your mom's death as alcohol related. Nate shouted, 'I had nothing to do with Maggie's death, but at least you got your son back! How would you like losing both Lucas and Celeste?'*

Lucas blurted, "Nate's a dirty rotten bastard!"

Yes, Grunge agreed with him. *He is.*

Ben approached the van, grinning at Lucas. Goblin was so excited to see him he squirmed in Lucas's lap until Ben opened the door and picked him up. "Goblin," he said. "Good to see you, little guy!"

After getting reacquainted with the pup, Ben placed him on the ground and turned to greet Lucas. "Since I know you don't go in for hugs, how about a handshake, Lucas?"

Ben reached into the van, clasped his right hand in his, and gently pulled him out of his seat, settling him down between himself and Goblin. "It's really good to see you, kid," he said, a broad grin on his darkly-tanned face. "Did you miss poop patrols out here?"

"Don't remind me," Lucas said, failing to keep his smile in place.

Ben said, "I still haven't found a way to recycle it."

That had been a running joke between them ever since Lucas had moved in at Wounded Arrow. Ben had talked about his neighboring rancher's herd of buffalo, explaining to Lucas that buffalo dung was unlike cow dung, in that it replenished the ground wherever it happened to fall. And he'd added that it was too bad dog waste didn't have the same properties. Or they could find a way to get rich off of the plentiful supply they had always been plagued with.

"How is the big guy?" Ben asked.

Lucas said, "There's been some complications with Grunge."

"Nate took him back to the fights?" Ben asked.

"Yes," Lucas said. "I'm afraid so."

Despite any disappointment he felt about the plight of Grunge, Ben placed a leather thong over Lucas's head. Once settled around his neck, Ben smoothed out the small eagle feather attached to the cord and slipped it inside of Lucas's shirt.

"You left this," Ben said, "Cora thought you should have it."

Lucas reached out and placed his hand over Ben's. "Do you really think I deserve it after I let Grunge down so badly?" he asked.

Ben glanced down at the rare show of affection by Lucas, his hand resting on his own. "Of course," he said, "how else are you ever going to be a Thunder Dreamer?"

Chapter Twenty-Seven

A flood of memories then washed over Lucas as he stood there:

Wolf settled Goblin at his feet, then withdrew a leather cord from beneath his parka. He slipped it around Lucas's neck and settled the three-inch long feather inside of his shirt. "That is an eagle feather, worn by one of the Shirt Wearers, American Horse. A sacred item. In the coming days, you're going to need it. You are supposed to be a special mediator."

He then remembered Grunge let out a soft whine. The big pit got to his feet and walked over to him. He stopped directly in front of him. The moment Lucas's hand came to rest on Grunge's head, he opened his eyes. Tears welled up in Lucas's eyes as he softly said, "Thanks, Grunge. Thanks for trusting me."

Wolf said, "Angry spirits were attracted to you when you disturbed the fabric of the Otherworld with your bitter outbursts. You were infected by these wrathful beings, who fed off of your rage and lent power to your tantrums. You must kick them out, send them packing, or they will torment you the rest of your lives."

Lucas stood there, reminded of the unseen strings that attached Grunge and him together. The two had an emotional bond that could not be broken, and yet Lucas had let the big dog down by not speaking up for him, by not championing him when he should have. "I tried," he said, "to tell Dad what Nate was doing, but Nate held something over Dad's head, something I can't tell you about."

"Biker code, right?" Ben said, frowning.

"I can't be a snitch," Lucas said. "But at church yesterday, I gave two-hundred dollars to pay off Nate's obligation to keep Grunge out of the upcoming fight. Some members of the club chipped in, and so, too, did Reason's dad, Rain Nelson, president of the Outlaws. Nate walked away with seven-hundred dollars."

Ben said, "This is not what Stone agreed to. Grunge deserves better than this."

"Nate," Lucas said, "might try to steal him back, Ben."

"If Nate pulls that," he said, "I'll just go get him back."

Ben gestured over one shoulder at the seven Natives gathered near his dog cemetery on the south side of his ranch. He then firmly added, "And I won't go alone."

***

As Ali and the three dogs joined them, Ben started walking down to the cemetery. He glanced back and said, "Come with me. Beef is taking your writer friend for a tour of the ranch. I am scheduled to hold a ceremony for a dog who recently passed."

A few minutes later, Ben introduced the Cheyenne dog handlers known as the Ghost Company to Lucas and Ali. Five of them were big men, heavily muscled and over six feet tall, their hair military-style short. The other Native wore his hair in a single braid trailing down his back. All six were dressed in black, which reminded Lucas of martial arts clothes, loose-fitting and easy to move in. All six moved with catlike grace as they gathered around a headstone there in the Wounded Arrow dog graveyard.

Lucas blinked in surprise when he saw a large Native rising from beside a grave to join the Ghosts. The big Lakota's salt-and-pepper hair was tied back in a braided tail, and he was dressed in dark jeans and a black duster. Colton Lone Wolf smiled down at Lucas, saying, "Ben informed us that there were some evil men wanting payback. It is a shame that those terrorists now want to exact revenge. In Mosul, our dogs prevented dirty bombs from being built by the Vipers. The Ghost Company is now retired. Three of our dogs are still alive, getting fat and lazy in the homes of three Ghosts who own them. Two are buried out here. And the sixth dog?"

Wolf gestured at the headstone. "Bear was a Brindle given to me by Pete He Dog of Pine Ridge."

"A Brindle?" Lucas said. "Like Grunge?"

Wolf said, "Grunge came from the same line that Bear came from. Same mother and father, just a different litter."

Lucas said, "This is Ali. You guys knew his dad, Khalid, captain of the Phantoms when you were all in Iraq, right?"

All six Cheyenne soldiers looked directly at the small, raven-haired Ali standing there nervously fidgeting. Lucas looked on as each of the Native men stepped forward to shake the kid's hand. Wolf said, "We would not be here if not for your father. You must be very proud of him. Your father is a legend, Ali."

Wolf's dark eyes swept the land to the north. "My sixth sense is telling me that amongst these headstones and these giant pine trees, we are very vulnerable. Hostile eyes watch us."

Ben chided, "Don't be so paranoid, Wolf. We've got bikers from five clubs patrolling the ranch and the pastures bordering my land.

We should be safe to bury Bear without interference from hostile forces." Ben pointed in all four directions of the compass. "Though you might have the creepy crawlies, to the south, we have the massive buffalo herd. To the west, we have the creek, and along its banks are several snipers perched in deer stands. To the east, we have the ridge, the woods, and Kooper Steading. Several soldiers of fortune walk those grounds. And to the north, is Salt Creek winding its way across the Nebraska plains."

"And," Wolf said, eyeing the tree line running along the bank of the creek a mile distance, "that is the direction I am getting the creeps from. Someone is watching us."

Ben placed the urn with Bear's ashes on the headstone, turning it until it clicked, indicating it was settled into place. He removed sage from a pouch around his neck. He used a lighter to burn the sage, sang a Native song in the Oglala Lakota language, the tongue of his people, and tossed pinches of the burnt sage into the four directions. He then removed an arrowhead from a thong around his neck. He placed the arrowhead against Wolf's chest. "May this open," he said, "the fabric of the Otherworld, so that you may give Bear a farewell."

Lucas remembered the story Ben had shared with he and Cora Red Cloud one winter night this past year: *"This talisman," Uncle Pete said, "belonged to Sitting Bull. It is a token of power that will shield you from the Dark Ones. It is endowed with big medicine."*

Wolf sank to his knees. "I can't see him," he whispered. "There are just clouds, shimmering like a misty rainbow. The big Lakota lowered his head, his huge shoulders shaking. "Bear is not there."

Yes, he is, Goblin sent to Lucas a foot away from him. *I can see him resting beside a mountain stream. Use the feather, Lucas. Guide this Native to his dog.*

Lucas stepped up behind the Native who mourned the passing of his dog. He removed the eagle feather from the thong around his neck, and placed it on the back of Wolf's neck. And both Lucas and Wolf gasped as visions exploded in their minds: *A black buck with a 14-point spread, burst through swirling threads of falling snow. The buck's antlers glistened, casting specks of power off into the moonlit trees. The buck continued to run through the winter night. When he emerged from the edge of the tree line, the morning sun greeted him. The buck approached a green land dotted with forests. Fireflies speckled his breast. Specks of lime-green whirled around his antlers as the buck walked up to a Brindle pit bull seated near a stream.*

"Bear!" Wolf called to his dog.

The dog bounded to the left, then darted to the right, and yet his paws never touched the waters separating him from his master. Bear gave one last heart-piercing howl his voice echoed across the rocks of the mountain and engulfed Wolf as he stood there, softly crying. "Bye, boy," the Lakota said. "I'll see you on the Otherside one day. You were loved greatly and will not be forgotten."

Bear barked one last time, then slowly faded from sight.

Chapter Twenty-Eight

Wolf rubbed his neck where the eagle feather had just been. "I seen him," the big Lakota said. He placed a large hand on top of Lucas's shaggy blond head, "thanks to this Thunder Dreamer. The feather that once belonged to American Horse holds great medicine."

The big Native soldier began to share with the rest of the Ghost Company all the things that they had seen. The six Cheyenne stood there, listening attentively, their eyes filled with reverence. Native medicine was not to be taken lightly.

Wolf caused all of them standing there to peer at him in alarm. He spread his arms to reveal the red dot dancing across his chest. "Told you I felt eyes upon us!" he whispered cryptically.

He knew at once it was the red dot of laser beam coming from the scope of a high-powered rifle. Rather than try to take cover behind the headstones surrounding him, Wolf spread his arms wide to let his enemy know he was prepared to take the shot that would end his life. The unknown sniper had him dead to rights, and his death by bullet was inevitable. A second red dot zeroed in on Lucas's chest.

He whispered, "Oh, no!"

Ben dove at Wolf, taking him down with a flying tackle. Goblin lunged up, planting his forepaws on Lucas's back, causing him to topple over to the ground. A second later, a hot lead projectile struck a granite headstone ten feet behind where he had been standing. The bullet shattered the granite, sending pieces in all directions.

The next few minutes were chaotic. Lucas could hear the crackle of walkie-talkies as the ranch came alive with former soldiers trying to communicate with each other at once. He could see the Ghosts had all vanished. He didn't even see them leave the graveyard.

Beef and Reason came from the north end of the ranch to check on Lucas there in the cemetery. Beef spoke quietly to Ben.

"Five of them?" Ben asked, his dark eyes straying to the creek some distance away to the north. "And caught by Cora?"

Before Beef could answer him, the four of them looked across the field in the direction of the creek where a female Lakota dressed in an Animal Control uniform was marching five young boys toward the graveyard. Cora Red Cloud prodded at two of the boys with a large .44 Magnum pistol. Lucas locked eyes with one of those boys being herded toward him. It was Jabar. Exchanging a puzzled look with Reason, Lucas said, "How the hell did he get released from detention? Judge Sully must be losing it to let him go after the crap he pulled yesterday."

Cora led the five boys through the arched opening of the grave-yard. Jabar and the four boys struggled with the zip-ties around their wrists. Wolf grinned. "Good thing my niece was here, Black Bull. Ghosts? American Vets? All guarding Wounded Arrow, and it took her to stop these terrorists. Too bad she didn't catch them seconds earlier. It might have saved me from having a coronary over being shot at."

Wolf glanced behind him to the Ghosts coming from the creek. All six soldiers carried the high-powered rifles that the assault team had been armed with. It was Beef who pointed out the obvious as the Ghosts brought the firepower with them into the graveyard. "That is some serious weaponry. You boys are in deep trouble."

Jabar snapped, "Moloch will protect us! We do his will!"

Lucas sneered at Jabar and said, "Just like he protected you from taking that dart to your forehead, right? Where was Moloch then?"

Beef asked, "Who supplied you with the guns?"

Lucas said, "Achmed Waziri."

Jabar spat over his shoulder, "Prove it, American! Besides, Waziri has diplomatic immunity!"

Beef herded the five boys out of the cemetery and walked them to his cruiser at the center of the ranch. Once the Ghosts had the guns loaded into the trunk of the cruiser and the boys secured in the back-seat, Beef drove them away from the ranch. Cora drove away as well. As she left Wounded Arrow, Lucas shared with the Ghosts all that had taken place at Khalid's house the day before.

Since each member of the company knew the Phantom captain who had escorted them out of Mosul when they had secured the x-rays machines, Lucas downplayed his role, foiling the assassination of Khalid, yet Ali shared that it was Lucas wielding his father's cane that left no doubt in the minds of the Natives that Lucas had stepped up to the plate. He would have liked to have spent more time with this company, but as the sun sank in the west, the Cheyenne soldiers began walking the perimeter of the ranch, pulling guard duty.

***

Wolf, Ben, Reason and the two boys sat around the blaze of a camp-fire situated between Ben's underground home and the dog barns. Wolf and the boys whittled at sticks to make marshmallow and hot dog skewers so that they could eat a fire-cooked dinner beneath the moon and the stars. Goblin ate more than half of the hot dogs Lucas burned over the fire. "He deserves a steak," Lucas said.

"Yes," Ali agreed. "He saved your life."

Lucas said, "But what made him do that? How did he know that a bullet would follow that red dot? Maybe my guardian angel guided him to do what he did to save me from getting shot."

Ali finished eating a toasted marshmallow. He said, "Angels are part of Islam. The Arabic word for angel means messenger. Angels share revelations from God. They gather a person's soul when they die. Islam considers angels, jinn, and demons to be different entities. Jinn were worshiped before Islam began. In ancient Arabia, they belonged to many religions. Zoroastrian. Christian. Jewish angels and demons were called jinn. Some scholars claim jinn were pagan gods who became lesser beings as other gods grew more important.

"Muslims identify the prophets as humans chosen by God to be his messengers. The prophets were instructed to bring the will of God to the people of all nations. Prophets are human, not divine. It was changed from Mohammadism to Islam, because it gave too much credit to Mohammad, a man, not god. Muslims believe that God sent Mohammad to preach the divine message to the world. He was sent as a prophet to human and jinn communities. Solomon was granted authority over the rebellious jinn. King Solomon forced them to build the First Temple. Islam says the angels were created on Wednesday, the jinn on Thursday, and man on Friday. The jinn became corrupt, and God sent his angels to battle the infidel jinn. Only a few survived, but with the revelation of Islam, the jinn were given a chance to find salvation."

Wolf said, "All religions are Man trying to figure out God."

Long moments of silence passed. The fire crackled. Wood smoke drifted up into their faces. Lucas shielded his eyes with one hand. Wolf turned his head to one side, allowing the smoke to slither off him and be on its way. Wolf said, "The Great Spirit AKA Wakan Tanka, is the supreme being among the Native American. He takes a personal interest in our lives. Wakan Tanka is the Great Mystery. The Ghost Dance Religion was founded by Wovoka, a Paiute. The Ghost Dance was meant to serve as a connection with traditional ways of life and to honor the dead. In 1888, Wovoka, the son of a medicine man, fell sick with a fever during an eclipse of the sun. Upon his recovery, he claimed that he had visited the spirit world and the Great Spirit told him the world would soon end, then be restored to a pure state. Natives would inherit this world, including those already dead. Wovoka called for meditation, prayer, singing, and dancing as an alternative to mourning the dead. This Ghost Dance spread to many tribes. Arapaho. Cheyenne. Lakota. Wovoka predicted white people would disappear. A Ghost Dance at Wounded Knee in 1890 was attacked by the Seventh Cavalry, who massacred unarmed Lakota people, fearful that their dancing would cause many more Natives to go into a murderous rage.

"The seven bands of the Lakota are:

"Sichaŋu, meaning burned thighs.

"Oglala, meaning they scatter their own.

"Itazipcho, meaning without bows.

"Huŋkpap, meaning camps at the end of the circle.

"Miniconjou, meaning plants near water.

"Sihasapa, meaning blackfeet.

"Oohenuŋpa, meaning two kettles.

"Lakota leaders were Sitting Bull, American Horse, Sword, Touch the Clouds, Red Cloud, Black Elk, Spotted Tail, and the legendary Crazy Horse from the Oglala and Miniconjou band.

"And the All Father, the Great Spirit, unlike this Moloch, has not once asked us to kill anyone who does not accept him as their god."

Chapter Twenty-Nine

It was past midnight when Reason loaded both sleep-dazed boys into the backseat of his van. After making sure they were both sprawled out comfortably as they shared the seat, he placed Goblin and Lobo in the passenger's seat. Reason turned to say good-bye to Ben and Wolf. "Thanks," he said to Ben, "for sharing the history of the ranch with me. I'll write up a piece for the Storm Haven site. Kids should read about the rescue work you do with these dogs."

Ben said, "Give my vets credit for the work they do out here. They often serve an ungrateful nation, and many take them for granted. It would do them wonders to be bolstered on the Internet with your story. Give them the credit they deserve."

Wolf stepped up beside the van. He placed a leather cord around Reason's neck. Patting the arrowhead dangling from it, he said, "The Thunder Dreamer is not easy to live with. Perhaps, the arrowhead of Red Cloud will prove to be a token of power to help in dark days ahead as you deal with Lucas and his anger. But this Ali?"

Reason waited for him to say more.

Standing there, shaking his head, the big Lakota offered Reason a deep frown. "So far outside the Sacred Hoop."

Reason said, "I'm sure Ali and his father have never had their faith described that way before. Both would prefer to live in peace with the rest of us. Moderates are extremely cautious not to be called heretics by Extremists. Or they will find themselves on a religious hit list. I don't know how conflicted Ali is over his belief, but I do know his father is a good man with a good heart."

Suddenly, a black Ford van went speeding past the front gate of Wounded Arrow, heading north and doing 90mph. Its headlamps lit up the roadway ahead, while twin red taillights marked its location in the swirling fog and the darkness surrounding it.

Once it disappeared over the top of a rise, its driver braked hard, gunned the van's engine, and turned around at the bottom of the roadway to come roaring back over the hill it had just descended.

At the wheel was Crow Harper.

The president of the Apaches cradled his bandaged stump at the end of his left wrist against his chest. His right hand was attached to the steering column with a length of chain, leaving him just enough room to steer the van. He cursed Waziri for cutting his hand off to free him from the handcuffs securing him to the dumpster. He cursed

Waziri again for forcing him to drive with him to cut a deal with the Powder King. The scraggily biker had pleaded with the man to drive him to the local ER to have a surgeon sew up his stump. But Waziri refused and kept them on track to purchase the Deep 9 powder he planned to destroy the US service dogs with.

Crow gunned the van and took it down the roadway, once more passing the gateway of the ranch. He fully expected at any moment to be blown to kingdom come, for the vest he wore was hooked up to a number of explosive devices. In his hatred for the man, Crow drove the van with reckless abandon. Waziri had ordered him to race up the driveway of the Wounded Arrow ranch, plow directly into the main dog barn. And then, Waziri would detonate the bombs strapped to Crow's chest. And four kegs of powder would be dispersed into the air, leaving the dogs inside the barn to die a slow, painful death as the chemicals evaporated the air in their lungs.

Crow glanced behind him to the four plastic drums filled with the deadly powder. The Arab man waved his hands above a wooden crate situated in the van beside the four barrels, uttering words in a foreign language. Crow hissed in terror as a green mist leaked out of the crate, leaving a crackling emerald cloud in the back of the van.

Crow whimpered as the crate behind his seat burst apart. Four wisps of green smoke coalesced into the air in the back of the van. Four brutish apparitions that could only be described as Middle Eastern ghosts appeared. All had scalp-locks hanging down the back of their clean-shaven domes. Stomping hard on the brakes, Crow brought the van to a halt in the middle of the road. He peeled out, heading back toward the gateway of the ranch. Crow was gibbering with terror as he crashed into the entrance of the main dog barn. Waziri, from some distance away, detonated the explosives strapped to his chest. The thunder of hell-fire followed. The van, Crow, and the four plastic barrels were ripped to shreds by the detonation and an enormous cloud of white dust filled the inside of the dog barn.

***

Goblin launched himself from the front seat, pouncing on the sleeping form of Lucas. *Wake up!* the pup sent. Lucas looked to the barn as the van exploded. Tears spilling down his face, Lucas muttered, "All of those dogs! All of those poor, damned dogs!"

He sat there watching the enormous white cloud burst from the bomb-shredded van and transform into a dragon with coal-black eyes and an open red mouth. The cloud-creature viciously hissed at the two dozen bikers who came running toward the barn. The beast dismissed them with a hiss, then slithered deep inside the dog barn.

"That demon," Ali cried, "is going after the service dogs!"

Lucas leaped out of the van, determined to rescue the dogs trapped now within it. Ben latched onto him. "But," he cried, "we've got to get the dogs out of there! It will kill them sure as hell!"

"No," Ben said, "it won't."

Lucas looked up at the Lakota dog handler in bafflement.

Ben said, "The dogs are not in there. Cora had me remove them two days ago. They are safe in the underground kennels of Kooper's Steading. And they are guarded well by the Ghost Company, who would die before they allowed anyone to harm those dogs."

Reason asked, "Kooper's what?"

"Steading," Lucas told him, his eyes locked on the smoldering barn and wisps of smoky white powder drifting in the air. "Old Man Kooper used to hold dog fights in an underground bunker. I found it when I lived here with Ben in foster care."

There came a cry from the yard before the demolished barn. Bikers there scattered as the cloud-dragon emerged from between two charred beams at the center of the front door. The creature's mouth opened in a vicious snarl. At once, blue-white lightning burst from between its jaws. Zephyrs of lightning passed above the heads of the twenty bikers, causing them to beat a hasty retreat to the nearby second barn.

The ghost-dragon turned its gaze on the field beyond the barn. It was the field of Ben's neighbor, a rancher who owned a large herd of buffalo. It was the field that lay between the dust monster and the US service dogs in the underground kennels of Old Man Kooper's former fighting arena. The dragon of particles and deadly chemicals began tracking the dogs by scent. The creature moved across the field beyond. There, gathered in a huddle, were a herd of buffalo, staring in alarm at the ghost dragon drifting their way. Lucas looked to the field and saw the ghostly dragon plow through strands of an electric fence in its path. A loud crackle filled the air. Traces of the creature's lightning sparkled along its wires. The strands of the fence snapped, leaving an open pathway for the dragon to pass through.

At the sound of the implosion, the lead bull of the herd turned to face the threat. Wolf cursed and started to run toward the herd, but Reason stopped the big Lakota and guided him over to his van. Ben and Lucas were quick to follow them. Inside the van, Ali looked to the smoldering barn and the four ghostly forms slithering out from between the burned boards of the barn behind it.

Ali said, "Those are the jinn we were talking about earlier. Waziri must have transported them across the sea and set them free here on American soil. They are far more dangerous than terrorists."

The four jinn drifted in behind the dust monster, their sights fixed on the herd of buffalo. Reason headed the van straight through the opening the dragon had left in the fence, then veered in between the buffalo and the cloud-dragon.

Wolf said, "Use the feather magic. The feather of American Horse was given to you for a good reason, Lucas. Wield its magic, or those buffalo are going to die!"

In the back seat, Wolf opened the door of the van and hopped out. Grunge bolted out behind him. The dog growled into the faces of the many buffalo inching their way forward. He nipped at the nose of the lead bull. The bull huffed a challenge to the ghost dragon.

"No, my brother," Ben said. Snorting defiantly, the bull buffalo peered up at the Lakota and wheeled around, his herd following him across the field. Springing out of the van, Lucas reached inside his shirt, latched onto the feather, and ripped it from the leather thong around his neck. He caught a quick glimpse of Reason honking on the horn to get the entire herd of buffalo to run back across the field toward the distant pasture.

Realizing the van was no longer between him and the demons, Lucas wheeled about, his eagle feather crackling with Big Medicine. A burst of multi-colored light streamed from his raised fist clenched tightly around the token of power. Each beam attached itself to the rainbow of color Ben had conjured with the arrowhead he held in his own clenched fist. And then, Reason was there, joining them, the arrowhead of Red Cloud clenched in his fist.

Light beams from all three tokens of power transformed into an explosion of glittering feathers, and a flock of eagles, hawks, owls, and ravens sped toward the white dragon in an aerial attack. Beaks and talons ripped through the beast's form, shredding its breast and horned head. Stunned by the bird barrage, the dragon reared back. The four jinn wielded green scimitars. They began to attack the magical flock of winged creatures. Lucas stared down at the eagle feather clutched in his hand. "How did I do that?"

Ben said, "The talisman I wear around my neck is the arrowhead that belonged to Sitting Bull, a token of power to shield me from the Dark Ones. It is endowed with big medicine. By activating your own arrowhead, you opened a doorway into the Beyond. What comes through it has to do with the images you conjure. Concentrate now to stop this thing."

Standing there, Lucas watched in horror as the cloud-dragon blew breaths of sparkling particles at the raptors. At once, owls, falcons, eagles, and hawks were caught in the blasts. Smaller birds fell to the sweeping blades of the four jinn who hammered them from the air. It was a terrible slaughter. Lucas knew the buffalo herd would be next. One whiff of the chemicals wafting from the dragon, and the buffalo would suffer an agonizing death.

Ben held the violet-glowing arrowhead up to the four directions. At once, a lavender-shaded field of force draped itself over him and Lucas. The warding encased them in its transparent shell as the dragon blew a frosty breath of the Deep 9 chemicals down at them. The violet shield took the brunt of the dragon's breath, caving in, repelling the smoky cloud so that its devastating particles slid off the warding. Lucas conjured images in his mind and let them loose with a shout.

Spectral creatures of the wild burst through the fabric between this realm and the Otherworld. Dozens of shimmering beasts closed on the jinn. Badgers, wolverines, wolves, cougars, bobcats, and deer made a full charge at mystical monsters conjured by Waziri. The wolves and cougars swept the four jinn off their feet. The badgers and wolverines closed on the spirit-warriors, mauling them, and with a pitiful wail, the four jinn retreated to the Unseen realm.

The dragon roared. A burst of snow-like crystals exploded from his mouth. The chemicals caused the shimmering beasts to disintegrate, turning them into sparkles that fizzled and dissolved as the turbulent cloud washed over them. Lucas swirled the eagle feather through the air. An image appeared on the ethereal plane of the Otherworld. An enormous supernatural grizzly charged through the rip in the fabric. The brawny brute plowed into the dragon, locking it in a savage embrace. The massive grizzly roared in fury and buried his fangs into the dragon's neck. He shook his shaggy head from side to side, but the dragon sent his claws raking through the bear, and he imploded into a sparkling mist.

Ben thrust his arrowhead before him and shouted, "Sitting Bull! Touch the Clouds! Gall! Crazy Horse!"

Four riders came hurtling out of the Otherworld behind him, war cries echoing across the field as they fixed the dragon in their eagle-proud gazes. Scintillating horses of star dust carried the Native riders. Sitting Bull thrust his spear into the beast's chest. Touch the Clouds drove his tomahawk into the dragon's skull. Seated on his glimmering horse, Gall sent his pulsating arrow into the chest of the beast. Thunder ripped through the clouds. Crazy Horse buried his knife in the chest of the dragon.

A moment later, the cloud dragon disintegrated and was no more.

As the supernatural battle took place, Reason stared in wonder at the sight of the four great Lakota war chiefs as they rode their horses made from star dust back into the Otherworld.

"So," Lucas asked, "how did I summon the bear? I just thought of him, all powerful and fierce, and he came roaring out of the seam in the fabric between the realms. Is that how I activate the medicine of the eagle feather. With my thoughts?"

Lucas kneeled between Grunge and Goblin as the two dogs nosed their way beneath his arms. He peered down at the eagle feather and it came to him then, that he was answering some sort of calling. Amazed that Ben had conjured Sitting Bull, Gall, Touch the Clouds, and Crazy Horse, Lucas was determined to learn how to summon such power. Goblin whined beside him and Grunge growled. Lucas placed the leather chord back over his head, and the eagle feather settled into place against his chest beneath his shirt, he hugged both dogs and kissed them both on their snouts.

***

That next day, Reason invited Ben and Wolf over to the house for breakfast. As a writer, he was fascinated that they had experienced a supernatural encounter. He asked why the four chiefs intervened against the beings Waziri conjured. Wolf explained that the Lakota were visionaries, that a visit by legends from the Otherworld were a gift from the All Father.

Lucas said, "Now that Crow is dead, what about my dad?"

Reason said, "The county attorney released your dad. However, Waziri escaped to the Middle East. As an ex-Delta Ranger, your dad has contacts overseas to help in the hunt. His flight left an hour ago. You're stuck with me until he returns. If it's any consolation, Ali got the worst end of the entire deal. While Khalid and your dad hunt for Waziri. Ali is to stay with your old foster parents, the Yardleys."

"Two to take on Waziri?" Lucas blurted. "What if Waziri and an army of extremists removes my dad from the face of the earth?"

Reason said, "Khalid is a highly qualified anti-terrorist agent. He will not take any unnecessary risks. They both know how dangerous this man is. Agent Raynes is joining them on the hunt."

"Great!" Lucas said. "An agent with an attitude! I feel better about this already!"

Chapter Thirty-One

14-year-old Alex Thorn stood in the alley behind the house. In the darkness, he resembled a Goth raccoon. Black face paint around his eyes. Black hair hanging in a tail down his back. Black trench coat swallowing his slender frame. He gasped when a small monkey skittered past him. The bug-eyed creature scurried up the side of an oak tree in the middle of the yard.

Alex crept past the tree, glancing warily at the creepy monkey, its black-eyed gaze on him as he sidled up to the house. Atop a layer of white powder, Alex had a yellow lightning bolt down the left side of his face. Earlier that day, Lucas had lectured him on the significance of painted faces: "Protects you from being recognized by demons! Native warriors painted their faces for battles. Every mark on the face had meaning. The hand symbol meant the warrior was great in hand-to-hand combat. The zig-zag across the forehead symbolized lightning. Red was war."

Lucas had enlisted Alex to do the sneaking he couldn't do. Since moving into foster care with Reason, Lucas had opted out of any lawbreaking activity, and burglarizing an old man's house was crossing a line. Therefore, Alex was out in the middle of the night trying to reclaim the two rings Lucas had given to the relic collector, Gus Howard. Alex was determined to get them back.

As he inspected the door before him, the monkey advanced on him across the backyard. Splayed against the back door of the house, Alex felt something brush against his leg. He cried out as a gray cat hurtled out from between his feet. The cat careened into the spindly monkey. Screeching, the monkey wheeled away to avoid claws. Put off by the fury of the cat, the creature ran back to the tree, scurrying up into its branches. The cat darted down the alley, disappearing into the night. Alex crawled through the cat door. He crossed a kitchen, and entered into a shadowy bedroom. He moved to a dresser against the far wall. He opened three drawers, revealing a cache of weapons resting on velvety pads in each drawer. The kid gaped at the assortment of pistols. He reached down, touching a gold cross. It snapped open to become a short sword.

A quick search of the drawers resulted in a frustrated sigh. Alex turned to the still form in the bed. Gus appeared to be asleep. Alex focused on the old's man's thin chest, his eyes widening in horror when he spotted the railroad spike buried in Gus Howard's breast.

Wheeling around, Alex darted out into the hallway. He barreled into the kitchen, his sights on the cat trap at the end of a slick linoleum floor. Alex was moving so fast that he slammed headfirst into the solid metal door. He saw stars. He saw blackness. He stumbled and fell, fighting not to pass out.

Suddenly, the back door struck the kitchen wall, causing the house to shudder. Nate Holland stood there before him, and Alex scrambled to his feet. The biker grabbed him by the throat. A voice came from the end of the hallway: "Let him go, Uncle Nate."

Struggling to breathe in the big man's vise-like grip, Alex turned to see a dark-haired girl stepping out of the kitchen. "Celeste!" he whispered, surprised to see Lucas's older sister standing there looking like a Vampire Mistress clad in her black duster. Her short raven hair gave her a boyish look, but nothing could tamp down the catlike glare in her she-lion gaze.

Celeste raised the tazer she held, driving the snapping prongs into Nate's neck. He did the funky chicken, crashing back into the wall. She removed a pair of handcuffs from her duster pocket. She placed one of them around Nate's right wrist and locked the other end to the floor radiator.

"Did you get the rings from Gus?" Celeste asked Alex.

"Gus is dead," Alex quietly said.

"What?" Celeste gasped. "Dead? How?"

"Someone," Alex said, "got here before me!"

Celeste sighed, sadly. As she spun him around toward the living room, Nate drew a .22 pistol from beneath his jacket. He aimed the gun at the chain of the handcuffs. Six shots rang out. Startled by the whizzing hot lead, Alex ran into the wall and slid to the floor, out cold. Unaware of Alex sprawled on the floor, Celeste tripped over the black monkey latching onto her. The creature then pulled her out through the back door.

***

Reason sat staring at his computer screen when Rumor sprang onto the edge of his desk. Startled by the cat's appearance, Reason tried to coax it to walk the last few feet and into his lap. Still ruffled from his encounter with the monkey, Rumor's widened eyes were fixed on the nearby open window.

Reason knew better than to attempt his hand at cat-wrangling. He knew that Rumor belonged to Gus Howard, a retired security guard

106

who lived down the street, and yet the cat had discovered the dog-trap in his back door and crept past the two dogs sleeping in the kitchen. Startled by the muffled gunshots from four houses away, Reason headed for the back door, dodging Lobo and Goblin who sprang up into his path. Peering through his screen door, he was startled when Celeste ran up to his house. "Gus Howard has been murdered!" she said. She then turned and ran off across his back-yard, a small black monkey trailing behind her. He hurried back into the kitchen and called Detective Tory to report the shooting.

Minutes later, Reason sat watching from his back porch, Rumor snuggled in his lap, Lobo and Goblin sprawled at his feet. Red and blue lights rotated from the nearby alley. A yellow flashlight beam cut through the shadows as Detective Tory approached the porch, a frown creasing his well-trimmed golden beard. He said, "I tried to check on Gus, but Alex Thorn refused to let me inside. He's inside Gus's house, armed with a gun. He wants to speak with you."

Reason said, "The kid hates me. I make him go to school. I make him stick to his contract. Why me?"

Beef said, "I called in there. Alex answered. I asked him who he trusted. Alex said his truancy tracker. That would be you."

Reason rolled his eyes and muttered, "Sweet Jesus."

Chapter Thirty-Two

At the end of a heated debate with Beef, Reason agreed to wear a bulletproof vest to appease him. Beef said, "Wear the vest, or we find another way."

The moment he stepped in through the back door, Reason slipped out of the vest and dropped it on the kitchen floor. "Alex?"

"The little bastard is in here!" Nate thundered from the front room. "The damned psycho raccoon!"

Cautiously, Reason stepped out of the kitchen to enter the living room, dimly lit by a table lamp. Nate was handcuffed to a floor radiator. Alex sat huddled in a recliner, tear streaks marring the war paint he wore. Reason looked down at the pistol. "Is that loaded?"

Alex tossed the gun on the floor. "No. I got knocked out. When I came to, I decided to stay put to explain to the cops that I didn't kill anyone. Nate didn't either. It was someone else."

Reason looked down at the cuff linking the biker's right wrist to the radiator. It held a faint glow to it. Nate gave another strong pull, yet sparks shot from the band of metal, causing him to cry out.

Alex said, "Just get me out of here, will you, Reason?"

"Working on that," Reason said.

Stepping into the bedroom, he stared in horror at the sight of Gus staked through the heart. He had known the man as a fellow writer. It seemed impossible that he'd died in such a gruesome manner, the railroad spike barely visible in the blood clotted around the wound. When he reappeared in the hallway, Nate lunged at him. The band secured to his wrist emitted a loud hum, and the biker was reduced to having some sort of spasm on the floor. It was then that Reason saw the maps above the wall beyond a computer work station.

Sadly, he shook his head. *Damn,* he thought, *to have a book just aching to get out, and then to have all that work cut short before it could be finished?*

He offered Alex a most sympathetic look. "Sorry," he said, "but cops will want to question you. Do you know Detective Tory?"

Alex nodded. "Known as the Viking when he rode with the Outlaws? Yes, he might nail me for being an accessory, right?"

Reason nodded, yet said nothing.

The sudden beep of the nearby phone caused the three of them to stare at the desk where it was situated. Reason bent forward to read the caller ID on the answering machine. "Is it Tory?" Alex asked.

Shaking his head, causing his long tangles to fall into his face, Reason said, "No."

Reason picked up the phone. "Hello?" he said.

Click! The caller hung up. Reason looked down at the answering machine. It continued to blink, indicating there were messages left behind earlier that night. Disregarding those for the time being, Reason called Beef, assuring him the situation was under control.

***

When Beef stepped inside the house, he had Lobo, Reason's award-winning sniffer with him. The pit greeted his master warmly. Beef offered Alex a sad smile. "You are to be taken into custody, kid."

Alex said, "I didn't murder Gus. All I did was sneak in through the cat door. What are you charging me with?"

"Depends," Beef said, pulling him up out of the chair. "Best case scenario, I'll return you home later. And worst case scenario? Lock up at DC. We shall see. What's the story on Gus?"

"Gus," Reason said, "has a railroad spike through his heart."

Beef moved over to Nate seated there on the floor. Studying the illuminated handcuffs binding him to the radiator, he produced a key from his belt pouch, then kneeled to slip the key into the slot on the cuff around the biker's wrist and opened it. Nate lurched forward, head-butting the blond detective. Beef staggered back. He fell to his knees. Nate ripped the pistol out of his holster. Reason sidestepped him, flinging his arm out, clotheslining Nate across his throat with his forearm. The biker flew off his feet. Reason sank to one knee, driving his right hand into Nate's nose with a palm strike. The pistol flew out of his grasp, and Lobo walked over to him, a soft growl burbling deep in his throat.

"Sheesus!" Alex cried. "Where'd you learn those moves?"

Beef fumbled dizzily with the radio at his belt, managing to say, "Back up." Seconds later, two cops came through the front door.

Nate was escorted away by two uniformed cops, while Beef led Lobo to the crime scene in the bedroom. Reason went to the kitchen to retrieve a wet wash rag. When he returned to the living room, he washed the paint off of Alex's face. Alex endured several swipes of the damp cloth. "Anything you can do for me, Reason?"

Reason said, "Your contract states four months of school attendance. You ditched me so many times, I can't recommend you as the poster child for my truancy program, Alex."

109

Tears welled up in Alex's eyes. "I know. I'm a royal screw up."

A few minutes later, Beef exited Gus's bedroom, Lobo trailing behind him. He turned to examine the maps on the wall. "Gus was writing a book," Reason said. "I know you can't involve me in this investigation, but unofficially, could I take a look at his files?"

Beef said, "Thanks, Reason. If we need a consultant to decipher the old man's writings, I'll mention your offer to my superiors."

Reason said, "Why do you have Lobo involved? Thought I made it clear, he was permanently retired."

Beef said, "I wanted to see if Lobo could find those rings. Rumor is they ended up here with Gus. However, Lobo didn't find them."

Beef turned to place Alex in handcuffs.

Just before stepping outside, Reason shooed Lobo out the door and said, "Let me know what you decide to do with Alex."

Chapter Thirty-Three

Cops could not tie Nate to Gus's murder, so they released him the next day. He had payback on his mind the moment he returned home. Celeste lay curled up in bed when Nate shoved her bedroom door open. He stood there, his bald head gleaming, his green eyes radiating rage. In an eerily quiet tone, he said, "Go over to Reason's and bring Grunge back here, now!"

Celeste said, "You will never put his dog in another fight. Lucas loves that brute, and to break his heart like that would be cruel!"

At 17, Celeste Holland was a force to be reckoned with. Having been through treatment, twice, she had battled her addictions to both meth and K2. She was now drug free, and as such, opposed to her Uncle Nate's business and how it might impact her future. She was disappointed that her father had chosen to leave the country to join Khalid and Raynes on their search for Waziri in the Middle East. Especially, now that she had just finished treatment in Omaha and ended up in the care of her Uncle Nate.

The good little Celeste had died the night her mom died. She had been hell on wheels ever since. Celeste dealt with her pain over the loss of her mom by using large quantities of drugs. Oblivious to the rest of the world around her, she started using any drug she could get her hands on to cope with her grief. She started with weed, but after a stint on probation where she had to give UA's every week, she had switched to K-2, the man-made substitute for weed. The agency keeping track of her did not have the finances to test for K-2, therefore, it never showed up on tests. She became addicted to the stuff, and used it consistently for the rest of that year, until her best friend, Crystal, suffered a collapsed lung from smoking one evening. She suffocated right there in front of Celeste.

After such a tragic experience, Celeste progressed to meth. She discovered that was a dead-end, too, one night when she smoked a potent batch cooked up by a member of the Den. Ripper, the biker who had produced the stuff, ended up dead that night. Celeste went to the ER, and spent the next four months at an inpatient treatment center. When she was released, her caseworker had her placed at her uncle Nate's home.

Once she was back in Havelock, Reason tried to reconnect with her, but Celeste refused to talk with him. In order to pay him back for being sent away, she targeted Billy Connors, his grandfather and his legendary stained-glass window. It was a central focal point of the Havelock, depicting a black dragon, red flames shooting from his mouth, and an emerald clutched in his talons. The Emerald's iconic window had been gifted to Billy in Ireland years ago. Rumor was that the old Irish gun runner was owed a debt by the Hidden Ones. Each shard of colored glass had been crafted by the hands of the Wee Folk to create a six-foot wide, eight-foot tall window. In a drunken fit of rage, Celeste pounded on it with a fist, but magic erupted from the window, leaving her unconscious on the sidewalk. Billy found her there.

When she came to, he said, "My window is a beacon for those braving the seas of the Otherworld. It is guarded by the Wee Folk."

Billy guided her past the mantle where the heads of seven stags looked down from the fireplace. They approached the bar on the other side. Beyond it was a wall-length mirror. When Celeste looked at her reflection in the mirror, she saw the tattoos on her throat and neck. The stag in the hollow of her throat had antlers that evolved into twin wolves snaking up on either side of her neck. The stag held a fierce gaze in his eyes, and the two wolves were facing sideways, their lips set in mid-howl. Billy said, "Those magical beauties were transferred from my window to you. They are talismans that will come to life when you most need them."

"Cool," Celeste whispered in awe, thinking she would be envied by her friends for sporting such unique tattoos.

With Nate standing there before her in her bedroom, Celeste was relieved when Ben Black Bull came to the house to confront Nate. The Lakota dog handler was the distraction she needed to slip out through the back door. Five minutes later, she stood before the huge stained-glass window of the Emerald Pub.

As she reached for the ornate handle in the center of the large oak door, the black imp appeared on the sidewalk beside her. "Why?" she gasped. "Do you keep following me, monkey?"

The bald-headed imp sent back to her: *Not a monkey. Mogrim, from the realm of Valasar. Jango is what my master called me before he was no more. Have you come to attend the White Council?*

Jango scampered across the sidewalk and ended up perched on her left shoulder. The mogrim reached out, his tiny fingers gently caressing her cheek. *Are you,* the little imp asked, *here to enter into a war that has been raging for centuries? Have you come to join the Servants of Light? If so, I claim you as my new master.*

Before Celeste could respond, the oak door before her seemed to open of its own accord. She peered into the shadowy alcove beyond. Celeste glanced down at the strange imp seated on her shoulder. Jango stared back at her, his overlarge eyes changing from dull black to a brilliant shade of blue. Celeste entered a room, complete with an oak bar on one side and a fireplace on the other. Jango chortled with glee. Celeste felt his tiny fingers tracing lines around the tattoos on her neck and lower face.

Old Billy Connors stepped up beside the fireplace, the cherry in his pipe illuminating the weathered features of his face. Dressed in a three-piece suit, his long, silver hair fell loose about his shoulders, while beneath his hawk-like nose was a thick mustache. His blue eyes pierced Celeste where she stood. The old Irishman said, "Star dust from my magically enchanted window got transferred into your DNA the night you tried to destroy my window. It reacted and zapped you. You carry the magic to become a Keeper of the Flame."

She looked into the old man's lion-like gaze and then behind Billy, where an oaken door swung open, revealing a round wooden table where a pair of white-robed women sat. Celeste stared at the two ladies in stunned surprise. "Cat? Cinnamon?" she said.

Cat's hair was purple. Cinnamon's auburn hair cascaded past her shoulders. The torcs at their necks glowed. Three huge grizzled men sat at the table across from them, one with white hair, the second with raven hair, and the third with golden hair. All three wore sleeveless Harley T-shirts, yet resembled Norse Vikings.

Billy said, "Havelock is known amongst the White Council. In our small suburb are Waystations between realms: The Emerald Pub. The Roaring Lion, owned by Cinnamon and Cat. The Trainyard Bar, owned by the Three Bears, Kodiak, Winter, and Griz. Mage Lords committed to battling the Unseen."

He took a drag on his briarwood pipe, then said, "My grandson has been dealing with that at-risk bunch of kids for the past ten years. Drugs. Suicide. Runaways. Truancy. Probation. Prison. Endless Celtic hoops that kids find themselves trapped in. So, he created a program to curb delinquent behavior. A virtual game, where kids can interact, using special electronic equipment. It is known as force feedback in gaming apps. There's an alternate dimension beyond the door to my Dragon Room. Reason created a game script that aligns with this realm. He submitted it to Game Wizards. They designed a virtual reality game that can be played with the use of a headset. I considered Lucas for the initial gaming session, but the boy's urges to go ape in a moment's notice make for an unstable guinea pig. I'm seeking someone with a calm demeanor to test the game."

The old Irishman puffed away on his pipe, creating a cloud of blue smoke. "In this realm, our cause is noble: Creating a virtual reality game that will help delinquent kids. In the realm beyond, there is war raging there that the White Council is now a part of. If you chose to join us, your true gifts will be awakened. You are much more than you know, Celeste Holland. You may have considered yourself a worthless little druggie a few months ago, but you have more potential than that. Will you join us and awaken your powers?"

Celeste said, "One would think that maybe I am still tripping after hearing you talk, and this tattoo is a little much to figure out. I came here tonight to get you to tell Nate that Grunge is off limits."

Billy removed his pipestem from between his teeth. "I'll deal with Nate, lass. All I ask of you is you think this over. Agreed?"

She gave a shrug, and said, "We shall see, Billy. We shall see."

Chapter Thirty-Four

A few minutes later, staring at the alley stretching before them, Celeste said, "Jango, I have a mission for you. Will you help me?"

When she reached Gus Howard's back porch, she listened to the sounds coming from inside. Police radio static. Robotic voices. Footsteps across the floor in the kitchen. Noises from the front of the house. Car doors slammed. An engine started. A fire truck drove off, a steady grinding of gears echoing in the night.

Celeste stood there with Jango seated on her shoulder. The small, bug-eyed creature stared up at Celeste, puzzlement in its gaze. She gently stroked the fur at the base of its neck. The mogrim chortled with glee, craning his small, bald head to the left and right, pleased with the attention Celeste was giving him. She whispered into his ear, then Jango leaped down and crawled in through the cat door.

Blending into the shadows, she listened intently as footsteps could be heard inside the kitchen. Jango came shooting out through the cat door. The back door opened. Detective Tory chased the mogrim across the yard. Jango wheeled around. Beef clawed at his holstered pistol. Before he could draw the weapon, Jango hurtled into him taking him to the ground. He perched on his chest, doubled up his tiny fists, and gave Beef a furious pounding.

By then, Celeste had slipped inside the house. She went directly to the computer workstation. Keenly aware that she was not alone, she listened several seconds to the murmur of two female voices coming from the bedroom. When certain the two forensic officers were busy going about their work, Celeste removed a thumb drive from the USB port on Gus Howard's computer. She slipped it into her shirt pocket when the red light on the answering machine caught her eye. Silently, she removed the machine's cord attaching it to the wall. She exited through the back door. The moment Jango spotted her, he sprang off Beef and scampered away, leaving the cop dazed from the beating he took. Tucking the answering machine beneath her arm, Celeste raced away toward the open back gate.

***

Rumor suddenly sat up, going from a sound-sleeping ball of gray fur situated on the edge of Reason's desk, to alert beast mode, letting out a guttural *meeoww!* A faint sound came from the kitchen, and Rumor stood up on all four paws. Still shaken from the murder of

Gus Howard, Reason opened his desk drawer and drew out a .380 Lorcin pistol. Back in the 90's, when his writing career first started he'd authored a book about a murdered female informant. Kelly Drake was an informant for Jessie Dalton. Having been responsible for dozens of narcotics busts, she had been shot at the Emerald Pub's outdoor café by Jack Holland of the Elder's Den. And that's when Reason stumbled his way into the middle of the conspiracy. After his book was published, he received a call at 3AM. The man asked, "You the guy who wrote that book?"

"Yeah," Reason answered.

"Where'd you get your information?"

"Why? What's it to you?"

"Well, the information in your book is fairly accurate."

"I wrote it as a piece of fiction."

"Truth is sometimes stranger than fiction."

"Any accuracies were purely coincidental."

"There is a network of people involved in that narc's murder. If they contact you one day, you're gonna want a gun."

Click! The caller chuckled and hung up.

The .380 Lorcin had been purchased that next week.

The pistol held before him, Reason quietly made his way into the kitchen. Lobo and Goblin stood on either side of Grunge. The dog curled back his lips in a growl. Stepping out of his bedroom, Lucas latched onto Grunge's collar. "Mind your manners, Grunger."

Reason lowered the pistol. He set it on the kitchen counter. He said, "Alex was arrested last night. After Beef grills him, he's gonna talk to you. Besides, two of my rings are still missing."

Grunge detected the anger in the man's words. His dark eyes met Reason's. They held each other's gaze for several seconds. Reason realized his direct stare was a challenge to the pit. He looked away. He raised one hand, his fingers tucked in. Grunge sniffed at his outstretched hand. "I reported Nate to Animal Control two months ago, when I found a dog wandering around. The pit bull was injured. Animal Control officer Cora Red Cloud took the dog to a vet to have its wounds tended. There was no proof Nate had abused the pit. By law, he was the owner, and the dog went back to him. Two months later, Cora informed me the dog had been found dead by Stephen's Creek. Nate's cruelty is difficult to prove. Dogs do not talk. And yet, some people do. I wrote the story for Storm Haven in regard to dog fighting. It made Nate look bad in the eyes of many readers."

A knock came from the back door. Reason snatched up his pistol from the counter. When he opened the door, Celeste stared down at the pistol. In a mock gesture of surrender, she raised one hand in the air, juggling the answering machine in the other. Reason placed the gun on the kitchen counter. Celeste handed him Gus's machine. She said, "Maybe it holds a clue as to why he was murdered."

She reached inside her shirt pocket and produced the thumb drive. "I know what Gus was working on. It will take those cops months to sort through his material. And even then, they won't have a clue as to what any of this means. How much do you know about paranormal activities? Ghosts? Demons?"

Reason simply stood there, holding the machine.

Lucas said, "It freaks me out, too, when she talks this way."

After setting out bowls of water for Grunge, Lobo, and Goblin, Reason joined Lucas and Celeste in the living room. The two were seated on the couch, the machine situated between them. The kid made himself at home, removing his shoes and socks. After drinking water in the kitchen, Grunge wandered into the living room and sprawled out before Reason, seated in a recliner.

"I'll be damned," Celeste said. "Grunge likes you, Reason. He's usually wary of everyone, but he completely trusts you, and that's a compliment coming from him."

The pit bull settled his chin on Reason's crossed feet, closing his eyes. A moment later, Lobo and Goblin came from the kitchen to sprawl on the other side of Reason.

Chapter Thirty-Five

Celeste pressed the button on the machine. After a sharp *beep!* a voice said: *"Gus? It's Colton Lone Wolf. I finished research on the ghosts of the Dead Kings. In the Hebrew Bible, Rephaim were a race of giants. The Israelites exterminated the inhabitants of Canaan, some large individuals. The Book of Joshua suggests that Og, King of Bashan, was the last Rephaim. His bed was 13 feet long! He was big! In Deuteronomy 2:18-21 Ammonites called them Zamzummim, meaning Buzzers, or 'the people whose speech sounds like buzzing.'*

"In Deuteronomy 2:11, Moabites referred to them as the Emim. They are mentioned in Genesis 14:5. The name translates as the dreaded ones. Ancient texts refer to the Rephaim as the Dead Kings. Many references to them in the Hebrew Bible suggest that ancient Israelites imagined the spirits of the dead as playing an active role in the lives of the living.

"The link between these Giants and Ghosts comes from the word, meaning to forsake. Gus, you're on to something! Dreaded Ones? Terrors? Dead Kings! I delved into the thing about Moloch. Leave it alone. You could unleash something that should be sealed away forever. Moloch was a Canaanite god who demanded child sacrifice. Moloch is based on the root mlk 'king'. There are a number of Canaanite gods with names based on this root, the name of a god surnamed the king, lord, ba'al, or master, instead of Melek which is also frequently given to Yahweh the god of the Jews.

"Remember how God asked Abraham to sacrifice his son, Isacc? Child sacrifice was prevalent. The gods of Canaan asked those who believed in them to sacrifice their children. Jeremiah 32:35: 'They built the high places of Baal, to cause their sons and daughters to pass through the fire unto Moloch.' 'Passing through the fire,' became the name for child sacrifices. In the Carthaginian religion, they burned children as an offering to Baal. There was a bronze statue, its hands extended over a bronze brazier, the flames which engulfed the child. When the flames burned the body, the mouth seemed to be laughing. The Carthaginians sacrificed 300 children! Moloch was made of brass. They put the child between his hands, and it was burnt." Colton muttered something inaudible, then *Click!*

Reason looked to Celeste. "Do you know this Lone Wolf?"

Celeste said, "Lakota dog handler, yet he has doctorates in both theology and psychology. His paranormal work with the Dark Ones of Pine Ridge made him the one professional in a five-state radius who didn't think Gus was a royal nut case."

Reason asked, "Who exactly was this Gus Howard?"

Celeste quietly said, "Gus was a Demon Hunter."

Reason allowed Celeste to stay the night at his place. She had come to him seeking a safe haven. If he'd turned her away, Nate might hurt. Reason would not allow that. He knew to keep her safe from Nate, he had no choice. As Celeste's legal guardian, Nate was a mean-spirited man who didn't take her in because of love. Celeste, as a ward of the state, came with special needs payments. Nate was taking in three-thousand per month, and all he had to do to earn that was to show up at each six-month court hearing, pretending to be the kind uncle who wanted what's best for his niece. Nate Holland was playing the system.

***

The next morning, after receiving a call from Beef down at the police station, Reason drove downtown to meet with him. When he arrived at the police station, he noticed the bruising on the left side of Beef's face. "Did you get into a fight?" he asked.

Beef grinned sheepishly. "You ought to see the other guy."

He ushered Reason into an interview room, and was greeted by Alex Thorn seated before them. Beef said, "The County Attorney is not going to charge Alex for Gus's death. Judge Sully is placing him on a suspended sentence to the Youth Center for trespassing."

Reason looked over at Alex. The raccoon was gone. The war paint washed away. The kid sat there, his long, dark tangles of hair hanging to his thin shoulders. He did not meet Reason's gaze.

The suspended sentence meant Alex had lucked out. Reason knew that Judge Sully only easily handed down six-month probation terms to first-time offenders but saved the suspended sentences as a scare tactic to repeat offenders. It was a wake-up call to the little criminals, letting them know they were on the edge of worse placements. It had a fifty-fifty success rate. Some kids left the courtroom in shock. Some wept with relief at the second chance. The others were too stupid to recognize mercy when it was offered. Reason had sat in court, exchanged sad looks with Sully as he said, "Sentence revoked," too many times. Reason labeled them Kamikaze Kids. Despite the trespassing charge, Sully was giving Alex a break with the suspended sentence.

119

So why, Reason wondered did the kid look so sad.

"Alex's mom," Beef said, "refuses to take him back. Per a phone call I had with her, she is flying back to her homeland in Wallachia. She is breaking the law by abandoning her son, but Alex's grandfather demanded she cut all ties with him. I tried to convince his mom she would be charged with reckless abandonment if she left him to fly overseas. But his grandfather commanded her to leave Alex here to fend for himself."

Alex sadly muttered, "My grandfather is of the Cingane, a clan of Gypsies. The Cingane have their own system. Cingane give you just so many chances to succeed. And then, if you fail, you are shunned. Grandpa Petrov has ordered me shunned."

Chapter Thirty-Six

After missing three months of school, Alex had been court ordered to Reason's truancy program. So far, Alex had refused his help. Reason knew at the rate the kid had been going, if it hadn't been the burglary, he would have stumbled his way into some other situation sooner or later. A knock came on the door of the interview room, and in stepped caseworker for the state, Connie Douglas, a slim, middle-aged woman with short-cropped blond hair. In the past, Reason had provided foster care for three state wards under her supervision. He liked her as she was one caseworker who went the extra mile for her troubled cases.

Connie said, "Would you take Alex in on an emergency stay?"

Reason gave her a puzzled frown.

"I get it," Alex said. "You don't want me either. I failed you, too."

Reason said, "Failed yourself! I gave you dozens of chances to prove to Sully you could comply with his attendance order. You blew all of those. In the past, I've taken in some of the most hard-core kids. Kids who reached the end of the line. Kids who burned everyone who had ever taken them in. I once took in a kid who had ran away from forty-six other placements. He remained with me for two years after his placement, not running once. In the course of ten years, I've taken in kids who hit me, kicked me, bit me, and spat on me. Each one I saw as the starfish I was going to make a difference with. I put up with what few foster parents ever would. I endured every assault. I never once called a caseworker and said, 'Come, get this little monster. I've had enough.'"

Reason peered into Alex's dark eyes for long moments, then said, "Alex of the Roma, a nomadic ethnic group of Europe. Romani are known as Gypsies. Not to be confused with Romanians. The term is derived from Egyptian. The Gypsies of your line, Alex, were exiled from Egypt as punishment for harboring the infant Jesus during Herod's reign in Jerusalem, when he had all male infants killed to keep the prophecy of a Jewish Messiah from being fulfilled. Another title of the Romani is Cingane, derived from a Christian sect the Romani were associated with in the Middle Ages.

"Alexander, born in Wallachia, Gypsy child of an American biker and a Romani archivist, grew up among a pack of wolves. His mother adopted an injured, pregnant wolf. She had a litter of seven pups. Alex was in charge of them for the next three years. Living in a Gypsy encampment, he and his pack roamed the wilds together. Alex loved his wolves. Then his mother moved them to America in an attempt to find his father. And Alex has been struggling to find his true center ever since."

Alex stared at Reason, his brow furrowed deep in confusion.

Reason said, "I am a writer. I research. Last year, when you were assigned to me through court, your mom refused to tell me about you. And so, I contacted your grandfather—"

"Grandpa Petrov?" Alex asked, incredulously. "You called him all the way over in Wallachia?"

"Yes," Reason said. "And he asked me to do one thing."

Alex sniffled. "What was that?"

"He asked me to restore your honor."

"My honor? I have no honor."

Reason said, "Why don't we see if we can fix that?"

Connie Douglas invited Alex to ride with her so he could gather up his personal belongings. Once done there at the Thorn residence, she would drive Alex over to Reason's house a few blocks away. Her second mission would then begin, for she had statements to take from Celeste Holland. Reason had shared with her why the girl had showed up at his house, and she was concerned for her welfare, and had been granted an emergency placement from Judge Sully.

***

Celeste Holland was court-ordered to remain with Reason, until her dad returned to the States. Celeste remained silent, refusing to say a word of protest at being placed with her least favorite truancy tracker. In the past, she defied him in her endless quest to get high. Now that she was clean, she found it ironic that she would be living with him. Lucas took the news just as hard. After hugging the dogs, he looked up at Alex. "You, Celeste, and I will have to get used to living with the new *warden*."

Reason overheard this from his place in the kitchen. He stuck his head around the corner, grinning impishly. "Oh, it could be worse. I could send you out to the backyard to do poop patrol."

Rolling his eyes, Lucas said, "Did enough of that out at Ben's ranch. Besides, I'd rather do dishes than use a pooper scooper. I call dibs on the dishes."

An hour later, after Reason fed the three kids on the Isle's pizza, he went to his den, slipping the thumb drive into his desktop com-

122

puter to snoop through Gus's files. Rumor planted herself in his lap. In seconds, the cat was purring as Reason stroked her beneath her chin. Seated nearby on a big couch, Lucas and Alex played a video game, keeping the sound low so as not to disturb Reason.

He had just opened the first file, when the dogs came into the den. Grunge head-butted him on the leg. Goblin sniffed at Rumor, sending the cat springing from Reason's lap. She leaped up onto the desk, peering at Lobo staring in at them from the hallway. Reason said, "We have guests. You and Grunge are related. Same sire and dame, different litters. That makes you brothers."

Reason held up the ring he wore and flourished it in the direction of Lobo. At once, Grunge and Lobo touched noses, and in seconds, the three dogs were settled in the den.

Chapter Thirty-Seven

Jango capered into the room. He carried a leather bag in his small hand. Smiling at the mogrim, Celeste said, "His name is Jango. I sorta adopted him after meeting him down at the Emerald."

Reason asked, "What's it got in its bag?"

He grinned. The words reminded him of Gollum's words in *The Lord of the Rings* when he and Bilbo were swapping riddles, he was immediately aware that the little black creature resembled Gollum. Reason took the bag from him. He loosened the drawstrings, turned the bag over, and dumped out two gold rings into the palm of his hand. Lucas said, "Jango got them from Gus."

Celeste read the screen: "These files have to do with a book Gus was writing. He believed Ring Smiths created four rings in Ulster in the 12th century. There was a slave trade inspired by Moloch. He and his minions abducted thousands of children. Sacred Bands were sent out to slay Moloch and his minions who could disappear. They became known as the Unseen Ones. Ring Smiths forged rings that allowed their wielders to see demons. The rings were given to: A Celtic Swordsman. A Saracen Lancer. A Hebrew Archer. A Norse Axeman. The four used the magic of the rings to kill Moloch's minions. However, Moloch escaped. The warriors were buried in Ulster: Ian McNial. Sara Ali. Rachel Abrahams. Ragnar Thorson, one of Beef Tory's ancestors. McNial, meaning Niall's son AKA Nelson, with your own last name. According to Gus, Beef and you are descended from these two ring masters who battled against evil. The rings passed to Billy Connors of the Emerald—"

"I have been a reluctant ring master all these years," Reason said. "Not taking up the battle as my grandfather asked me to do. As a boy, he took me to the Grand Lodge of the Templars, where men in white robes performed a ritual. I refused to join the Templars. Instead, I became a writer. One evening, I received a package from the Irishman. It contained the rings. He urged me to stand up as a Templar. Even though I scoffed at him, I took to wearing one of those rings. Whatever I set my mind to: Writing. Dog training. Youth work. Investigating. The ring empowered me to pursue them."

Reason fell silent, his tale having been told.

Lucas and Alex stared down at the two rings he held.

Celeste said, "Perhaps it's time you allow others to share what you consider a burden. After all, what could it hurt?"

Mange, warlord of the Den, sat there in his old Ford van parked in the shadows on Logan Avenue. From his vantage point he had a straight shot, one-hundred yards to Gus Howard's backdoor. His night-vision goggles turned the outside world into green images.

Seated beside him, Nate said, "You've had the place covered for the past two days. Still no rings? The Arab paid us to find them. What the hell happened to those rings? Got both places covered. The dead geezer's. The Writer's place."

A flashlight beam suddenly bathed Gus's back gate in a lemony aura. The flashlight went out. Two boys opened the gate and entered into the old man's yard. Mange whispered, "Golden Boy and Gypsy Kid are back!"

Having snuck past Reason, Lucas crept into the den and stealthily removed two of the rings from the chest where Reason kept them. Quietly slipping out through the backdoor, he handed one of the rings to Alex and said, "The railroad spike driven through Gus's heart was a creepy way to go."

Alex said, "It creeps me out totally. But what do we know about demons? Or weapons to use against them?"

Lucas said, "It was you who told me about all the weapons."

Alex said, "The Cingane fashioned silver bullets to slay vampires with. So, maybe these special-made weapons in the hands of two ignorant kids could kill a demon."

"Don't call me dumb, Alex! Told you names piss me off!"

"I said, 'Ignorant,' not dumb!"

Lucas shrugged. "What did Reason mean by these Templars?"

Alex said, "Founded in 1119, the Poor Knights of Christ was the most skilled fighting units of the Crusades. After the First Crusade in 1099, Christians made pilgrimages to the Holy Land. Saracen bandits slaughtered them in the hundreds. In 1119, King Baldwin of Jerusalem created an order to protect these pilgrims. He granted them a wing in the ruins of the Temple of Solomon. The new order took the name Templar Knights. They were the advance troops in the Crusades."

But by then, their talking ceased for they had reached Gus's bedroom Wearing the rings, they chose not to turn on the lights. As they entered the bedroom, they froze.

Chapter Thirty-Eight

Lucas and Alex knew they were not alone. Someone was lurking in the shadows. The bed before them was stripped of its bedding, but there was a spot left behind by the blood from Gus's chest. Lucas felt a warm breath on his neck as Waziri said, "I am a Saracen who has a direct bloodline to the Gate Keeper, Mohammad Bin Aziri. In the 10th century, he opened a portal in Bagdad. My family has served the Ghost of this Dead King ever since. On a Babylonian cylinder seal representing child sacrifice, Moloch is listed as the abomination of the children of Ammon. Moloch is the term for child sacrifice."

He moved swiftly, driving the knife directly in through the collar of Lucas's jean jacket, slicing through the shirt beneath. The sharp point scraped on metal, skittering away. An electric shock traveled up the blade of the knife and into Waziri's hand. Lucas, who had slipped his hand up between them at the last possible moment, spun out of his grasp, revealing the glowing green ring he wore.

Waziri snarled, "The ring has protected you!"

Alex threw a punch, planting his fist in the center of Waziri's face, sending the man down to both knees. Lucas reached into Gus's chest of drawers. His hand closed on the hilt of a bladeless sword. He picked it up. A humming came from the hilt. A lavender blade sprang from the mouth of the falcon engraved on the hand guard. Alex latched onto Lucas and herded him back down the hallway and outside the house. As they ran toward Reason's house, they glanced back to see Mange in his van, staring into the eyes of a figure with slanted catlike eyes beside his door. The tall, bald figure reached through the biker's window and pulled him outside his van. He sank his canines into the biker's neck. He inhaled, sucking the life out of Mange, causing his eyes to loudly pop. His soul sailed out through his eye sockets, and the creature captured a remnant of his soul. He roared, "Moloch, King of Dead Ghosts is back!"

The roar was reminiscent of a lion on the plains of Africa. As Lucas and Alex ran, a primordial instinct kicked in and had them wanting to be up off the ground, out of harm's way. Lucas craned his neck and looked to the sky. There, moving across the moonlit horizon, was a mob of Mongol warriors riding winged-horses.

Lucas cried, "Demons!"

"Yes!" said Celeste as she appeared on the front porch. "Get inside the house! And hand me that sword, Lucas!"

Amazed that the boys obeyed her, Celeste took the violet-bladed sword in hand. She knew from months of working for the old relic collector that he had an arsenal of exotic weaponry in his bedroom. She'd heard the demon hunter speak about tokens of power that could ruin a demon's day. Gus said, "Our struggle is against forces of evil. Take up the sword of the Spirit, for the sword knows its moves. Allow it to lead."

Celeste's tattoos of the twin wolves and stag pulsed with a blue light. The stag peeled away from her neck, changing into a white creature. It bowed its head and dropped to its knees. Celeste quickly mounted the stag. It lurched to its feet, raking the air with its antlers. The twin wolves peeled away from her face, materializing as creatures sparkling with blue light. The violet sword raised in her right hand, Celeste gestured toward the demons, and the wolves moved like quicksilver, flashing through the midst of demons, avoiding their rising and falling blades. The pair killed dozens of demons in a burst of savage fury. Celeste rode the stag into the mob, wielding her purple blade. She slew demons in great numbers.

A war horn was winded within the demon ranks. The demons jerked on the reins of their turquoise steeds, wheeling away from the sweep of Celeste's blade. Celeste sat on her mount, her luminous blade wavering in the air before her. The wolves spun away from the demons and took up guarded positions on either side of the stag. She gasped as a small, muscular figure appeared there, striding boldly out of the mass of demons. He stood barely five feet tall, his furry chest and shoulders rippled with corded muscle. He had the body of a human and yet the face and head of a yellow-eyed goat.

"Baphomet!" Jango snapped.

The goat-headed demon cackled, "Yes," his twin horns upon his head glistening. "Fire gods from the Otherworld! My master and I returned! Our banishment is ended! May I serve you, Lord? You need sustenance to come into your full power? It has been hundreds of years since we've walked this plane. Follow me, Lord. I have a feeding ground with an endless supply of mentally ill, deranged, sex deviates, murderers, rapists, psychotics, the dregs of society. I have staked out the State Prison."

Beef came running down the street. "Hands in the air! Now, put your hands in the air!"

Beef lowered his gaze to Mange sprawled in the street next to the van. It appeared his eyes, had been sucked into a powerful vacuum sweeper. Moloch drew a long knife from a sheath at his side, the blade glowing red. "Drop it!" Beef ordered, raising his gun in a two-fisted grip. Moloch lunged at him, the knife extended before him.

Beef fired.

The red-hot lead projectile sped from the muzzle of the gun and punched a hole in the breast of Moloch. He staggered off balance from the force of the bullet, and yet he recoiled quite suddenly, and came on, the blade a red blur in his grasp.

Beef fired his remaining five bullets at point-blank range, each one striking Moloch in the center of his chest. Sidestepping to avoid the blade, Beef felt his attacker brush past him. Moloch stumbled forward. At the end of four paces, Moloch wheeled back around, an angry scowl on his face. He sucked in a gasp of air. He spat, sending all six bullets from his mouth. Beef recoiled as the projectiles hit him with terrific force, punching him off his feet.

And suddenly, Jango was there between the Ghost of Dead Kings and Beef. He launched himself at Moloch, using one fist to pummel him upside his head, while bringing his other hand down in a swift chop, sending the knife flickering out of his grasp. The fight that followed was lightning-swift as the two combatants erupted into a whirlwind of brutal attacks. The two fighters exchanged dozens of strikes, punches, and kicks. Both appeared to be evenly matched.

Moloch delivered an overhand strike down at the shiny head of Jango, when the mogrim ducked, swerved to the left, wheeled back to the right, and threw a swift uppercut into the chin of Moloch. The blow was delivered with such brutal force that his head snapped back. Jango followed through with a punch to Moloch's throat. The King of Dead Ghosts dropped to one knee. Jango prepared to finish the fight when the horde of demons came down from on high. Jango went down beneath them, barely avoiding their swords.

The mob of demons were so preoccupied with trying to slay the fast-moving mogrim they failed to notice Reason helping the fallen detective to his feet. Beef stumbled across the street, weaving his way onto the lot. Reason glanced back to see Celeste stand before the pack of demons. Dozens gathered around Moloch, weakened by his brutal beating he'd taken from Jango. Baphomet drew a shiny black blade from a sheath behind his left shoulder.

Celeste gave a nudge of one heel, and the stag turned at once. Followed closely by the two wolves, it carried Celeste to the center of the vacant lot. While the wolves took up guarded positions in front of Reason and Beef, the stag darted out in front of Celeste, dipping its head and digging the ends of its tines into the ground. An eerie violet light skittered down the length of its antlers, slithering into the grooves it had created in the earth.

Crackling with magical powers, the violet-shaded force evolved into a shimmering field. An enormous, transparent bubble formed around them, creating a haven of safety for those within. Baphomet struck the warding, his sword skittering off the barrier. Baphomet, repulsed by the shield, attacked the warding in a furious rage.

Celeste moved to the center of the lot, tapping her sword at the iron grating that created an opening to the sewer system below. Glancing once more at the enraged demon attacking the warding, she slashed at the grating, her blade slicing through each bar of iron like a hot knife through warm butter. Pieces of it fell inward and clanged loudly as they struck the concrete floor of the tunnel seven feet below them.

Reason slowly lowered himself in through the opening and down into the dark depths below. Celeste took a hold of Beef's forearm and gestured to the hole in the ground before them. Beef kneeled down, hovering above the tunnel. "You're not staying to play hero!" Beef said to Celeste. She snorted, "Oh, hell no! Once that warding is dispelled, I would die seconds later!"

She gestured at the stag and wolves with her glimmering sword and quietly said, "Return to me."

Beef looked on in stunned amazement as the three creatures swiftly faded into ghostly images. They drifted through the air in a blue smoky haze, and returned to their places on Celeste's neck and face, becoming tattoos once more. She dropped down through the opening at her feet, her violet blade flaring brightly in the darkness below. Beef did not hesitate to follow her.

Chapter Thirty-Nine

Reason and Celeste stood in the center of the nine-by-seven-foot corridor. Both of them peered up to the hole above them, expecting at any moment to see demons come hurtling down at them. Celeste lowered her gaze, locking eyes with Reason. She noted the ring he wore. "Is your imagination stretched out of proportion yet? Not every day an author encounters live ghosts or demons."

Reason glanced up at the hole in the ceiling of the tunnel. "Will that force field hold?"

As if answer to his question, there came a loud ripping sound from the air above them. The blackness inside the tunnel suddenly became illuminated by traces of lemony light as the transparent force field had been shredded. A moment later, the goat-head of Baphomet appeared in the hole in the ceiling above them. "And now," he cackled, "your souls will quench my thirst!"

Jango removed a green gem from his belt pouch. He pressed on one if its facets, producing a solid clicking sound, and tossed the fist-sized jewel directly up at the fire god's astonished face. "Holy shit!" Baphomet cried out in alarm as he hastily withdrew from the opening, catching the pulsating gem with his front paws. The goat-headed being tossed the green jewel away from him as fast he could, the gem sizzling as it left his cloven hoof. A sudden explosion came from above them. A brilliant emerald light flashed across the opening, and a swirling cloud of green swept Baphomet off his hoofs, its fierce force carrying him away. Jango launched himself down the tunnel. Reason fell in behind the mogrim as he scurried down the dark depths. He said. "Only four blocks to the north, the tunnel comes out the Burlington rail yards!"

As Celeste and Beef broke into a run, Reason frowned. Despite the fact that nothing had made sense since the moment he tried on the ring, he wondered if he was losing his mind. Ghosts of Havelock boys. Demons who fed on inmates at the State Pen. Two fire gods who had instigated child sacrifices. It was all a little much, even for Reason's writer's imagination to handle.

Keeping pace with Celeste, he said, "I know I sound crazy even asking this, but did we really just escape the attack of two gods?"

"Gods," Celeste said. "A figure of speech. In truth, Moloch and Baphomet are demons, fallen from grace like Lucifer. If you study Canaanite gods, you will find many are merely demons who conned unsuspecting men and women into worshiping them. That battle of the Song Lord in Heaven? Lucifer rebelled against God, and he and one third of the angels mounted a coup. God cast them out of Heaven. Demons have been a pain in the ass ever since. Attention whores! Lucifer, Moloch, Baal, Baphomet, Mot, Seth, Ishtar, Dagan, Tiamat, and Marduk. Demons set themselves up as gods to the folk of the Middle East. In time, they became known as gods, demanding the sacrificing of children. In those days, any man who pleased his god by freely giving up his own child to be burned at his god's altar was truly a worthy man."

Reason asked, "Why did they demand kids to appease them?"

"Innocence," Celeste answered. "Children were prized for their innocence and purity, very appealing to these demon gods."

Reason said, "I don't buy that. I've been doing youth work most of my life. I've known some dastardly evil kids. Self-centered and mean-spirited kids. Besides, weren't wives and children considered by Male-dominated Hebrews as chattel? Personal property? In Old Testament times, Men were the dominant figure of all households, while women and children fell under the category of doves, lambs, and sheep, simply personal property."

Celeste said, "It has to do with the first-born sons. Remember the story about Abraham and God demanding he sacrifice his son? The Canaanite gods used psychological warfare on their worshipers, in order to control them and make them faithful subjects. If any man was willing to burn alive his own son to please his god, that man was a follower. First-born sons inherited their father's legacy. It was a big deal to sacrifice him to a god demanding his death, a way to prove his loyalty."

They neared the exit of the tunnels. Jango sprang out of the tunnel. He scampered around the pond beyond, and skittered up the trail to the train tracks running through the train yards. Reason and Beef followed the mogrim. "We need to seek shelter," Celeste said. "A safe-haven where no demon will dare to tread."

"A church?" Reason asked. "Churches are a turn-off to demons."

Celeste said, "Churches have been compromised in the past. We need to head to Sanctuary. There, no demon will trespass for there is a Guardian there who has sent dozens of them wailing back to the Unseen Realm."

Reason asked, "And where is this Sanctuary? And who in the hell is this Guardian?"

Celeste offered him an impish smirk.

And Reason and Beef stared at her as she said, "The Emerald Pub. Your grandfather, Billy Connors. With him, we'll be safe."

Chapter Thirty-Forty

Alex followed Lucas into Gus's bedroom. "What are you doing?" he asked as Lucas rummaged through Gus's drawers. "We're just kids! We're not demon hunters!"

Lucas's hand closed on a hand-crossbow inside the drawer. "These demons killed my sister! They took out Reason and Beef! They are gone, Alex! So I'm gonna kill every last one of them!"

Alex reached down into one of the drawers and pulled out a short sword. He snapped, "This is just a plain, ordinary sword! What makes you lamely think it can be powered up?"

Lucas said, "They will activate the moment we need them! If they are not magical, why would Gus have collected them? Look at my ring! It's already lighting up!" He held his free hand up.

Alex's eyes widened as he saw that the ring Lucas wore was glowing. "Look at this!" Lucas said, pulling the eagle feather from beneath his shirt. "Magic knows magic, Alex!"

The eagle feather of American Horse he wore around his neck was pulsing with a blue light. The boys gasped when Billy Connors stepped into the room, his gaze locked on the words engraved on the stock of the bow and the blade of the sword. Reading them intently, the Mage Lord said, "Morrigan? Herne? According to Gypsy lore, Morrigan is a battle-maiden. Mór-Ríoghain, means queen of phantoms. She appears as a raven. She encourages warriors to do brave deeds and is associated with the Irish banshee, meaning woman of the fairy mounds and the barrows of Celtic kings. Herne has the antlers of a stag on his head. Your Gypsy kin, Alex, equate Herne, the Hunter with the Celtic god Cernunnos, Lord of Wild Things."

Alex said, "What happens when we face these mad-dog demons, and no magic comes to life?"

Lucas snorted, "That's not going to happen, Alex!"

And Alex muttered, "Famous last words."

***

Waziri led the two fire gods onto Ballard field, a swarm of demons trailing behind them. Green-skinned, frog-faced goblins. Bug-eyed, pug-nosed boglins. Sparkling, transparent demon-wolves. "I need an altar," Moloch rasped. "I need to feed in my weakened condition on blood and hearts! The younger the better!"

The cat-eyed Moloch peered at the team of boys in the middle of a glow-ball game on the ball diamond fifty feet in front of them. Unaware of the demons leering at them as they threw phosphorescent baseballs back and forth across the field, the twelve boys continued to play. The brightly glowing balls zipped here and there, their luminous light only going dark when a boy caught one. No sooner did one boy snag a ball from the air, then a second kid tossed another, creating lines of fluorescent red light as the balls soared back and forth between them.

"Their hearts will feed me," Moloch said, smirking at the boys in their white uniforms.

The team of boys shrieked in terror. Overwhelmed by demon horror rolling over them in waves, four of the boys wet their pants. Four more took off running. "Herd them!" Moloch ordered. "The stone fireplace ahead of us in the park shall serve as an altar for the sacrifice!" And so it was that six members of the glow-ball team were forced to run before a mad pack of demons from the ballfield to the playground of Havelock Park.

***

Billy Connors led the way through the dark streets of Havelock. "They are ahead of us," he said. "Moloch needs to feed on souls in order to recharge after lying dormant for many long years. Only in his weakened condition do we have a chance at stopping him."

Lucas hefted the handheld crossbow. He detected an aura around the head of the quarrel, so he assumed it was endowed with magic.

Running beside Billy, he asked, "What do you know about these evil spirits? Living with Black Bull this past year, I have witnessed these wicked entities. I've seen the tokens of power used by Ben. There is a battle being waged by forces from the Otherworld. Wolf named me a Thunder Dreamer. But I have no clue how to summon magic with Gus's weapons."

Billy shook back the long strands of his silver hair and narrowed his eyes. "I see you wear Reason's rings, so let's just hope you are fast learners."

With a soft growl, he said, "Don't look so afraid, lads. Be brave. I will help lead you through this battle."

Lucas, Alex, and Billy entered the park, coming to a stop fifty feet from the demons inside the playground area. Blinking his slanted, cat eyes, Moloch reached out and stopped his goat-headed companion from charging forward. "Beware," he hissed. "See the engravings on the bow and sword? The marks of Herne and the Morrigan! Celtic legends? This stinks of Merlin and Taliesin! Curse druids, bards, and mage lords!"

Moloch gestured with one hand. At his command, a mad swarm of goblins came howling across the playground. They were no more than three feet tall, but there were so many of them swinging swords above their black, greasy hair, that the mob of small folk were about to shred the three who faced them. Billy reached down and helped Lucas raise the crossbow. He fired it directly at the charging goblins. The quarrel sprang from the bow, sending out a barrage of ravens into the faces of the goblins. As the flock of birds slammed into the swordsmen, they evolved into a black-cloaked woman, wild tangles of black hair spilling down past her shoulders. She landed on bare feet, twin swords whirling above her head. Fountains of bright green blood jettisoned through the air as her blades slithered into the ranks of the pug-faced goblins.

Alex whispered, "The Morrigan!"

The Morrigan sprang into the middle of the goblin horde, her swords whipping around her in a flurry. Dozens of the greasy-haired warriors died, leaving wisps of black smoke drifting through the air as they evaporated, vanishing from sight.

Moloch cast a barrage of icy-blue shards at the Morrigan. The particles of luminous sparks struck her, and she froze, one sword raised above her wild strands of raven hair, the other falling from her grasp. With a long, wail, the Morrigan disappeared, leaving behind a scattering of blue sparkles.

Moloch gave a command, and a company of boglins ran through the ranks of the decimated goblins. They were larger than their goblin cousins, standing five feet tall with broad shoulders and thick arms. Their heads were shaved with the exception of a single scalp-lock. They were all armed with spears, and they ran directly at the three dogs. "Alex!" cried Lucas. "Activate your sword!"

With terror in his eyes, Alex watched the boglins picking up speed as they raced across the playground. Upon hearing Billy growl in defiance, Alex swung the sword up to defend them. And the ring on his finger connected with the emblem of the owl engraved on the hilt of the sword. "Ouch!" he cried as a flash of light erupted from the engraving of the owl. The explosion of light stung his hands, yet he kept his grip on the hilt and looked on in wonder as a greenish-black illumination slithered down the length of the blade and shot from its tip. At once, a shiny black owl emerged from the ball of green light, and with a *Swap!* of his wide-spread wings, the raptor launched himself at the charging swarm of boglins. The moment the owl careened into the spearmen, he evolved into a black-cloaked, hooded figure, wielding twin daggers. The hooded one rose up to a full seven feet tall, and with a whirl to the right, he took out three boglins. Wheeling away from the fallen trio, he lashed out at four more of the foes, leaving tendrils of smoke in their wake, his blades slashing into them, sending them to the Otherworld.

Flinging one dagger overhanded, he skewered one spearman, then heaved his second dagger into the breast of another. The two boglins evaporated, leaving this world to hurtle back to another plane of existence. The hooded man clapped his gloved hands together, and with a crack of white lightning, a longbow appeared in his hands. With a flurry of rapid movement, the large bowman fired off a dozen fiery arrows, leaving a red spray trailing through the air before plunging into the breasts of twelve more of the boglins.

Screaming in rage, Moloch raised one fist, and from it sprang a burst of fire that evolved into a winged serpent, wildly twisting and crackling as it sailed toward the large bowman. The moment its fiery fangs closed on the breast of the hooded man, the hood fell down about his shoulders, revealing the antlers he sported on his head.

"Herne!" said Alex as the antler-crowned bowman vanished in an explosion of dazzling green light. "The charges on each relic have run out! What's the plan now?"

"Payback for my sister!" Lucas snapped, angrily.

Chapter Forty-One

Alex gestured at the team and the two fire gods. The boys all wept hopelessly, certain they were about to die. Lucas said, "What do these demons want with them?"

Billy said, "Their still beating hearts will be ripped from their chests that the fire gods of the Canaanite faith can be fully restored."

Lucas snapped, "To hell with these weirdo gods!"

He raised his fist and from the ring on his finger a beam of scintillating light shot through the air, striking Moloch directly between the eyes. He wailed in pain and crumpled in Baphomet's grasp. The smaller demon staggered beneath his weight and they both collapsed there on the playground. "Did," Lucas whispered, "I do that?"

He looked down at the ring now glowing a bright green on his finger. He then felt a firm hand close on his shoulder. "Not bad for not knowing what you were doing, lad!" said Billy. "Just think, if you had a little training, you would be a force to be reckoned with!"

The Irishman raised a black staff in his hand. A blaze of white-hot lightning spat from the end of the oaken staff and struck the two fire gods. They were engulfed in a blue fireball that rendered Moloch and Baphomet unconscious. With a yelp of terror, the terrified team of boys ran down the alley north of the park. Watching them flee, Billy said, "The stories those young lads will be sharing with their parents. Poor lads will more than likely need therapy."

There came a shimmer beside Billy. All five mages of the White Council appeared there in the park, their black staves blazing. Cat, Cinnamon, and the Three Bears sent waves of blue fire washing over their prone forms. The old Irishman offered Lucas and Alex a weary smile. "Off to home, lads," he said. "I heard that you are staying with my grandson, Reason. He'll be worried about you."

"Reason is alive?" Lucas asked. "What about my sister?"

Billy said, "Alive and well. Both wondering where the hell you two are. Head home, now."

Tearing up with relief, Lucas followed Alex out of the park.

***

Khalid was furious. His fury changed to disgust, then sickness. Had his emotions been displayed on a multifaceted jewel, his soul would have been illuminated like a glistening rainbow. The shades of his aura were so strong, he put forth an incandescent blue glow that shimmered from the top of his turban-covered head to the tips of his military-style boots. He was afire with an inner light, and he stood there muttering foul curses. "We killed the wrong man," he said.

Kneeling beside the body, Stone used the silencer on his pistol to peel back the hood from the face of the man gunned down only seconds ago. Raynes gasped when she saw the man's eyes staring vacantly at the ceiling overhead. "Not Waziri? How is this so? We've trailed him since he left the airport back in Chicago!"

Still kneeling beside the dead man, Stone glanced up at Khalid. "Waziri pulled a switch on us. It could have been back in the States, or in Paris. Somewhere along the line, Waziri passed the tracking device off to this man. We've been blindly following this honing device from the States over here to the Middle East."

The three of them looked at each other, knowing how badly they had failed. It had been decided back at the Omaha airport how they would handle Waziri when they caught up to him. It wasn't a matter of if Waziri lived once he reached the Middle East, but how long he would be allowed to do so.

The quicker they accomplished their task, the safer the world would be. Waziri needed to be put down. Stone and Khalid had been in complete agreement over this, with Raynes being conflicted on the grounds she was an agent of the US, and as such, assassinating enemy combatants was not to be taken lightly. In truth, she knew it happened all the time overseas; it was just that she had never had to make that decision herself. Nor to carry it out.

The three of them had joined forces back in Lincoln to track down Waziri, with the understanding that the man was to be arrested for attempting to destroy US military dogs at Wounded Arrow. As an agent of Homeland Security, Agent Raynes had secured an agreement with Khalid and Stone that the end of the road would not result in a dramatic shoot-out. Back in the US, as they chased the man they thought to be Waziri from one airport to another, her goal had been to arrest him quietly without incident.

During the week they spent in the States, trailing the man they assumed had been Waziri, Raynes had shared with the two men her own emotional attachment to the man. Stone and Khalid had listened in respectful silence as Gloria revealed the greatest heartache of her life. Her own parents, as emissaries to Africa, had been in the World Trade center on 911. Both had been killed when the planes struck the buildings. In that one terrorist attack, Gloria had lost her parents.

And although, Waziri could not be tied to any involvement of the bombing of the World Trade center, she knew he was a member of the terrorist network who brought death to innocent victims like the three-thousand that had died during the 911 attack.

Gloria had joined Homeland to counter terrorist movements and be responsible for enforcing the laws that shut them down. Only she was committed to doing her job in a legitimate manner, nothing outside the box would be acceptable to her.

While Khalid and Stone took a hardline stance against showing mercy to Waziri, they did agree to abide by Gloria's terms during the first stages of the hunt. And yet, all agreements to bring Waziri in alive, were abandoned once he'd left American soil. Since it was made known he had flown back to the Middle East, Waziri was to be eliminated on sight in order to put a stop to his terrorist activities. In the end, ironically, it had been Agent Raynes who had fired the fatal shot. And yet, she killed the wrong man.

"We need to get a cleaner team in here," Khalid told them both.

Stone stood up, removing the silencer from his pistol. He moved swiftly down the tunnel-like hallway inside the tomb they were in. "Call in cleaners," he said. "But any second now, some unassuming tourists are going to discover our victim's body. We should be long gone by then."

Nodding in agreement, Khalid slipped his own gun back into a shoulder holster beneath his jacket. He went to one knee beside the corpse. After several seconds of searching through his jacket pocket, he produced a small red gem.

Stone and Gloria exchanged curious looks as Khalid tossed the gem down on the stones at his feet. At once, the red, dime-sized gem shattered and a roiling cloud exploded from its fragments. As the rippling reddish smoke parted, an iron gateway was revealed, complete with a lion-headed knocker at its center with an iron ring in its mouth. "What are you doing?" cried Stone as Khalid reached through the smoky tendrils before them and pulled on the ring in the lion's mouth.

"Getting rid of the body," Khalid responded.

The elaborate gate made no sound as it swung open, revealing a sunken garden beyond. Inside a circular pit was a round wooden table where a pair of white-robed women sat in deep discussion. The ladies looked at Khalid standing there within the gateway. Surprised by the appearance of the gate, the two cats seated before the fountain at the center of the garden, bounded over to confront Khalid.

"Padraic! Eddie!" said a woman at the table. "He is friend, not foe! That would be Khalid, our emissary from the Middle East! And come just in time to advise us what to do with our problem!"

Stone stared at the two dark-haired ladies in stunned surprise. Cat and Cinnamon, owners of the Roaring Lion bookstore in Havelock gestured at the prone body sprawled directly behind Khalid. "Billy?" Cat said. "Be a dear, and please clean that up."

Chapter Forty-Two

Tamping out his briar pipe in the shadows at the far end of the garden, Billy Connors rose to his feet. As he approached the gateway, he gently scooted the two cats out of his path so he could approach the body. He wore a torc around his neck, and it glowed as he reached down and drew the dead man back through the gateway. The Mage Lord carried the man into an alcove to one side of the garden. When he returned to the garden, he was shadowed by the Three Bears.

Looking at Stone, who looked completely lost staring at the three large men, Billy said, "Our hometown of Havelock is known amongst the White Council. In our suburb are waystations between alternate realms. The Emerald Pub. The Roaring Lion bookstore. And the Trainyards Tavern, owned by the three Bears, Kodiak, Winter, and the Griz. All are magic users of significant power, who are committed to battling the Unseen who are bred of Darkness."

"Wizards and witches?" Stone said.

Billy nodded. "That is one name for them, but trust me, they are much more than that. And it appears, they need our help."

Cinnamon told Stone, "Waziri summoned the two demons. They are back, not yet in their full power. It was your daughter, Stone, who came to Billy, seeking his help. Billy confronted them at the park, creating two imprisoning gems to anchor their souls, in order to dispatch them to another realm. Since you are at the Valley of the Kings, place these gems inside the vault of Tutankhamun, where Moloch and Baphomet can be imprisoned for good."

Griz rumbled, "What is this Valley of Kings?"

Cinnamon said, "Also known as the Valley of the Gates of the Kings. It is a valley in Egypt where, for 500 years tombs were excavated for the pharaohs. The valley stands on the west bank of the Nile. It contains 63 tombs and 120 chambers. In modern times it became famous for the discovery of the tomb of Tutankhamun, with its curse of the pharaohs. Khalid has managed to open a pathway for us to send the souls of the two demons into this tomb."

Cat looked over at Billy. He shrugged and asked, "What about the Dog Soldier? Don't you think we should consult with him?"

Kodiak said, "Wolf is dealing with a strange castle that has appeared out near Wounded Arrow. He has left us in charge of the anchoring gems. I don't think he would oppose this plan."

Khalid stood in the corridor of the Great Pharoah, listening to a hushed debate between the six members of the White Council in the garden before him. Behind him, Stone began pacing up and down the corridor, while Raynes stood there looking baffled as to how Khalid had managed to open such a rift between realms. She was not easily accepting things at face value and wondered how it was that Stone seemed to be dealing with the situation so well.

She was still overwhelmed with the fact she had shot and killed the wrong man. After several long moments of more debate between those in the sunken garden, Griz lumbered over to the gateway, two glowing fist-sized gems in his hands. He handed them to Khalid. The massive, golden-haired wizard said, "It took a lot out of the Irishman to subdue those two. As it was, the Bears called on Odin, Thor, and Freya to help imprison Moloch and Baphomet inside the jewels. Handle them carefully, Khalid, Lord of the Sands."

Kahlid tucked the two pulsating gems into a leather pouch depending from his shoulder by a braided strap. He then nodded and turned away from the gateway.

Inside the sunken garden, Cinnamon heard the loud, angry hiss of her two cats, Padraic and Eddie. She turned to watch the two felines launch themselves at the mob of small figures racing past the council table, their overlarge eyes fixed on the slowly closing gateway between the realms. "Fair Folk children?" Cat asked, in puzzled tones. "Are they rebelling against their Queen!"

With a swift flick of her staff, Cinnamon sent a sapphire fireball sailing across the chamber, directly toward the mob of wild-haired fairy children, all racing toward the closing gateway. The brilliant ball of blue light struck the gate in front of them and dozens of the little figures ran directly into the center of the phosphorous flaming sphere. With wild cries of dismay, the fairy folk struck the barrier and were hurtled back into the garden. Some fell in stunned heaps upon the floor, while others dropped to their knees, holding their small hands out in a gesture of surrender. Some bowed their heads and wept openly, ashamed of their own actions.

A snigger of wicked laughter came from one wild imp, his strands of dark hair trailing over his bare shoulders as he dove through the closing gateway. Following behind the shaggy-haired imp, a child-like figure with the face and head of a coyote sprang up from the floor, slipping in through the gateway just inches behind the imp. And just as the gate was inches from closing, cutting off one realm from the other, a tall, slender red-haired boy tucked and rolled, as he, too, passed through from the garden and into the Valley of Kings.

The three misfit Fair Folk children danced around Khalid who stood in the center of the corridor, protectively holding the leather bag that contained the two gems imprisoning the souls of Moloch and Baphomet. The Saracen's brow furrowed deeply as he named the fey creatures of myth that capered around him, saying, "Puck. Loki. And Coyote the Trickster."

Coyote snatched the bag, causing the strap to snap. With a burst of laughter, he tossed the bag to Puck, whose large blue eyes sparkled with mischief. He caught it and took off racing down the long corridor. Loki, red hair streaming, took off running behind Coyote and the blue-eyed Puck. The three continued to play a game of keep-away even as they sprinted toward the open gateway at the end of the tunnel-like hallway.

"Damn them!" Stone snapped, drawing his pistol from the holster beneath his jean jacket. Raynes armed herself, as well, and yet before the two could pursue the small beings, Khalid said, "Put your guns away. Bullets can't harm them. They are just having fun. Once we catch up to them when this tunnel ends at King Tut's tomb, we can explain why we need those gems back."

Stone growled, "Fun with gems that holds the souls of demons?"

Khalid said, "Puck, also known as Robin Goodfellow, is a nature sprite. He is well-known among the English, the Welsh, the Celts, the Norse, the Swedish, and Iceland, with the term pixie originating from the diminutive of Puck. In mythology, a trickster is a character in a story which exhibits a degree of secret knowledge. Tricksters are archetypal characters who appear in the myths of many cultures. They violate principles of natural order, playfully disrupting normal life. Often, the bending of rules takes the form of tricks. Tricksters can be cunning. In Norse mythology, the mischief-maker is Loki. In many Native American mythologies, the Coyote stole fire from the stars. These fey jokers are Puck, Loki, and the Coyote."

"Come," Raynes said, "let us go explain to these tricksters that they are playing with fire. Let us bring reason to the unreasonable."

A few minutes later, the three of them approached the cavern-like opening into the chamber beyond the shadowy corridor they were in, when Raynes said, "They've removed the gems from the pouch, and they are playing a very dangerous game of catch with both of them!"

A concerned look on his face, Khalid ran the last few steps into the tomb of King Tut, where Loki had just thrown one of the gems to Puck, who was suddenly jostled by Coyote. Khalid, Stone, and Raynes looked on in horror as the gem tumbled out of Puck's small hands and fell toward the hard, cold stones of the floor.

And all three tricksters spoke in unison, saying, "Ooops!"

***

Khalid, Stone, and Agent Raynes came rushing into an underground tomb. Before them, three small figures stood cowering in one corner of the chamber, trapped there by the goat-headed Baphomet. Loki, Puck, and Coyote quailed in terror as Baphomet glared at them with his goat-like slanted eyes and inched his way closer to them.

Behind the fire god, shards of the broken imprisonment gem lay scattered where Loki had dropped it onto the stones of the tomb's floor, allowing the soul of Baphomet to escape.

"Tricksters?" Baphomet growled. "The dark gods of the universe sent Tricksters to the tomb of Tut in the Valley of the Kings? Where is the gem that holds Moloch's soul?"

Cringing like terrified children, Loki, Puck, and Coyote let out pitiful cries as Baphomet conjured up a handful of glistening black snakes. Clutching them in his hand, he raised them above the heads of the three lesser gods. Each snake had long fangs that dripped with poison so vile and harsh, it sizzled as it fell to the stones of the floor.

"Stop this!" Khalid shouted as he stepped over the glittering shards scattered beside the gem that imprisoned the soul of Molech, for it did not break and shatter when it struck the floor. It was still intact, with the soul of Moloch trapped within it. Unaware of the gem on the floor between him and the sarcophagus of the boy-king, Tut, Baphomet continued to advance on the three lesser gods.

Swinging his black walnut staff up above his head, Khalid whispered a spell, and brought the black staff down hard on Baphomet's horned head. Thunder rumbled from somewhere outside the tomb in the Valley of Kings, and sheets of blue lightning rained down on the fire god even as he tormented the three lesser gods. Bolts of thin shafts of the lightning struck each snake, ripping them from the fire god's hand and pinning them to the floor. Each tendril of the wicked blue lightning penetrated the heads of the snakes and tore through their long, slender bodies, killing them within seconds. Enraged, Baphomet cast a barrage of fiery pellets at the Mage Lord, ripping the staff from his grasp. Khalid was struck in the chest and hurtled back off his feet. He slammed into the sarcophagus of the dead boy-king, then flew back against the stone wall beyond, striking it with a sickening thud.

Baphomet drew a dagger from relics hanging on one wall of the tomb. Stone Holland swept up Khalid's staff. A burst of green light shot from the staff, hammering the fire-god back against the wall. Loki, Puck, and Coyote scampered out of the way. In one last attempt to ward off the magic washing over him, Baphomet lashed out, a dispersal spell flickering weakly on his fingertips. And yet, before he could activate his own magic, an explosive concussion plowed into the fire-god with crackling green fire. Engulfed in the emerald shades of power, Baphomet collapsed there on the floor of the tomb. Stone turned and watched as Billy Connors stepped in between the realms, his sizzling staff held before him.

Loki let out a shrill giggle, gesturing at the unconscious fire-god with a one-fingered salute. Coyote and Puck danced around his prone form, kicking at the incapacitated Baphomet. "Stop!" Billy said. "You three tricksters have done enough damage!"

Offering the Mage Lord contrite looks, the three lesser gods crept out of the chamber of the dead boy-king. In seconds, Billy conjured a second gem of imprisonment and with a flourish of his hands, re-captured the soul of Baphomet.

Raynes picked up the leather pouch from the floor, opening it so that Billy could place both gems inside. The old Irishman walked toward the shimmering portal connecting the tomb with the dragon chamber back at the Emerald pub. He said, "If I had the power, I would teleport the three of you out of the Valley of Kings and back to the Emerald, but that is beyond me."

Dazed, Khalid asked, "What will you do with the gems?"

Stepping through the portal, Billy said, "Place them in a secure place out at Wounded Arrow. Someone from beyond, has conjured a castle that was designed to hold the souls of the two fire-gods."

With that, Billy Connors was gone.

Chapter Forty-Three

Reason seated himself in a high-backed booth in the Emerald Pub. He picked up the steaming cup of black coffee situated on the table in front of him, sipping it slowly. He smiled and thought of his grandfather who had sat in that very booth for over forty years, sipping at his own cups of hot black coffee. Billy Connors once told him, "I've settled for the lesser of two evils, one being the booze, the other being the bean that makes goats kick up their happy feet and dance after they've consumed a score of the little black beans!"

In contrast to the days Billy was an alcoholic, his coffee-drinking mellowed the Irishman, proud owner of the Emerald, considerably.

Reason studied the Emerald's rustic woodwork, its white-washed walls, oak beams, high-backed booths, and tall stools situated before a bar with brass foot rails. Tapestries on the walls depicted castles, and dominating the west wall, was a red banner with three black lions wearing gold crowns. The most eye-catching sight in the pub was the enormous stained-glass window at the front of the building, facing out onto Have Ave. The dragon carrying the lime-green emerald in its talons had cost the old man a pretty penny. Reason remembered the first night he'd set foot in the pub. Billy met him inside the entrance. He'd said, "I'd like you to watch the meeting from a surveillance console in my office. Maybe you can detect if you're r telling it true or lying."

Old Will Connors had then led him to his office at the back of the pub. Tall and scarecrow thin, Billy's snow-white, collar-length hair trailed back over his ears in wavy wisps, and the tips of his thick, white mustache were waxed and twisted into tight curls. To add to his noble appearance, the old Irishman wore an expensive three-piece suit, but as Reason looked into Billy's ocean blue eyes, he detected a dangerous rage roiling beneath the surface of his regal-looking exterior. He reminded him of an old, gruff lion.

"I know you are reluctant," he told Reason, "but perhaps by you watching from a distance, we can resolve this issue."

The issue was, Reason at 13 had gone to a party. During a bust of said party, Reason had a collision with private investigator, Jessie Dalton, and a drug dealer named Brooks. In the aftermath of their floundering around in a shadowy kitchen, Reason had snatched up what he thought to be his leather jacket. Instead, he came away from the party with the jacket of Brooks. Later, after hiding out in a doghouse behind the party house, Reason discovered a strange blue key in the pocket of this jacket. Jessie tracked him down, and there at the Nelson house, the private detective had shared with the boys and their mother, Rose, that the key belonged to a safe-deposit box at a Havelock bank. Inside the box, was evidence that would solve the murder of Jessie's informant named Kelly Drake. Jessie warned the Nelsons that Brooks and Jack Holland, who may have murdered her, badly wanted this key to prevent the evidence from falling into the hands of the local police.

Reason, plagued by a bad case of oppositional defiance disorder, refused to cooperate with Jessie and stubbornly kept the key. Jessie enlisted Billy Connors to talk sense into Reason. Using the pub's security system, Billy saw right through Reason's lies.

Jessie had escorted Reason into the pub. Patrons looked up from their meals to stare at the rugged-looking owner leading the boy across the room. Reason walked over and stood beneath the heads of seven deer mounted above the mantle. The numerous strands of tiny, green lights wrapped around the antlers of the bucks caused them to resemble fireflies floating above their heads. Reason shifted his gaze and peered at the wooden plaque on the mantle beneath their chins. Reason turned to face Billy.

It all played out inside of his head as he sat there:

Reason asked, "Is that the plaque the Sinn Fein gave you? Mom said the IRA were terrorists, yet you believed they were patriots, and you sent money back to Ireland to finance their war against British oppression. Mom says you're the King of Scoundrels, the great Irish Godfather of Havelock"

"Godfather!" Billy snorted. "Do you know your history? Nelson means Neal's son, which is derived from Niall, High King of Ireland! You've got the blood of kings in you! Your ancestor founded an Irish dynasty. Niall's raids into foreign lands in the third century resulted in Saint Patrick coming to Ireland. He became a great saint, yet you fall so short of what you could be. It's tragic and disappointing."

Quietly, he said, "Tell me, lad, do you have the key that Jess needs to solve this murder?"

***

Only later did Reason find out that Billy was his grandfather, and Rose's estranged father. In Billy's checkered past of running guns and other nefarious deeds, one deed came back to haunt him. He broke away from the IRA and as a result of this, his wife was killed in a car accident in Ireland. Due to her death, Billy turned to the bottle, and Rose had wanted nothing to do with the old Irishman ever since. Rose did, however, allow her two boys to establish a relationship with the man and though she never forgave him for her mother's death, she was cordial to William Connors, the Godfather of Havelock.

Tonight, as previously planned by Billy, Reason came down to the Emerald. He was greeted by members of his brother's boxing team, who served as Billy's bouncers. Doug Kaluza, Tony Menefee, and Joe and Tony Mendoza. The four had retired from the ring but stayed on there at the Emerald as security staff. Although Boone had walked away from the MMA years before, he still stayed in touch with the four Havelock tough guys. Tall, blond-haired Doug greeted him at the door. "Welcome, Bossman," he said.

Dark-haired Tiger handed him two ornate keys. Reason glanced down at them, finding one to have a rampant lion on its end, while the other was adorned with the same emerald that dominated the window of the pub. The tiny gems inside the lion's eyes were blue, while the emerald was a deep green. Before Reason could examine them, the Mendoza brothers ushered him into the dining hall of the pub and seated him before the massive fireplace.

Joe Mendoza said, "As secrets go, the boys and I have had a hard time keeping this from you, but tonight, despite Billy's mysterious absence, the Emerald Pub is being deeded over to you."

Doug pulled a chair out from the table opposite of Reason. Tiger came from the bar, carrying a bottle and two shot glasses. He placed one glass down in front of Reason and moved around the table to place the other one before Billy's usual spot at the table. He then opened the rather ornate bottle, with a label depicting a dragon connected to a knight by the lance driven into its side.

"A shot of Dragon's Breath," Tiger said, pouring from the bottle and filling both jiggers to the brim, "to seal the deal."

Doug stared down at the golden liquid and said, "Now, although Billy's not touched a dram for over 40 years, and I know how you feel about spirits, Reason, but to make this official, indulge us."

Placing the keys on the table next to the jigger, Reason stared down at the swirling gold liquid for several seconds before picking it up. He killed the drink. He had never tasted anything like it in his life. The gold liquid stirred images that rose slowly like a fish rising sluggishly in murky waters. He saw in his mind's eye: *The marble statue of a lion-man in the tall spire of a castle's tower. In his raised fist, an emerald pulsated with an inner light that sent shimmering rays shooting across a lush landscape, dappling a forest beyond with sparkling light beams.*

The second swallow of the liquid stirred a second image: *A silver dragon soared across a stormy sky, lightning crackling all around her outstretched wings.*

The third wash of the gold liquid going down his throat produced an explosion of images: *He was mounted on a black stallion. In his hand he held a glowing blue sword, and he was dressed in some sort of black leather armor with a roaring lion emblazoned on his breast. A swarm of antler-crowned warriors with florescent braids of hair surrounded him, and Reason raised his sword and he swung . . .*

He sat his shot glass down with a solid *clink!*

Doug said, "That brew of Dragon's Breath comes from the Inn of the Howling Moon in Valasar. Delivered by Creed Blackstag, Bard Chieftain of the Order of the Lion."

He gestured at the keys. "The emerald key opens the door to the Emerald. The lion's head opens the door located in the back room of the pub, beside the sign, which states, '*Here, there be Dragons.*'"

He tossed a pen to Reason and slid the deed across the table in front of him, and said, "Sign it and the Emerald is yours."

Silently shaking his head in disbelief, Reason signed his name to the deed. Doug, Tiger, Tony, and Joe shook his hand, and left, saying they would see him tomorrow evening, serving as security staff. All four of them told him to say hello to Boone for them the next time he called. That night, Reason became the new owner of the Emerald Pub, but he wished Boone was there to help him manage the place. His brother had gone off to Scotland nearly a year ago. Although he called home at least once a week, Boone now lived in an ancient castle in the highlands of Scotland. He was doing research on their family line that included the MacAveys, a royal family in Scotland.

Several times, Boone had urged Reason to move over there with him, but until Reason located their missing grandfather, he refused to leave the Emerald behind.

Chapter Forty-Four

Reason was greeted by a large, heavily panting pit bull that came bounding into the Emerald. It was a beautiful dog, with black fur masking his face, and the same black fur trailing down his back, blending with his broad white chest. All four of his paws were black, as well. The dog gave him a gentle head-butt, proceeding to slobber and drool all over his pant leg as its head came to rest on his leg.

"Well," he said, "nice to see you, too, Lobo."

Lobo let out an excited whine as Beef Tory came through the front door of the pub. The bearded man sporting a long, braided pony-tail, approached Reason and placed an item on the table in front of him. Beef took a seat across from him, grunting as the rambunctious pit bull tried to scramble up into the booth and join him. "Manners, Lobo. Remember your manners."

Reason peered down at the black bandana. He proceeded to pet Lobo as he settled down beside him. "Lobo's nose-work," Beef said, "led me to Stone Holland's place. That bandana belonged to Lucas."

Reason said, "The bandana and the baseball bat. I just put two and two together. And the kid's temper."

He paused, took another sip of his coffee, then said, "Evidently, Lucas came here for payback."

Beef asked, "This had to do with Billy sending those two gems through the portal? Gramps did involve his dad in this mess, so you think the kid came here seeking revenge?"

Reason said, "He brought a baseball bat with him for some reason, and I don't think during the wee hours, he was playing ball. Granddad has been missing for two days now, and tonight I learned that he deeded the Emerald over to me."

He slid the deed across the table. Beef studied it a moment, then said, "The new owner of the Emerald, wow." He looked to the oak door at the end of the hallway. "You think Billy went in there?"

Reason's gaze lingered on the doorway leading to the chamber beyond. "Whatever lies beyond the 'Dragon Door,' I don't think Billy would consider using it under any circumstances."

Beef asked, "Even if he used it to escape the Holland clan?"

"It crossed my mind," Reason said, solemnly.

"So," Beef said, "do you want me to track the kid down, get him alone somewhere and ask him what he was doing breaking in here, or should I put the same question to Nate?"

Reason shrugged. "I can't see the Den doing anything this serious. If the other clubs found out they'd harmed Gramps, they would shut the Den down in a rapid heartbeat. They all respect that old Irishman. But the kid coming in here to cause mischief?"

Beef said, "I know you don't want to believe it, having him in your care as a foster kid, but I don't have the same feeling about this little hot-head Lucas. He can be a menace."

At the mention of Lucas's name, Lobo gave a low whine. Reason nodded as if the dog had silently communicated with him. "Lobo, it seems, has the same opinion of the kid as I do. It was Lucas who rescued my dog from Nate when he tranqued him and stole him. El Lobo thinks pretty highly of the temperamental kid."

The two sat in silence for long moments. Reason sipped at his coffee, gently stroking the head of Lobo. He said, "Maybe he's in there, Beef. Maybe he discovered a reason to enter the second chamber. Has he ever said anything to you about what lies beyond? He shared a few secrets about the Dragon Room with me."

Beef said, "Secrets?"

Reason asked, "Ever heard of virtual reality?"

"Virtual, what?" Beef asked.

Reason said, "Alternative realms. Virtual gaming? The computer-generated simulation of a three-dimensional image can be interacted with by a person using special equipment, such as a helmet fitted with sensors. Augmented reality systems are considered a form of VR that layers virtual information over a live camera feed into a headset giving the user the ability to view three-dimensional images. A person using VR equipment can interact with virtual features."

Beef said, "Sounds like a cool system. But what does this have to with why Gramps is missing?"

Reason said. "Gramps discovered a way to be involved in my youth work that has just been approved by Judge Sully at juvenile court. It took a lot of legal wrangling, and case studies by therapists and psychologists as proof that it might succeed."

Beef asked, "What does juvenile court have to do with gaming? Video games are frowned upon by therapists, psychologists, and a lot of parents. Grand Mobile Killing Fields doesn't inspire most kids to rise to become responsible adults. Why would Judge Sully be asked to condone gaming here at the Emerald?"

Reason smiled. "Says the cop who has been doing surveillance on the bad guys and rotten hombres from the sidelines?"

Beef's laughter caused Lobo to stare at him. "All I know about kids, I learned from trying to stay one step ahead of one troubled boy back in the day when he ended up with that damned key."

Reason said, "The things that plague at-risk kids is what I've been dealing with for the past ten years. Drug abuse. Teen suicide. Runaway and throw-away kids. Anger and rage management. Probation. Institutions. Parole. Prison. All just endless Celtic hoops that kids find themselves trapped in with the juvenile court system.

"So, Gramps proposed a new program, using one kid as a test pilot to instigate a video program that not only curbs delinquent behavior, but builds self-esteem and character through leadership skills. Something new in the field of youth work."

Looking down the hallway to the oak door, Beef's eyes opened wide as he realized what Reason was now talking about. "Wait a sec," he said, "Gramps doesn't even know what this secret chamber is all about, and yet he approved of you putting a kid in there? Not even knowing what plane of existence that kid would end up on?"

Reason said, "I'm not sure, but based on what Gramps shared with me, I created a game script and submitted it to Game Wizards, and they designed a virtual reality game that can be played with the use of a headset, connected to that room by a single cord. Judge Sully was really pleased when I got involved in youth work. In pitching this VR game designed to help delinquent kids, I presented all the programs to help kids. Scared Straight. DARE. Big Brothers. Big Sisters. Foster care. Group homes. Drug treatment. Juvenile Justice spends millions each year. I just proposed to Sully a method to boost a kid's self-esteem through a role-playing game that will build leadership skills. If a kid wins the game, to save and rescue an entire new realm, what kid wouldn't be intrigued by that?"

***

After speaking with Beef at the Emerald, Reason and Lobo returned home, where he found Grunge and Goblin sprawled beside Lucas in the den. Reason placed the baseball bat on his desk, making certain Lucas saw it.

Purposely ignoring the bat, Lucas asked, "So, have you made a decision on which kid will test pilot the game?"

"Not you," Reason said. "You're still on probation, so not a likely candidate. Besides, during the time you've lived with me, I watched you play video games. You flipped out whenever you didn't win,

152

and if a challenge became too overwhelming, you threw your controller against the wall. You're not the most patient gamer."

Still purposely ignoring the bat, Lucas asked, "Is it Alex then?"

Reason said, "Alex Thorn is your best friend, so maybe you can encourage him to keep his cool when he sits down behind the console tomorrow afternoon."

"Yes," Lucas said, "I can tell him not to have blow-ups like I do."

"Good," Reason said, noting that Lucas stared intently at the bat. "That would be a great help on your part. Alex will need a lot of support if I am going to make this gaming therapy a success. And yet, there is something else you could help with."

"Me?" Lucas said, squirming uncomfortably in his chair.

Reason smiled. "You know I told Beef, that deep down you really had a heart. He did not believe me. But I tried to convince him that my dog loved you. Always a good sign when a dog accepts you."

Lucas glanced over at Lobo sleeping beside Reason. He looked down to Grunge and Goblin snoozing at his feet. "Yeah. Dogs know what's roiling around inside a person."

The long-haired youth worker was always three steps ahead of him. Reason said, "I was a conning, manipulator as a kid. I had defiance disorder. I'm surprised I lived through all the tirades I put my brother through. He wanted to pummel me senseless. I was a major brat of the worst kind. Don't think you invented that mode. I'm ahead of you there, bud. You can't bullshit a bullshitter."

Lucas shook back his shaggy, blond bangs with a quick flick of his head. "What are you accusing me of?"

Reason said, "We were just having a friendly convo about my new virtual reality game to be played by Alex down at the Emerald, the pub owned by my grandpa, Billy Connors—"

"Who you know I hate with a mad-dog passion," Lucas said.

Reason said, "Question is, how bad do you hate him? He's been missing for two days."

Lucas went into full meltdown mode, a defensive move that Reason was prepared for, for he'd seen his performance many times while fostering the volatile kid. He simply sat there as Lucas exploded out of the chair, snatched up his baseball bat, and left the den in a major huff. All three dogs peered curiously at Reason as the back door slammed loudly. "Damn," Reason said. "Temper, temper."

Chapter Forty-Five

Tucking wild strands of his blond hair beneath his black bandana, twelve-year-old Lucas Holland slid from the shadows and into the moonlight. He imagined himself a Ninja pirate, dressed all in black and creeping around at 2AM when no cars or people were in sight. He stealthily raised the wooden baseball bat he carried, moving back to the edge of the sidewalk, giving himself plenty of room for what he planned to do.

Before him, the Emerald took up the entire block at the center of Havelock Avenue. The Irish pub was a legendary steak house there in the small suburb. Patrons included Irish railroaders, Husker football fans, and dozens of biker clubs on Poker runs, fund-raising for one good cause or another. The entire rough crowd were all drawn there by its home-brewed ale and its fine Nebraska beef.

Lucas faced the huge stained-glass window that dominated the pub's front wall. It was a central focal point of the business district, depicting a black dragon in flight, red flames erupting from his mouth, contrasting sharply with the green emerald clutched in his talons. He could have sworn the flames slowly unfurled as he faced the building. If he squinted just right, he detected a slight flutter of the dragon's wings. He froze there on the sidewalk, creeped out by the emerald pulsating with an eerie green light within the six-by-eight-foot window.

Old man Billy Connors should have never interfered in his dad's business. The old Irishman had placed Stone Holland, president of the Elder's Den, in deep trouble. Since teaming up with the anti-terrorist agent, Khalid, Stone had gotten in way over his head in his hunt for the extremist, Waziri. Someone needed to arrest the man, Lucas just didn't want it to be his dad. Besides, now that Waziri was still in the States and not in the Middle East, Lucas knew his dad was on a wild goose chase. And now that Billy had captured the souls of Moloch and Baphomet, imprisoning them inside of two gems, the old Irishman had sent them through a portal to the Valley of Kings in Egypt. Billy placed Stone in danger by sending their entrapped souls through the portal. Lucas was determined to get even with the Irishman for putting his dad's life at risk.

He dug down inside his jean pockets for one of the black rocks he'd stuffed them with earlier on his way down to the Avenue. He plucked out one sleek, black stone, tossing it up into the air a few times. Remembering what his Uncle Nate had said about putting a bullet from his .357 directly through Billy's prized window, Lucas determined he would beat his uncle to it. He thought about stealing Nate's big pistol, but he knew he'd probably get caught and throttled for such an infraction, so he resorted to the next best thing besides bullets: Rocks.

Satisfied that the one he'd selected would do, Lucas tossed it up into the air, took hold of his bat with both hands, and swung at the falling rock with all his might.

Thock! The satisfying sound echoed up and down the Avenue, bringing a smirk to his face, and his powerful swing of the bat sent the rock flying directly at the illuminated window.

Prrrrrrfht! was the sound that came from the panes of the colored window as the rock struck it. Where Lucas expected shattering glass and a domino-effect of complete destruction, figuring the entire window would cave in, he blinked in astonishment. The rock struck the glass, and was literally sucked inside the stained-glass window.

"What the holy hell!" he gasped, staring at the ripples that passed through the entire artistic creation. In the aftermath of what he expected to be a satisfying crash, he stood there watching the dragon shudder as the warbled, rippling effect flowed over it. Lucas tried another rock. He tossed it high in the air, swung the bat two-handed, and *Thock!* sent another sleek, black rock at the stained-glass window of the Emerald. *Phhhhrrfring!* echoed shrilly in his ears.

He blinked again as this rock, too, vanished within the deep greens of the emerald clutched in the dragon's talons. The same ripples spread swiftly across the face of the backlit window.

This time when they reached the dragon's flames, there came an airy *Poof!* And the flames flickered as if they had been splattered by cold water. "No way!" Lucas growled. "No way in hell!"

He gripped the baseball bat in both hands, swung it back and over his shoulder, and charged at the window, determined to shatter it to smithereens. The bat struck the glass with considerable force, passed completely through the window, and the momentum of his charge, carried Lucas forward and on into the pub.

He landed opposite the stained-glass window on a bearskin rug before an enormous stone fireplace. He cringed and closed his eyes, fully expecting the entire window to come crashing down on him, showering him with a bright burst of colored glass as it shattered into a million pieces.

But when he opened his eyes, the window behind him remained intact. Not even a crack to show he'd come through it. Lucas's brow furrowed deeply. He shivered as he realized he had just passed through the multi-colored glass without a scratch. He shivered again, just thinking how he should really be plucking slivers of sharp glass from his skin, and yet there he stood, unharmed.

He reached up, removing the bandana from his head, golden hair spilling past the collar of his black T-shirt. He used the bandana to wipe the sweat from his brow, and tears from his cheeks. He couldn't help himself. No way he could have fallen through that window without breaking it or cutting himself to bloody ribbons.

Blinking away tears to clear his vision, Lucas looked to the seven stag-heads mounted above the fireplace mantle. Streamers of green Christmas lights hung from the antlers of the proud-looking deer, resembling fireflies drifting through the darkness of the pub. Just beneath the mounted stag-heads was a wooden plaque, one that Lucas had heard so much about growing up in Havelock, the Irish-Catholic community founded by Irish railroaders back in the 1800's. The oak plaque was engraved with words and sported two perfectly round bullet holes above the words. Those holes had been left there by another Havelock kid, determined to take Old Billy Connors out of this world. From the story Lucas had heard, the old Irishman refused to involve the Irish mob in an act of revenge for a young girl that the boy had fallen in love with.

That was the mushy part of the story that hardly interested Lucas. But he did, however, like the part that the boy had stolen that same gun earlier that night while car-shopping. It just so happened that the gun had been used to murder the young girl that the boy demanded vengeance for. The kid used it to try and shoot Billy late one night. He had failed, yet left behind two bullets in the plaque above the fireplace. The ballistics had linked the gun to the murderer.

Hesitantly, Lucas raised his hand to touch the bullet holes. Being only 4 foot 10, he had to stand on his tiptoes to reach the plaque. As he did, he read the words of the plaque out loud: "Dedicated to William Connors for his service to the Sinn Fian."

He said, "Sin," pronouncing it the wrong way, and seconds later a gruff voice came from the shadows at the back of the pub: "Shinn Fayn, lad. It means, 'We Ourselves,' in Northern Ireland."

Old Billy Connors stepped out of the blackness just beyond the pub's pool tables. Dressed in a three-piece suit, his long, silver hair fell loose about his slender shoulders, while beneath his hawk-like nose was a thick, white mustache. His amazingly blue eyes pierced Lucas where he stood, nailing him in place.

The old Irishman asked, "Do you have a quarrel with me, lad?"

Unable to muster any words that would make sense, Lucas searched the room, frantically looking for an escape route. To the right of the fireplace was a dark hallway stretching toward a round oak door standing closed at the end of the ten-foot hall.

Above the door was another wooden plaque that read:

Here, there be Dragons.

A strange light leaked out from beneath the door and slithered into the hallway, illuminating its walls with a greenish light.

Lucas turned and ran toward the door.

"Don't!" Billy shouted at him. "Don't you dare go in there, boyo! I swear to you, no good thing will come of it!"

Ignoring the old man's ranting, Lucas pulled on a rusty door latch, swinging the door open. The fresh scent of mint washed over him and a slight breeze ruffled the strands of his unruly hair.

Keenly aware of the solid footsteps behind him, he ran through the doorway, and the door slammed shut behind him, cutting him off from this world and sending him to the next one beyond.

Chapter Forty-Six

Lucas found himself standing in a round, stone vault with an array of stained-glass windows taking up the entire front wall of the chamber. He counted six windows, with an oak door beneath them. It reminded him of Saint Patrick's church down the street from the Emerald, with its ancient stonework, its oaken doors, and its own windows, usually illuminated by candlelight.

Twin birch trees stood on either side of him, their branches creating a framework for the window-like screens in the front wall. Swift movement behind the first window on his immediate left caught Lucas's eye, and he stared in amazement as the shadowy forms of two dragons slammed into each other, locking together in fierce combat. One beast was sleek and black with green eyes, while the other was white as snow with deep blue eyes. Flames burst from the mouths of the beasts as they tumbled through the skies, disappearing from the view that the window-screen allowed Lucas to see.

Looking at the second window, Lucas saw a bird's eye-view of a massive castle under siege by a vast horde swarming across its greenway. Thousands of antler-crowned warriors converged upon the fortress, while above the high towers of the besieged castle black banners unfurled, revealing a winged, white lion.

The third window showed a herd of wild horses fleeing across a wide-open plain, their eyes wide in terror as sleek, black wolves pursued them. Hundreds of horses appeared there on the screen before Lucas. He cringed as the dark beasts drew closer behind the steeds. Suddenly, a pack of shaggy gray wolfhounds sprang up from the long grasses, and hounds and wolves crashed into each other, while the horses ran on, their lives spared by the attack of the noble dogs.

Lucas looked over at the fourth window where a company of child-like figures drew swords from sheaths depending from their shoulders. The impish warriors were cloaked and hooded in black leather. As each blade was drawn, a brilliant display of multicolored light burst at the base of each sword, and like electric eels slithering beneath the surface of dark waters, scintillating colored hues of blue, green, red, and violet traveled down the length of each blade.

"Those wee woodland imps," came the voice of Billy moving into the chamber behind him, "are the Jewel Folk."

Lucas wheeled around, his blond shaggy bangs whipping wildly as he turned to face the Irishman. Rumors of Billy's cruelty whirled through Lucas's mind, especially the one where Old Man Connors once caught Reason stealing pop off of his loading dock, and put a knife to the back of his knee and threatened to hamstring him, making his own grandson a cripple for the rest of his life.

Lucas bolted and ran, placing distance between himself and the old man. "No!" Billy shouted. "Don't. Go. In. There!"

But Lucas swung open the door beneath the windows. He darted through, pulled the door closed behind him, and ran into what could only be described as a Hobbit hole.

In full flight mode, Lucas passed through a rounded room, lit up by a small, cozy-looking fireplace to one side of the room. A cheery blaze crackled inside its hearth, yet its bright red glow was enhanced by a row of lanterns lined up on the mantle above. In each globe of the lanterns were lime-green specks of light that cast a green aura about the rest of the room. He noticed a teapot on the table between two high-backed chairs situated before the fire, then glanced down at a small figure seated there. At the sight of the fair-haired kid racing through the den, the tiny fellow let out a startled yelp.

As Lucas ran past him, he muttered, "A Hobbit! As if dragons weren't bad enough? And I don't even do drugs!"

Skidding to a stop before a round green door, he reached for the latch and heard the small fellow behind him say, "Not a hobbit, but Chaykin, lad! Chaykin of the Jewel Folk fame!"

Without bothering to even look back, Lucas pulled open the door and sprang outside onto the porch situated before an enormous hill. In fact, both the porch and the round green door were directly in the center of a large mound of earth. "Holy Moses!" Lucas gasped as he ran beneath the luminous fireflies flittering through the evening air and listlessly drifting through a woodland clearing. Only these fire-flies were as large as doves, their tails lighting up so brightly that the surrounding trees were splotched here and there by a lemony haze.

A horn sounded from the distant woods. The sound of galloping horses came from deeper in the hills beyond the clearing. Lucas scanned the darkened trees, his heart beating loudly within his thin chest. He wished he'd carried his baseball bat with him, for being armed against whatever was coming seemed to be wise. He had trespassed into a different realm. He was certain there would be consequences even if he had been trying to escape from Old Billy.

His eyes were drawn to a flicker of red flame at the end of a path-way winding up the wooded hillside just opposite of the one he'd exited. A tall, pale figure mounted on a large black elk sat there, a fiery sword held above his head. The rider's long, silken dark hair danced wildly about his shoulders in the night wind. His red eyes matched the fire of his blade, and as they locked on Lucas standing there on the porch, he felt a malicious rage and hatred pass through him as though the pale-skinned rider had cast a spell at him.

The dark-haired swordsman spurred his mount into a run. The elk sprang down the path, carrying his rider down the hillside. As the black elk picked up speed and brought the swordsman closer, Lucas could see that his bare chest and arms were covered in blue tattoos, a mix of predatory beasts, tiger, panther, bear, all dominated by a horned devil inked across his thick chest.

Each tattooed creature emanated a strange bluish glow as the rider closed the distance between them. Like an arrow sent swiftly down the hill, words were sent by the tattooed swordsman: "I was drawn here by your rage, boy! Your anger and the fires and storms, shone like a beacon in a dark night, drawing me to you like a lodestone! And I have come to feast upon your soul!"

Lucas suddenly found himself surrounded by a small pack of white wolves. Green eyes glowing, all nine of the beasts turned to face the approaching swordsman, fierce growls of challenge rising to meet him. The black rider raised his fiery blade and snarled, "White Wolves of Masgar dare thwart me? This is my hunt!"

Lucas shuddered at the word *feast*. He had already been alarmed by the swordsman's claim that he had come to eat his *red-hot soul*. He did not like what that implied, since he figured the rider was speaking anything but figuratively. No, Lucas surmised that the rider meant to literally eat his soul, though he had no clue how he intended to do that. He immediately thought of Mange and how Moloch had drained him of his soul, and he shuddered to think that this swordsman intended to do the same thing to him. Suddenly, the entire clearing between the two massive hills lit up with a brilliant light, and Lucas turned to see a small band of hooded warriors riding horses down into the clearing. As the riders formed up on either side of the swordsman, slender glowing swords appeared in their hands. One of the hooded riders said, "Sheen of the Fife! The Stealth are here to serve!"

Sheen of the Fife gestured wildly with his flaming blade and beckoned with his free hand, saying, "The wolves are yours! But the soul of the boy is mine alone!"

Chapter Forty-Seven

Standing there within the semi-circle of the wolves, Lucas heard the haunting trill of pipers from the far end of the vale. Above the bag-pipes a pleasant voice rose in song:

Kissed by the sun,
embraced by the morning,
the Forest sheds
her cloak of night.
She slips into
a gown of mist,
she wove herself,
by morning light.

In amber rays,
the Forest dances.
In hidden glens
within the hills.
Barefoot, she glides
through open meadows,
tip-toes her way
past silver rills.

Her gown of mist,
trails behind her,
fluttering in
the morning wind,
adorned with gems
and sparkling jewels,
the rising sun,
did surely send.

The song ended and a herd of dainty black stags appeared on the slope in the distance. The tiny sable stags were no bigger than fawns, and yet they each sported a full rack of glistening antlers. All of the creatures had large blue eyes that glowed with a strange illumination. The herd of stags gracefully bounded down the green slope, scattering leaves in their wake. Within the mad swirl of colorful leaves, child-like riders appeared on the slope. To Lucas's surprise, all of the wee riders were mounted on dozens of the dainty black stags. At first, he thought the riders were small boys, but then he saw that beneath their long, black riding coats, they were clad in leather armor and heavily armed, with sheathed swords strapped to their saddles. Most of the small folk wore their various shades of long hair either loose or in single, braided tails, but some wore wide-brimmed, deep-crowned hats adorned with jewel-encrusted broaches or bright red feathers.

It was a strange company for sure, and Lucas was quite startled when one little rider let out a riotous whoop, sending the entire band galloping down the distant hillside. The stag-riders rode in loose formation, their black mounts leaping in chaotic patterns across the valley floor. All at once, like a flock of swooping swallows, the wee riders formed an orderly charge directly toward where Lucas stood.

Suddenly, their leader, the long tails of his coat flapping wildly, rode hard toward the green mound. Lucas noted that beneath his long coat, the small fellow was dressed in shiny, black leather armor. He wore a black beret, adorned with a single red feather, and the locks of his raven hair swirled back over his slender shoulders, revealing gold hoops dangling from the lobes of his ears.

When the diminutive rider was a mere twenty feet away, Lucas could see that he had a tiny, upturned nose, a slight cleft in his chin, and freckles on his dimpled cheeks. The rider brought his mount to a halt, sprang from his saddle, and landed in front of the white wolves. While his stag raised its head and gazed at Lucas with its blue eyes, the wee rider removed his black beret and dropped to one knee, declaring, "Greetings, Advocate of Woodwalkers! The Black Foxes are at your service! I am their commander, Peyton Ring!"

Peyton Ring kneeled, strands of hair swirling down on either side of his brow. He rose to his feet and drew twin swords from his stag's saddle sheaths. Both blades were illuminated by a violet light that reminded Lucas of a winter sky before nightfall. He looked on then as the entire company of stag-riders drew their own glowing blades and shouted, "Hail, Advocate of Woodwalkers!"

Stepping in between two of the wolves, Peyton leaned forward and whispered, "Lad, now would be a good time to retreat inside the Lodge. If we should lose this battle, you will be on your own."

The small woodland warrior wheeled around and remounted his stag. He then joined the twelve other Black Foxes as they advanced upon Sheen and his Stealth allies. The fight that ensued was brutal. Sheen's fiery blade swooped down to be met by the shimmering jewel-blades of Peyton Ring, his violet swords deflecting the fire-blade of the dark-haired swordsman.

Lucas could hear the snick and flick of blades as the small riders were met by the hooded band of warriors. The worrying blades of the Black Foxes rang, sending shrill echoes off into the black trees.

He had watched many sword-fighting movies back at home, *The Lord of the Rings, The Thirteenth Warrior, The Kingdom*, and *The Princess Bride*, but never had he seen the speed and skills displayed now by the Jewel Folk, their moves so graceful and fluent that it was more like a well-rehearsed dance rather than a bloody, savage battle.

The Stealth were swiftly eliminated by the glowing blades of the Black Foxes. Some died with silent screams, others fell with loud gasps or pain-filled grunts as the shimmering blades of the Foxes slithered in past their guards, or sank within their bodies, spilling them from their saddles.

Peyton forced the elk to back up as his own small steed sprang up so that he could exchange sword strokes with the wielder of the fire-blade. The woodland warrior delivered dozens of loops and whirls of his flashing blades, yet they were deflected by Sheen as he parried each attack. With a loud bellow, Sheen's elk mount skidded to a sudden stop, lowered its head, and with its antlers, caught and lifted Peyton's stag, tossing both high into the air. Peyton somer-saulted backward, landing ten feet away on his feet. His black steed, however, struck the ground hard and collapsed into a crumpled heap, the blue glow slowly leaving its eyes.

Stirred to wrath by the loss of his steed, Peyton started back across the clearing, but before he could renew his battle with Sheen, the swordsman drove his fire-blade into a hapless Fox closing with him. The fiery blade crackled as Sheen lifted the sword-skewered warrior up and out of his saddle. The Black Fox screamed in agony then as the red blade literally sucked his soul from his small body. Looking on in horror, Lucas watched as the Chaykin's face melted, his eyeballs popped, and his body collapsed like a wet paper sack, dropping to the ground with a wet-sounding *thwack!* Laughing wildly, Sheen withdrew his blade from the dead warrior, and sent the blade cleaving into a second rider within his reach. This small Chaykin died horribly, too, his body flopping to the ground like a landed fish as the fire-blade sapped his soul from him.

Sheen took out four more of the Jewel Folk before Peyton finally reached him. And then, the wielder of the fire-blade was knocked from the back of his elk mount as the Chaykin sprang up high and barreled into him, slashing and hacking with his jewel-blades.

Sheen landed on his feet, his sword sizzling as he fended off the small swordsman's twin blades. Finding himself hard-pressed to win against the highly skilled Peyton, Sheen removed his left hand from his hilt and with a wild gesture, he cast a spell at his fierce attacker.

A strange blast of force blew Peyton off his feet, sending him cartwheeling across the clearing, his violet blades flashing as he rolled to a stop before the wolves.

Lucas could see that the little swordsman was dazed by the blast. He had dropped his glowing swords, and as he pawed frantically at them, Sheen came on, his flaming sword raised above his head, his eyes locking on the great, noble beasts moving to defend Peyton.

Chapter Forty-Eight

Lucas shouted, "No! Don't kill the wolves!" He then ran between two wolves on either side of him and snatched up the violet-shaded jewel-blades. "No, lad!" cried Peyton. "You don't stand a chance!"

A shimmering blue field of force appeared between Lucas and the falling blade of Sheen, stopping the flaming sword from descending. A tall, well-built figure suddenly moved in front of Lucas and said, "Sheen, return to the Shadow Realm!"

Sheen was flung backward by the large figure, who shook his shaggy-maned head. Sheen and his fiery blade were then gone, vanishing into an ethereal cloud at the edge of the forest.

The hulking figure turned to stare down at Lucas. He had the large body of a man, yet the head, the face, and the long, scraggly mane of a lion. His smile was dazzling, and the light in his blue eyes caused Lucas to cringe as the lion-man fixed him in his gaze.

"Tawn," said Peyton, rising to his knees, "Chief Messenger of the One. Is this the Chaykin Advocate?"

Tawn shook his head, his mane trailing over his huge shoulders. "No," he said. "Not this one."

A movement across the clearing caused Lucas to look to the elk as he moved to stand over Peyton's fallen stag. Lowering its head, its rack of white antlers glistened in the moonlight as it sniffed at the dead stag. As Lucas watched Tawn approach the elk. The lion-man ran a hand down its flank and said, "You are free. Go. Run the forests again, no more to serve such a master."

With a soft *chuff*, the elk sprang away, vanishing into the night. Tawn kneeled beside the fallen stag. Peyton staggered to his feet and moved to join him. Smiling down at the raven-haired Chaykin, Tawn reached down and placed his hand on the head of the dead steed. A strange green mist drifted out between the fingers of the lion-man's hand. It swirled round, evolving into a thick emerald cloud that slow-ly covered the entire body of the small, black stag.

Lucas actually gasped when he saw the ethereal form of the stag settling down on the prone body, blending with the undulating mist, now sparkling with tiny bursts of lime-green light. With an audible *click!* the soul of the fallen stag entered back into its body, and the once-dead creature's eyes blazed a bright blue as he lifted his head, staring up at Peyton, now kneeling beside the lion-man, tears of relief streaming down his face.

The white wolves darted across the clearing, reminding Lucas of excited puppies as they whined, each garnering attention from Tawn. Some rolled over on their backs, exposing their stomachs to the lion-man, while others burrowed their heads into his outstretched arms as he hugged them to his massive chest.

Studying the lion-faced man, Lucas noted the gold hoop hanging from the lobe of one ear, barely concealed by the silvery white strands of his mane. The beast-man was dressed in a leather vest and pants, yet he was bare-chested, his bare arms rippled with muscle. He reminded Lucas of his dad, who had similar proportions when it came to physical appearance. It occurred to him that this beast-man was a warrior who relied on his muscles to conquer his enemies.

Tawn peered in alarm at the western sky. "Drakvoren is coming!" he said. "The Drak?" Peyton said. "Coming here to the Lodge?"

Tawn's eyes locked on Lucas. "The Drak is drawn here because of him. He radiates rage, and distress. He's a walking wound that desperately needs healing."

Peyton said, "If he is not the Advocate of our kin, send him back, Tawn. There is really no other recourse."

The Chaykin moved to Lucas, retrieving both of his jewel-blades. "Sorry, lad, no offense, but you cannot stay. Boyos, you must ride from here now!"

Vaulting into their saddles, the Black Foxes rode out of the clearing and away into the vale beyond the Lodge. The white wolves trailed behind them, and within seconds, the band of Jewel Folk and wolves vanished into the dark night.

With one last glance at the western skies, Peyton led Lucas to the porch of the Lodge. Lucas asked, "What is the Drak? Why is it coming here because of me? He's a dragon, right?"

But Peyton pulled open the large, round door of the underground haven, pushing Lucas inside. I'm sorry, lad," he said, sorrow in his eyes, "you are not the one I have come here for. You must return to your realm. It is far too dangerous for you here. Your raw emotions attract evil beings, and I'm afraid you would be a magnet. Nothing for you then, but to go back to your world."

A thunderous roar came from the sky beyond the vale. Peyton glanced back, alarm in his eyes. Lucas looked past the lion-man to see a dark dragon coming swiftly through the sky, angry flames bursting from his open mouth. Peyton stepped into the Lodge behind Lucas and pulled the round door closed behind him.

Lucas looked across the den to the fireplace where Billy Connors stood beside the Chaykin Lucas had startled when he'd ran through the Lodge. "Sorry," Billy said, "the wild child got past my guard. He should have never trespassed into the realm of Valasar. I should have been a bit quicker on my feet."

Suddenly, a deafening roar erupted from the outside in the forest.

"Sweet Jesus!" the old man gasped in alarm.

As he and Peyton hurried to the round window overlooking the clearing outside, an answering roar exploded from the grove beyond the window. It had a deep, throaty harshness to it, and reminded Lucas of the roar of an African lion. He imagined that Tawn was now battling with the dragon, and he had little hope that he would win such a combat. Bright flashes of red light illuminated the panes of the window glass, and while Billy and Peyton were distracted, Lucas made his move to escape.

He darted across the den, his sights set on the oak door he'd come through to enter this realm. As he raced past the fireplace, he looked at the Chaykin now seated in one of the high-backed chairs, a leather map clutched in his hand.

Impulsively, Lucas snatched it up, crumpling it up in his grasp. "At least, I'll have proof," he whispered as he reached the door. "Hobbits with glowing swords! White wolves! Tawn the Lion-Man! A dragon named Drak! When Alex laughs at my story, I'll just shove this map in his face as proof I've been here!"

Chapter Forty-Nine
Realm of Valasar

Dusk banked above the radiant Oakwood Kings, drifting for several moments on gentle currents. Winded from his long flight, the hawk wearily glanced down at an opening in the treetops beneath him. He passed over it, then circled back and plunged down between the branches. In graceful spirals, Dusk descended into the glen below, settling down beside a pond. Dropping the pouch he'd carried for so many miles, he said, "Tanner Silvertree of the Jewel Folk?"

A moment later, a shaggy-haired woodland imp stepped into the clearing, his black leather vest and breeches blending with shadows beneath the trees. He stood barely three feet tall, and with his silky raven hair trailing over his tiny shoulders and gold hoops glinting in the lobes of his pointed ears, he greatly resembled a young gypsy boy out to do mischief. But as he peered at the hawk, the fierce look in his blue eyes and the feral grin on his dark, elfin features, caused him to appear far more dangerous than any wild kit of rogues or gypsies. Dressed in his black leathers, belted at his waist with a thick band of leather, Tanner looked very much like a skinny, rambunctious eight-year-old boy. However, he carried an arsenal of weapons on him that no child would ever be skilled at using. Two short swords, a dagger, and four small throwing knives.

Dusk said, "Famed Legend Weaver of the Jewel Folk, bright gem among the Chaykin race. Huntsman sworn to prevent Demons of Shadow from invading Valasar. Those are your titles, true?"

A troubled look on his face, Tanner nodded.

The hawk said, "You, as Legend Weaver, have access to the royal archives. Your knowledge as a historian is needed. The matter is urgent. The Keeper of the Lodge sent you this." He dipped his head and plucked up the pouch. "Here," he said, dropping between them. "Open that. The ring inside will take you to the Lodge. Swiftly."

Eyeing the pouch warily, Tanner said, "I'm leery of magical devices. Especially any token of power the Keeper sent. It's rumored his tokens came from a hoard cursed by the dragon Drakvoren."

Dusk said, "Is not the Keeper of the Lodge a fellow Chaykin? Certainly, he would not offer this token if it would send you to an unknown void. Those at the council need to hear your testimony."

Dusk looked down to the pouch on the ground between them. Tanner picked it up and opened it. As he stared down at the green gem that rolled out into the palm of his hand, Dusk told him, "The last messenger to carry that did not fare so well. The owl died upon arriving at the Borderlord's keep, peppered with darts by a flight of Morgoth who pursued him through the Northlands! But he managed to deliver that vision-gem sent by Lord Kennon of Hickory Hall."

Dusk fanned one wing, gesturing at the pond. "Toss it into the waters, if you wish to see why this council has been called."

Tanner did so, and as the green gem sank beneath the waters a tapestry of visions appeared on the surface of the pond:

A company of white-cloaked knights herded a group of young boys directly into a mass of branches piled high on the crest of the hill. Another youth, a crown upon his blond head, stepped forward, a flaming torch in his grasp. A maniacal gleam in his eyes, he said, "Children of Star Fire, my Lords of Night have found you guilty, and this fire shall consume you and end your demon-inspired talents!"

As the vision faded, Tanner stood there, greatly unsettled. "For these boys, it is too late, but the Borderlord believes that I can change the fate of other lads who suffer for this same crime?"

Dusk said, "It is why he has called for this council. If you wish to know more, simply use the ring to teleport to the Lodge."

Tanner said, "I told you, I'm not inclined to use magical devices."

Long moments of silence passed between them.

Tanner refused to meet the hawk's gaze.

Dusk peered down at the bright red leaves floating on the mossy surface of the pond. "These leaves," he said, "resemble translucent jewels fallen from the crowns of the Oak Kings. How ironic! I came here searching for a gem among Jewel Folk, fallen from the grace of the king he once served. Farewell, Tanner."

Dusk then launched himself from the roots of the oak and soared away, leaving the Chaykin staring down in bewilderment at the ring in the palm of his hand.

There beneath the Oakwood Kings, Tanner stood bathed in the pink light filtering through the branches above him. The sun was setting beyond the forest far to the west. Trying to keep at bay the images of the young boys the vision-gem had shown him, he held the summoning ring up, snorting in disgust at Dusk's suggestion that he use it. After all, the ring was a token of power. Magical items were too unpredictable. Especially a teleportation device which had the potential to whisk him away to unknown voids, and cause him to disappear. Forever.

Tanner slipped the ring into his belt pouch. A faint sound came from the nearby stream ten yards away. There the forest grew thick, yet a slender pathway snaked down out of the trees, connecting with a bridge spanning the gentle flow. Tanner scanned the mist above the stream. A company of white-hooded riders emerged from the trees beyond the bridge. Their ghostly white steeds appeared float as they moved onto the bridge. The lead rider barked a command, bringing the band of riders to a halt. "Woodwalker," the man said, drawing back his hood, revealing his bearded features and short red hair. "I am Sir Balan Dane, Commander of the Knights of Flame. I hail from Kallador. King Rannen wishes to speak with you about your investigation into the bloodline of the Kings of Erin."

"*Investigation?*" Tanner said, puzzled.

"Yes," Sir Balan said, smiling pleasantly. "As a record keeper and archivist to King Ronan, you know the legends of the heroes of old! Ah, the tales you could tell! Share a fire with us! Let us discover the treasure trove you store inside your head, Legend Weaver!"

Scanning the faces of the other riders, Tanner did not like the cold, hard stares they offered him. "I think not," he replied.

"I must insist," Dane said, and a moment later a band of winged creatures descended into the clearing. Each had the muscular body of a man, but the face of a bat. Shaggy manes ran from their foreheads to the napes of their necks. "Morgoth!" Tanner spat in disgust as the beings dropped down beside the stream.

Tanner ripped his twin jewel-blades free of his shoulder sheaths. He erupted into a deadly whirlwind, his blades glimmering with lime-green light. Turning and spinning, he executed a series of lightning-swift strikes that caused the creatures to reel back. One Morgoth sprang forward, his blade descending in a killing stroke. Twirling one sword above his head, Tanner parried the blade, yet was driven to his knees by the brutal attack. Blocking a second stroke with one raised blade, he thrust upward with the other, driving it into the Morgoth's breast. The bat-faced being burst into lemony flecks that vanished with a loud hiss.

Tanner slid his swords back into his sheaths as Balan Dane and his Wardens engaged in combat with the rest of the Morgoth. He darted off the trail and veered into the mist rolling down the slopes of the wooded bluff before him. At the top of the bluff, he glanced back, listening. Swords clashed. Voices of the riders were muted by the fog. Slipping off the main trail, Tanner darted onto a slender deer trail, where he heard a low hiss. Tanner peered up to see a Morgoth looming before him. A tall, dark figure stepped out of the shadows, intercepting the creature, his bright blue blade snaking out and under the chin of the beast so swiftly that the Morgoth's head went sailing away, its red eyes resembling hot coals whirling through the air.

Tanner looked on in wonder at the lean, raven-haired Elf standing before him, his blue jewel-blade lighting up his handsome features. This Elf with his long, unruly tangles of black hair, was tall, broad-shouldered, and wore a sleeveless vest, leather breeches, knee-high boots, fingerless gloves, and leather bracers. "Creed Blackstag," he said. "You refused the summoning ring Dusk offered you? Then allow me to escort you away from here."

Creed gave a sharp command and a pack of white wolves raced off through the undergrowth. He led Tanner away between the trees. They moved down an S-shaped curve. Soon the forest closed in around them. Creed brought them to a path between the trees. Pressing the jewel embedded in his sword hilt, he sent blue light spiraling down the length of the blade, illuminating the massive boles of the forest titans around them. In the luminescent glow, the giant trees resembled pillars supporting the leafy ceiling of a forest cathedral. They made camp in a small glen beneath these trees.

"No fire," Creed told Tanner. "The wolves will keep you warm."

Tanner fell asleep, a wolf on either side of him. When he awoke the next morning, he kneeled beside the stream running through the glen. Dressed as he was in his sleeveless vest, he saw his reflection in the waters, the tattoo of a snarling lion covered his right shoulder, while a dragon wound itself down from his left shoulder. On his right temple was the tattoo of a rampant wolf. He offered Creed a look of reproach. "Is this your work?" he asked, rather testily.

Ignoring Tanner's scowl, Creed said, "Ravenhawk asked me to apply the talismans. You will need them in the days ahead, for there is a boy coming to you from Outside. To serve as his guardian, the lion, the dragon, and the wolf will aid you greatly."

He smiled and added, "His name is Alex Thorn."

Chapter Fifty
Havelock

Alex Thorn crept out of the alley across from the Emerald. He was well aware of the temper of Reason's grandfather, Billy Connors. The cantankerous old Irishman had once thrown a bucket of water on him when he had sailed past the pub on the front walkway on his skateboard. The shock of the cold water caused Alex to crash into the trash can situated near the pub's driveway, and Billy had chewed him out as he hightailed it away from the Emerald, offering the old man a one-fingered salute to show he did not appreciate the dousing.

At 14, Alex was lean and five feet tall in his socks. His long raven hair fell to his shoulders, and due to his mother's Cingane bloodline, he had smooth-complected skin. He was a good-looking kid, with a dimple in his chin, and large, brown raccoon eyes. He could have been a model, yet he used his good looks to charm his way through the juvenile justice system due to delinquent behavior.

It was 9PM. He stood there in the alley, peering at the illuminated window of the Emerald directly across the street from him. Alex had an appointment to meet with Reason there, but he didn't want to have a confrontation with Billy Connors. The Irishman's irascible nature grated on his nerves. And out of respect for Reason, he didn't want to lip off to the old man.

A harsh whisper drifted out of the alley behind him: "Alex of the Roma, a nomadic ethnic group. Romani known as Gypsies, not to be confused with Romanians. The term Gypsy comes from gypcian, derived from Egyptian. This title owes to the belief that the Romani were itinerant Egyptians."

Alex stood there, seeing no one. It was as if the raspy female voice came from out of thin air. There were four dumpsters lining the dark alley, with the brick walls of two adjacent buildings taking up either side of the long, dark lane running back to the end of the next block. The voice said, "In fact, the Gypsies of your line, Alex, were exiled from Egypt as punishment for harboring the infant Jesus during Herod's reign in Jerusalem when he had all male infants killed to keep the prophecy of a Jewish Messiah from being fulfilled. Another title of the Romani is Cingane, derived from a Christian sect the Romani were associated with in the Middle Ages."

Alex snapped, "Show yourself!" Soft laughter echoed between the buildings.

A chill ran down Alex's spine. He frantically searched the entire confines of the alley before him and still could see no one.

The speaker continued: "Little Alexander, born in Wallachia, the Gypsy child of a Romani archivist and an American biker boy. His mother adopted an injured, pregnant wolf, and she had a litter of seven pups. Little Alex was in charge of those pups for the next three years, living in a Gypsy encampment of motor homes. He and his pack roamed the wilds together. Alex loved his wolves. And then his unwed mother moved here to America. Alex was eleven, and he has been struggling to find his true center ever since."

Alex said, "How do you know these things about me?"

He peered hard at each of the dumpsters. He narrowed his eyes and stared at the blackness as if willing someone to appear there. But there was no one there. "Alex's mom," the unseen speaker said, "refused to take him back. She flew back to Wallachia, abandoning her son, because his grandfather demanded she cut all ties with the rogue. Cingane give you just so many chances to succeed. Grandpa Petrov ordered you shunned, didn't he?"

The words wounded him, reminding Alex of what he'd lost this past year. His mother's leaving the States stirred up a lot of sorrow inside him. The unseen speaker said, "Control your feelings, Alex. The thing that hurts you the most will become your worst enemy."

Control my feelings? Alex thought. *Exactly what Reason told me last night in regard to being a player on this new game he designed.*

And as he stood there, peering hard at every shadow before him there in the dark alley, he recalled the words that passed between them before Reason accepted him as a foster placement months back: Alex said. "I failed you, too. I'm nothing but a loser."

"Failed me?" Reason said. "Failed yourself! I gave you a hundred chances to not skip school. You blew all of those. Don't con me with the 'loser' line, to make me feel sorry for you. Because I don't."

Reason knew what he was doing. In the past, he had taken in some of the most hardcore kids. Kids who had reached the end of the line. Kids who burned everyone who had ever taken them in before. He once took in a kid who had ran away from forty-six other placements. He had remained with Reason for two years after his placement there, not running once. In the course of ten years, he had taken in kids who had hit him, kicked him, bit him, and spat on him. Each one he saw as the one starfish he was going to make a difference with. And he did, putting up with what few foster parents in the system ever would. He endured every assault, every stab in the back, every failure those kids brought upon themselves.

And he never called it quits. Never once called a caseworker and said, "Come and get this little monster. I've had enough."

It just wasn't in his nature to quit.

During that meeting they had in order for Alex to be accepted into his home, Reason said, "You've got potential, but somewhere along the way you lost hope. I tried to steer you down the right path, but you sabotaged all my efforts. When you were assigned to me through juvenile court, I contacted your mom. Your mom, however, refused to talk about you. So, I called your grandfather in Wallachia. And he asked me to do one thing: To restore your honor."

"My honor? Then I have failed him," Alex had said.

And Reason had said, "Why don't we see if we can fix that?"

***

Two luminescent orbs suddenly appeared high up on the building on the left side of the alley. Bright blue, they appeared to be floating through the night air. Until Alex realized he was peering up at a pair of glowing eyes. The owner of those eyes was perched on a rusty metal sign. Twenty feet below the faded sign was a door that had once been open to the public for weekly haircuts by some long-dead barber who plied his trade there in the railroad town of Havelock, keeping the rail yard crew shorn and shaved back in the day.

"Jango?" Alex said as he looked up at the monkey-like being perched on the sign. Seated there on his haunches, the small, spindly creature sprang to his feet. Alex watched the demon-monkey nimbly scamper down the building. The bald-headed, big-eared little acrobat landed on bare feet on the pavement close to the sidewalk where Alex stood. Never quite sure of the monkey thing's intent, Alex took two wary steps back and away from the grinning creature.

Jango plopped himself down at the mouth of the alley. He turned his small head to the left and right. He blinked, his large blue eyes reminding Alex of the eyes of an owl. It suddenly occurred to him who had been speaking to him. "Celeste?" he said, "what is this all about? Why did you tell me all those things?"

Celeste appeared behind Jango, slipping from the shadows. Her laughter rang out. She then said, "To prep you for the gaming session taking place over there in the Emerald tomorrow, young Alex Thorn. I was told you needed a nudge on a subject that might needle you. I was told to push the matter in order to trigger off your mad emotions. I would say, I did a good job at that, right?"

She stood there, looking like a Vampire Mistress all clad in black leathers. Her short raven hair gave her a boyish look, but nothing could tamp down the catlike glare in her she-lion gaze. In the hollow of her throat was the tattoo of a stag, its spread of antlers connecting with tattoos of twin wolves creeping up either side of her neckline, their snarling mouths ending evenly below her jaw line. Alex could have sworn the intricate tattoos flickered beneath her pale skin.

Celeste Holland was a force of nature and older sister to Lucas. Between the ages of 13 and 17 she had been a troubled delinquent with a severe addiction problem. Alex knew that Reason had pulled out every stop in his youth work arsenal, to save her from herself. But in the end, as her truancy tracker, to keep her from heading down the road of self-destruction, Reason had signed the paperwork to get her admitted to the treatment program in Omaha.

Although Celeste still carried a grudge against Reason for performing the intervention that resulted in her admittance to the treatment program, she was now determined to see that her little brother did not follow in her footsteps. She had made that very clear to Alex the first time she'd met him, when she threatened to put his lights out if she ever caught him giving Lucas drugs.

Celeste said, "In order to win this game, you must master your emotions. You were not the first choice to be first player."

Alex said, "I wish you would make sense, instead of speaking in these stupid riddles. I still don't get why you had to bring up all that stuff about my history. Besides, who else was Reason considering being the player?"

A burst of laughter came from Celeste. "Not Reason. He chose you. No, the old man wanted to put Lucas in the hot seat."

Consternation placing a furrow in his brow, Alex said, "Why not? I mean, weren't they just looking for some kid to use as a guinea pig for this project? Lucas has probably played way more video games than me, so why not him?"

Celeste said, "Little Luke is a whirlwind of rage. If Reason hooked him up to the censor meter, the needle would go into the red-rage mode. Little Luke is a powder keg just waiting to explode."

Alex looked across the street at the stained-glass window of the Emerald. "Meter?" he asked. "Is there more to this game than just sitting in a chair and putting on the headset?"

Celeste shrugged. "You shall see, won't you? Go. Go now."

Jango used one hand to shoo Alex across the street. He peered down at the creature and Jango showed his rows of sharp white teeth, causing Alex, to quicken his pace as he crossed the street.

As he pulled open the door to the Emerald, laughter echoed up and down the avenue, but when he looked back to the alley, Celeste and Jango were gone into the night.

Chapter Fifty-One

Reason greeted Alex as he entered the pub. He had heard the Emerald had been deeded to him by his grandfather, the Irishman Billy Connors. He appeared against the backdrop of the pub's fireplace, where green Christmas lights illuminated the heads of seven stags, their wires entwined within their antlers. Reason wore his dark hair long. He was dressed in jeans and a black Harley T-shirt. Alex looked to his muscular forearms. Reason had trained under his brother who once had a career in Mixed Martial Arts, and Alex was impressed that he could handle himself in most situations.

"Sorry," Alex said. "I am late."

Reason nodded. "Did you know my grandfather's been missing for two days? The Holland clan—"

"No," Alex said, not meaning to interrupt him. "Not Lucas. It ain't in him to do such a thing. But Nate? He's a different story."

Reason ushered him over to a nearby booth. "Beef Tory is over at the Holland's confronting the Den. He purposely left me out of their church meeting, due to a former altercation I had with Nate."

Taking the seat he offered him at the table, Alex said, "Something to do with him promoting a dog fight. I heard you sent him to the ER that night."

Reason said, "You shouldn't believe everything you hear. But yes, on account of my tussle with Nate, Beef didn't want me to join them at the Den's clubhouse. My grandfather got himself crossways with the Elder's Den, as well."

He crossed the floor to the bar, retrieved two bottles of pop from the fridge, and returned to the booth, handing one to Alex. "Beef is appealing to the Den to tell him what they know about where gramps is. If they don't get this resolved, my dad, Rain Nelson, is going to be at war with the Den."

Alex opened the bottle and took a deep swig. He belched softly and listened as Reason said, "Did I ever tell you my family history? Beef Tory is a former member of the Outlaws, a club run by my dad. Beef quit the club years ago when Rain went to prison for killing Daws Holland. When Rain was released from prison, he asked both of us join the club, but I, a youth worker, and Beef, a detective, were not interested. So, Rain took on a new cause. He and his disbanded club members started breaking up dog fights in Nebraska. And last week, when Ben Black Bull asked for help out at Wounded Arrow,

Rain called on the Outlaws to help stop that whacked-out extremist, Waziri, from killing US service dogs sheltered at the dog ranch. The attack on the dogs was stopped, but Waziri vanished."

Alex gestured at the wooden plaque mounted above the fireplace. "Billy had ties with the Irish Republican Army back in the day. Maybe Billy's old crew came to pay him a visit."

Reason said, "An ancient grudge if the Irish came calling. We are on the right trail with the Den as our prime suspects."

Alex tore his gaze from the bullet-riddled plaque given to Billy by the IRA back when he was running guns for the Troubles. He said, "Check Lucas off your list. The hot-headed little maniac is my best friend. I would know if he'd harmed Billy. I know about the baseball bat he left behind here at the pub two nights ago. He meant to use the bat on the Emerald's front window to smash it to pieces."

"But," Reason said, "Billy stopped him, took away his bat, and simply sent him on his way? Is that what you're telling me?"

Alex reached inside his jacket, pulling out the map tucked inside the inner pocket of the coat. "The last Lucas saw of old Billy is him talking to two little leprechauns inside of that room."

He gestured at the oak door at the end of the hallway with his free hand. There before the door was a sign with words engraved deep within the wood: *Here, there be Dragons*.

Alex scooted the map across the table to Reason. "He swore what he saw in that chamber had nothing to do with the virtual reality game. The sappy-headed boy claimed he was teleported to another world. He swore he was chased by your grampa for trespassing into the Emerald."

Reason spread the map out on the table, and studied the forests, castles, and rivers on the face of the leather map. "Valasar?" he read at the bottom of the drawing. "Where did you get this?"

"Lucas," Alex said, "nabbed it out of a hobbit hole."

He laughed, pointed a finger at his head, crossed his eyes, and said, "Loony and loopy. Despite all of this planning and preparation for me to be the test pilot your new VR game, Billy wanted Lucas to be first to try this game, not me like you wanted."

Reason pointed to the right of the map between them. There, sat a small black box with an armband attached to it by a series of wires. "Why would gramps want to interfere in my planning for my game? I mean, that is why you came here tonight, right? So I could connect you to the machine that would gauge your emotions, to actually test the limits of your temperament in order to get the best results for when you actually play the game. Sadly, Lucas becomes enraged when gaming doesn't go his way. He would blow that needle into the red, and Judge Sully overseeing this project would deem my virtual game a failure. I have to prove that it changes a kid for the better, not the worse. Billy wants my game to succeed, not fail."

Taking another sip of his soda, Alex pointed down the hallway to the door. "What if he's in there," he said, "with the dragons?"

***

As Celeste neared the far end of the alley off of Havelock Avenue, Jango let out a hiss of warning as a band of small, hooded figures came at them from out of the shadows. He sprang forward into the band of black-cloaked figures, his razor-sharp talons taking out the first four warriors. The stag tattoo on Celeste's neck came alive. The luminescent stag launched itself through the air, raking its glistening antlers to the right and left as it plowed into the hooded swordsmen coming at Celeste in a mad rush. The wolf tattoos on her neck came to life. The two scintillating beasts careened into a dozen of the impish warriors armed with short swords.

Celeste drew her twin short swords from sheaths hidden beneath her long, black duster. Both blades shimmered with a violet light, a sparkling purple that traveled up and down the twin swords.

Going on defense, Celeste parried over a dozen sword strokes delivered by the swarm of warriors, and although they were well-trained bladesmen, they did not stand a chance against Celeste when she switched to offense. With wild loops of her swords, she cut them down one-by-one, her guardian beasts serving as distractions, while she ran the swordsmen through with her whirling, twirling blades.

The last to survive the assault was subdued by Jango, who looped an arm around the warrior's throat and yanked off his hood, revealing the creature's frog-like face. He struggled briefly, trying to break free of Jango's hold, but Celeste slid her left hand blade beneath his chin, saying, "Why have the Nazarawnee broken the laws of Valasar and crossed the boundary between the realms? Answer me, and I will give you a swift death. Answer me not, and I shall bind you and turn you over to the White Council!"

The frog-faced Naz spat at her, then cried out as Jango slashed his claws down one side of his face, leaving four deep wounds that bled black blood.

179

Celeste used the tip of her sword, tapping it beneath its chin. "Answer my question, Naz! Or answer to the Council!"

At the mention of the Council, the Naz hissed, "We were on the hunt. King's Blood is strong with he who was just here with you. He needed to be stopped from crossing through."

"Alex?" Celeste said in confusion. "Yes, I know of his Cingane Gypsy heritage, but what do you mean by King's Blood?"

The Naz cackled, "The line of the Lion Lords of Valasar, that is his destiny. If he is allowed into the realm, he will restore the fallen Wizard-Warriors of Kallador. We were sent so that did not happen."

"Who," she snapped, "sent you?"

The Naz closed his yellow eyes and shook his head. Celeste glanced over at the luminescent stag at her left shoulder. The spirit-beast stared back at her silently. Tracers of green scintillating light marked its majestic form. Celeste looked to her right, where the twin wolves sparkled with a bluish light. They, too, stared silently at her. Her eyes traveled to Jango, and the monkey creature grinned at her. She quickly made up her mind and drove her left hand sword directly into the Naz's chest. "I kept my promise, didn't I?" she said, almost sadly.

Just before it passed, the Naz whispered, "My thanks."

***

Inside the Emerald, Reason and Alex looked toward the Emerald's stained-glass window to see bright flashes of light flickering beyond the colored panes. Staring at the flickering bars of green and red lights coming from the alley across from the pub, Reason moved to investigate. As he and Alex made their way across the street, both skidded to a stop as Celeste drove her sword into one small fellow's chest, both clearly horrified by the ruthless act on her part.

A moment later, the stag and wolves melded into her neck and chest, becoming simply tattoos once more. She had just turned to Jango when the boy lunged at her from the shadows. He was young, slim of build, and appeared to be a fifteen-year-old kid. He wore his red hair in braids. Clad in leather armor, gauntlets covered his wrists, and fingerless gloves were on his hands. He wielded twin daggers. One was bright red, the other pulsed with green light.

A maniacal gleam came to his eyes as he lunged at Celeste. There came a soft thumping sound as Jango pummeled the kid senseless. The boy fell to the ground, his daggers clattering on the sidewalk.

180

Celeste wheeled around and looked on as one-by-one the slain Naz warriors vanished with loud *hisses*!

Reason raised his brow. "Celeste? Green stag and blue wolves? A Gollum-like creature? And now, this kid with the glowing knives. Just what in the hell is this all about?"

Before she could explain any of this to him, the slender reed of a kid sat up. He looked at Alex and snarled. "You have the King's Blood! I was sent here to eliminate you, Mage Lord! In a realm where magic is outlawed, only the outlaws shall wield magic! You belong to the line and the House of Erin! Accept your fate. Allow me to extinguish your flame and send you to the Beyonder Realm."

Alex said, "What drugs are you on? House of Erin? What the holy hell is your deal, kid?"

The red-haired boy said, "I am Hunter Synn, son of Cain Synn, warlord of Mint, the Elven kingdom in the Whispering Timber! I am destined to slay wizards and any who trifle with magic!"

He snatched up one of his daggers and lunged at Alex. Hunter Synn was in full-blown attack mode. Suddenly, he cried out as Jango leaped up, placing him in a sleeper hold, and the would-be assassin fell to the ground unconscious.

Chapter Fifty-Two

Celeste spoke quietly to Reason as the two of them sat before the fireplace inside the Emerald. "My entire life changed on the night I came down here seeking revenge on your grandfather for the lecture he gave me on addictions. In a drunken fit of rage, I pounded on his stained-glass window, but magic erupted, leaving me unconscious on the sidewalk. Billy found me there. He said, 'My window is a beacon for those braving the seas of the Otherworld.'

"When I looked at my reflection in the mirror beyond the bar, I saw tattoos of the stag and twin wolves on either side of my neck. 'Those magical beauties,' Billy said, 'were transferred from my window to you. They are talismans that will come to life when you most need them. It is your destiny. You were called to this long before you were born. Will you become a new Keeper of the Flame? Our hometown of Havelock is known amongst the White Council, the Tuatha De Dannan, the Unseen Court, the Sidhe, and the Web of the Wise. In our suburb are Waystations you will need to travel through to join the Order of the Flame.'"

She stopped, her story ended. She looked at Reason expecting a barrage of questions. But he sat there, a look of bewilderment on his face. Seated beside Celeste in the booth, Jango embraced her, wrapping his skinny arms around her. Celeste smiled down at the black-furred mogrim and patted him gently on his bald head. Jango purred like a kitten.

Reason said, "What is with this kid assassin sent here to do a hit on Alex? Do you think he came through the Dragon Room?"

Reason and Celeste looked up in surprise as Beef Tory and five members of the Elder's Den came through the front door of the Emerald. Beef carried the baseball bat Lucas had left behind in the pub two nights past. Nate Holland was less than pleased that Reason accused the Den of having to do with his grandfather's mysterious disappearance. The five bikers lined up at the bar, glaring at them.

Beef said, "I suggested that we meet with Gypsy in private outside of the Den's clubhouse. I did not call the meeting to have a fight. I just want answers. Gypsy, as a former member of Reason's dad's club the Outlaws, I figured you would show him respect."

Nate angrily snapped, "With Stone off on his special ops mission, I am in charge. Instead of Gypsy, you should have talked to me. Instead, you accuse the Elder's Den of harming the old Irishman?"

Everyone there turned to look as Lucas barged through the front door of the pub, Grunge and Goblin trailing behind him.

"Sit your butt down, Uncle Nate!" Lucas said, pointing at the empty chair directly behind Nate. Lucas said, "Grunge!"

And the big Brindle pit bull planted himself directly in front of the biker and growled softly.

Gypsy fixed a stern glare on Lucas. "Tell us how these two men ended up with your baseball bat, Little Luke."

Stepping up beside Grunge, Lucas said, "Remember the last time that old man insulted dad? Uncle Nate said we ought to shoot out his colored window? You know, with his .357?"

Gypsy remained cold-stone sober as Beef looked across the table at him. "Well," Lucas said, placing his left hand on Grunge's head, "I knew better than to destroy such an expensive window, knowing that stained-glass must have cost gobs and gobs, and so I—"

"Luke," Gypsy said, "if you incriminate yourself, you will pay in more ways than one. Understand, kid?"

Lucas swallowed hard, yet managed to nod. "Yes, sir. See the reason my bat ended up with Old Man Connors is, I was in back of the Emerald, on his loading dock, smashing cases of beer to pay him back for insulting dad. Billy caught me. I dropped my bat and ran!"

Slowly, Gypsy closed his eyes, sighing in frustration.

Lucas could not tell Gypsy and Nate that Billy had transported the gems containing the imprisoned souls of two fire gods over to the Valley of Kings, where his dad had been on a quest to find Waziri. If he told his uncle the story about Moloch and Baphomet, Nate would demand he take a drug test. Or send him to the looney bin. If he could, however, convince Nate that he'd been paying Billy back for insulting his dad, they would be proud of him. Breaking beer bottles sounded better than failing to shatter the stained-glass window. It was a lie he was willing to tell over the disappearance of the Irishman.

Beef narrowed his eyes. "You didn't assault Billy?"

Nate said, "What do you take my nephew for, Tory? He wouldn't hurt the old man. We'd have retribution from seven clubs down on our heads if we touched the Irishman."

Reason fixed his gaze on Lucas. "So, Billy caught you smashing bottles with your bat. And he just took it away from you?"

Turning his head slightly so he could face his foster parent, Lucas nodded slowly. "Yes. See, I slipped and fell when he came out onto the dock, screaming like an Irish banshee. I dropped my bat, then tore out of there as if the hounds of hell were nipping at my heels!"

He paused, refusing to break his stare down with Reason. He then added, "Billy was alive and well, and madder than hell when I left him. Swear to God. Swear on my dead mother."

"Luke?" Nate gruffly growled. "Enough of that!"

Looking admonished, Lucas said, "But since Reason is convinced that Billy's vanishing act happened because the Den had something to do with it, I am telling the truth of what actually happened."

Looking to Beef, Nate said, "You satisfied? Is the Den in the clear on the missing Irishman?"

Beef said, "We're through here." He looked beside him to Lucas. "Thanks for the explanation. Guess we owe you an apology, Gypsy."

Gypsy said, "What was the insult? How did Billy insult your dad, Little Luke?"

Lucas froze. If he cringed or showed the slightest hesitation in giving Gypsy a believable answer, he was toast. Not only in trouble with the Den, but he would lose the trust Reason had placed in him since coming to live in foster care with him.

"The foster care thing," Lucas said. "Billy said that dad wasn't a very good dad. He said that I'd been in three different placements since him and mom had that fight at the lake. First, the Yardleys. Then Ben. Now with Reason. On account of me being in so many homes, Billy said dad was a loser."

He paused, his nostrils distorted for a touch of believability, and said, "I couldn't just let that go now, could I?"

Chapter Fifty-Three

The next night, Alex sat at the table before the Emerald's fireplace. Reason had arrived only minutes ago, and though he thanked Alex for showing up there as he'd asked him to, he seemed distracted as he set up the gaming devices needed to play the VR game.

He mentioned his angry prisoner. In keeping with his role as a private investigator, he handcuffed Hunter Synn and set him on a chair in the storeroom. After the boy's attack on Alex, Reason called Beef to arrest the dangerous kid and place him in the detention center. He couldn't set him loose on the streets of Havelock, not after his bizarre behavior. Celeste and Jango sat in a booth near the fireplace, watching Reason hook Alex up to the game apparatus.

"This is just a test run," Reason explained as he handed him a headset made of shiny leather. "We want to gauge your mood during play and test your ability to keep your cool during some of the most challenging quests. The boss fights will be the trickiest. If I made them too easy, you'd get bored. If I made them too hard, you might never want to play the game again. But if—"

"So," Alex said, "is Lucas in the clear on this Billy thing?"

Knowing that Celeste, too was concerned about her little brother, Reason said, "Maybe," as he handed Alex a silver torc, which he placed around his neck. It was fashioned with Celtic runes around its length and made to resemble the torcs worn by Irish chieftains. He next handed him leather gauntlets attached to fingerless gloves. Alex slipped them on and flexed his fingers, tapping one gauntlet with a finger and then reaching up to touch the torc.

Reason handed him a long, leather case. "The torc serves as the mood meter, gauging your emotions as you face each challenge. The gauntlets are laced with super-sensitive electrodes which enhance any movements you make during game play. And this?"

He reached inside the leather case and withdrew a gem-encrusted long sword with a red leather hilt. He gave it a few test swings, and the metal blade whooshed through the air, resembling a real sword.

"Psychologists," Reason told him, "wanted more fluff added to the game, so they suggested a magic wand or a rod of power in order for you to subdue enemies. But I ruled out, and we ended up with a nice slice-and-dice sword."

"Doesn't that," Celeste said, "border on the violence all these experts are complaining about? Bloody guts and swords?"

Reason said, "Cain did not kill his brother with a sack of fluffy feathers. And the pen might be mightier than the sword but Goliath was not killed by David with a pen. No battle was ever won without blood and guts. So, I compromised. Whenever the game calls for sword work to overcome an obstacle or defeat a boss, the end result is sparkle dust. All enemies are filled with sparkling dust. Once Alex skewers them, they explode in a burst of purple sparkles. I jokingly suggested the enemies burst with Skittles, but game designers shot that down. Skittles is a trademarked candy, therefore it would have been a copyright infringement."

Celeste stared at him. "Skittles? You're kidding, right?"

Reason laughed. "Here," he said, handing Alex the last item in his arsenal. It was a pair of VR glasses, that resembled the round-lensed glasses popular in the Steam Punk world. "Those will light up your world and take virtual to the next level. Carefully, snap them into place on the headband, and slip them over your eyes."

As Alex busied himself with the items he had been handed, Reason walked over to the game console situated on a table ten feet behind Alex. He gave a few gentle tugs on a cable attached to the gaming box. The black cable ran from the console, down the hallway, and directly in through the door which had been opened just a crack to access the chamber beyond.

"This is the lifeline," Reason told Alex. "This is the cable that is hooked up to Billy's Dragon Room, the place where all the bells and whistles are infused into the game."

He paused, before adding, "Collin Young and I snuck in there one day when we were kids. What we saw in those six windows is what gave him the idea for this game. He's been toying with this whole concept for the past ten years. It took Collin Young and a team of geeks three more years to design and place the concepts within the parameters of a game."

Celeste asked, "Where is Collin now days? I heard he won some prestigious awards for game design and moved off to Callie."

"Yes," Reason told her, tweaking the console for a round of game play. "He's known in gaming circles as the White Wizard, a title which amuses him. Nerd that he is, Collin always did march to the beat of a different drummer. He will certainly win another award if this game is successful."

Alex turned around in his chair, headset in place, gauntlets on, and sword in hand. He peered at Reason through the round lenses of the VR glasses he wore, and said, "What do I get for being the very first player? Super Geek of the Year award?"

"Hopefully," Reason said, grinning, "you shall be transformed."

Fortunately, Alex got what Reason was saying. He knew from being a client in his truancy program this past year that Reason was determined as a youth worker to change, restore, and encourage kids in his path by any means possible. Alex had read all of his books, each one action-packed thrillers that had an underlying message that empowered troubled kids, inspiring them to make the best of their lives, to turn negative situations into positive ones, and to build self-esteem. Alex knew from late-night talks that Reason had grown up on the streets of Havelock with his own behavior problems. At 10, Reason had been diagnosed with Defiance Disorder and ADHD. At 12, he received his first probation sentence for breaking into the Emerald pub, years before he even knew it belonged to his grandfather. Ironically, Billy Connors had demanded that the cops perform drug testing on his two young burglars, Reason Nelson and Vince Young, and the two kids had tested positive for THC.

As Reason had shared with Alex all of his kidhood antics, he had said for all the things he put Boone and his mom through, he was lucky to still be alive. Reason claimed everything Boone knew about his own youth work, he'd learned from dealing with him. In fact, some of his major outbursts had instilled in Boone a stubborn determination to never give up on him.

And now, Reason had taken the same stance and was driven by the same never-give-up attitude. Alex had seen this drive in action when watching Reason deal with him, and especially Lucas, who could push anyone's buttons. Transformation is what Reason hoped this new virtual reality game inspired in troubled kids, and Alex's own self-esteem was bolstered by the fact that Reason had chosen him to be the first test pilot of his creation. He sighed and prepared to be transformed.

The moment Reason hit the switch on the game console, Alex found himself hurled directly into the Dragon Room. Huge purple bubbles burst before him as he fell forward. He passed through them, somersaulting head over heels, and landed on soft, mossy ground in a sunlit forest. Alex was dressed in a black leather shirt, black vest, black trousers, high-top black boots, and a black duster.

He thought he had stumbled his way into a Ren Fair.

Chapter Fifty-Four

It was the howl that set Alex's feet to running. It came from the misty woods behind him. A high-pitched, wavering howl that caused his eyes to water. Alex flicked his scraggly black bangs out of his eyes and peered hard at the trees behind him. Silvery clouds of mist drifted there like luminous dragon's breath, shimmering with bursts of light. The howl came again. It was closer this time.

Alex picked up speed, his slender legs carrying him down the trail leading away from the woods. As he ran his unruly tangles of hair trailed over his shoulders, while the tails of his black duster fanned out behind him like a set of wings. The fear coursing through him spurred him on to run like the wind.

An answering howl erupted from the trees to his right. The copse of fir trees was some distance away, still he could see dark shapes beneath shadowy branches. He saw glimpses of pointed ears. Long snouts. Green glints of narrowed eyes. Vapor trails leaking from open mouths. Flickering flashes of emerald shot out from beneath the trees, the luminous green eyes of a dozen black beasts streaking toward him. "Wolves!" Alex gasped. "But not wolves of Wallachia! I sense no friendliness in these beasts!"

He slid down an embankment, and almost plunged into the swift flow of the river separating him from the distant bank ten feet away. He skidded to the very edge of the narrow river, tottering there five feet from the black waters racing past him into the woodlands. Fallen leaves crackled behind him. Twigs snapped. He turned his head to watch as the pack of beasts gathered on the berm above him, menace in their gazes. Fierce growls came from them. They bulked up their shoulders, hunched their legs beneath them, and prepared to launch themselves over the berm and down to the river bank.

The opposite bank was too far. If Alex leaped he would land in the middle of the swift flow, cold waters closing over his head. When he surfaced, he would have to swim madly for the distant shore as wolves splashed into the waters around him. He glanced back one last time. The emerald eyes of each beast served to illuminate their bulky bodies, and what Alex saw caused his breath to come out in one ragged gasp. Where he expected to see thick patches of black fur, he saw roiling clouds of pitch-black smoke curling around within the framework of each beast. They were not wolves at all, but some hybrid created of shimmering black vapors.

And yet, they had vampire-like fangs protruding from both upper and lower jaws, and looked capable of tearing him to pieces. The words escaped his lips before he could stop them, and Alex gasped, "Demon wolves!"

A quiet voice came from his left: "An apt name for them, but in this realm of Valasar they are *sleeth*. They hail from the Vale of Shadows, and are a cross between demon and wolf."

Alex looked down to see a long-haired woodland imp stepping in between him and the wolf-beings. The small fellow stood three feet tall. He was dressed in dark leather slacks and sleeveless vest. His bare arms sported the tattoo of a lion on his right shoulder, while a dragon covered his left shoulder. The raven-haired imp glanced back at Alex, revealing a tattoo of a rampant wolf on his right temple. Fierce blue eyes nailed Alex as he snapped, "Stand back, lad, lest I cut you with my blades!"

He reached over his shoulders in a cross-draw, sliding twin short swords out of leather sheaths hanging down his back. The two swords were two feet of shimmering steel. The luminous blades reminded Alex of sunlight shining through green leaves, for up and down their lengths the blades sparkled with tiny pricks of bright emerald light.

The pack of advancing sleeth reached the bottom of the incline. Alex asked, "Are you a leprechaun?"

"Quiet, lad!" hissed the wee warrior. "I'll need my wits about me once they close for the kill! Not leprechaun. Simply a Chaykin."

Alex whispered, "A what?" He looked on in total amazement as the small swordsman hurtled forward into the ranks of the charging beasts, his shining blades raised above the flying locks of his black hair. The Chaykin danced. It was not so much a battle of swinging, hacking, slashing, and chopping, but instead a series of graceful moves. This wee woodland warrior wielded his twin blades with great skill. Each time he struck one of the sleeth surrounding him, they vanished with airy poofs.

Alex was glad that they had not been wolves. Born in Wallachia, this Gypsy child had grown up among a pack of wolves back in the old country. As he watched the Chaykin wreaking havoc among the sleeth, he was glad he was not actually killing beasts of flesh and blood. It would have greatly saddened him. With a downstroke of his right hand blade, the small swordsman ended the battle, sending the last smoky creature out of the fight.

Waves of shimmering power undulated on the bank above the Chaykin and the Gypsy boy. A tall, dark figure appeared there, stepping through a portal. The Chaykin said, "Sheen of the Fife, former warlord of Mint, fallen from grace with your king."

The warlord was dressed in black robes, with strands of white hair tightly braided along the sides of his narrow, pale face. He offered the two below him a sardonic grin. "Tanner Silvertree? You meddle in my affairs? Who is this boy?"

Tanner said, "He is the catalyst that shall be your downfall. In him flows the King's Blood!"

Sheen laughed a brittle sound that caused Alex to stiffen. He did not like the dark scowl he offered him. The white-haired warlord's eyes glowed with maniacal glee. He snickered, "The Gypsy boy fears me. I can smell the magic on him. Its scent is that of apples doused with cinnamon, flavored by Autumn magic. It crackles around his aura. He does not yet know of the power within him. I must strike now before it is awakened."

Sheen of the Fife swiftly launched himself over the berm, a silver long sword flickering into his grasp. He was met by Tanner. The Chaykin's twin blades fended a dozen attacks as the two exchanged sword strokes too quick for any eye to follow.

Despite the rapid-fire sword strokes of the Elf swordsman, Tanner gritted his teeth and hissed, "Give it up, Sheen of the Fife! For all the legends about you, you could never best me!"

Sheen pursued his attacker, backing the small warrior to the edge of the riverbank. The two worried away at each other, their shimmering blades darting in. Slithering out. Slanting up. Poking. Pickering. Flickering from left to right, all to no avail.

Still, both the Swordsman from the Fife and the wee warrior of the Chaykin continued their duel there on the banks of the river. Alex caught a glimpse of a white burst of power as Sheen cast a spell down at Tanner. Although the Chaykin kept his concentration on his most aggressive opponent, the tattoos on his face glimmered to life. Wolf, dragon, and lion rose up, forming a network of scintillating lines, each magical creature meeting the speeding ball of light thrown by Sheen. Dragon, lion, and wolf served as wardings to deflect the ball of light before it connected with Tanner's face.

The spell fizzled and plunged into the dark waters of the river. Alex looked down in horror as the surface of the black waterway turned to a sheet of ice, locking the river in a freezing embrace. He could only imagine what such a spell would have done to Tanner. A horn sounded in the distance. Sheen faltered for a second. Tanner slapped his left hand blade down hard on the swordsman's blade, driving it point-down into the bank at their feet. Sheen attempted to free his sword, and Tanner slammed both blades down onto Sheen's sword, ripping its hilt from his grasp. His sword now wavered in the air, buried in the bank at his feet.

A series of horn blasts rippled through the woods.

Sheen wheeled away from Tanner's whirling blades. Swiftly, he raced back up the bank and mounted a steeds waiting behind him. He rode then to join a large dark horde in the vale beyond the river. Alex followed Tanner up the bank. The two stood looking on in wonder into the deep vale below. There at the center of the valley, rode a howling mad company of riders, long, pale hair dancing wildly upon their heads as magic sizzled from their glowing blades. There were hundreds of them. "Dark Elves of Loch Sheeann," Tanner said "Yet, the battle appears to be evenly matched," he added, directing Alex's attention to a pair of riders appearing on the hillside to the right side of the vale. There a slim, golden-haired Elven lady sat clad in white armor, her hair short, her gaze eagle-proud. She rode a white steed. "Lady Kerrin Skye, Priestess of the Unseen War," Tanner said.

To the left of her rode an Elf with unruly tangles of black hair trailing over his shoulders. He was clad in black armor. On his breast was a rampant stag, its antlers forming a network that resembled an entanglement of briars. He was mounted on a gray horse. "Creed Blackstag," Tanner said. "Wolf Lord of Shadow."

Riders poured out of the tree line behind the two. Swords flashed. Wolfhounds shot from between the trees. A company of white wolves joined the hounds. Tanner said, "Creed leads the clans of the Gypsy-Born. As well as the Companies of mercs: Legion of Sorrow. Badgers of Mosk. Wyverns. Red Sabers. Golden Spears. Twelve Lords. Wizard's Kin. Mad Boys. The entire host rides to war."

Alex's eyes narrowed as Lady Kerrin Skye drew a glowing sword from a sheath at her slender waist. It pulsed with red light and small, fiery balls of amber shot from the tip, sizzling as they cleaved into the ranks of the Dark Elves closing with the company of riders. A blue sword appeared in Blackstag's hand, and the Elf cleaved into the dark swarm. Tanner said, "*Thane* and *Silverflame* forged in the Dwarven kingdom of Quain long ages ago. Blades that have slain thousands of demons. Ancestral blades of the House of Skye and Stag. They came to defend you, Alex of the Gypsy-kin. Because of their intervention, you are safe for the moment. Come. We must leave these woods behind."

Chapter Fifty-Five

Tanner slid his swords into his shoulder sheaths and sprang down onto the ice. Alex took followed him. He skidded across the ice, then followed the Chaykin up onto the other bank. Two trails intersected there. One snaked its way into a jumble of briars. Tanner chose the path leading up into the trees. He said, "I am Tanner Silvertree, descended from an Elven Queen and a Dwarven King. Famed Legend Weaver of the Jewel Folk."

He then quoted a poem:

King Graenor of the Dwarf Folk,
kneeled beside a moonlit sea,
and there he pledged his heart,
to a fair Wood Elf Queen.

Defying Ancient Law,
beneath the stars they wed.
The first forbidden union,
their vows in secret said.

Then one autumn morning,
to them was born a son.
And two races of the Fair Folk,
became joined as one.

Thus began the Legacy of
the Children of the Woods.
Bright shining Forest Gems,
a race misunderstood.

For Dwarven sages wise,
and Elven priests of Light,
proclaimed these small folk,
were demons of the night.

Alex said, "It would have been simpler had you said you were a leprechaun. What is a Chaykin? A child of both Dwarf and Elf?"

"Yes," Tanner replied. "Children of the Woods, long before I was born, Elven priests declared that the interracial marriage between

Queen Chaylendriel and King Graenor was a sacrilege. Any child born as a result of their wrongful union was condemned. During the Crusades, small folk were declared demon-spawn and they were ruthlessly hunted by Elven and Dwarven Crusaders.

"But then one day, King Finn of the Elven Kingdom of Mint and King Bronn of the Dwarven Kingdom of Quain, found their Host of Kings, trapped in a siege by a vast demon horde from the Shadow Realm. The Horde outnumbered the Host of Kings and yet when all seemed lost, seven wind-ships appeared in the sky above the fortress. These wind-ships landed on before Mint, and their crew of Chaykin, armed with jewel-blades, waged war on the Horde and soundly defeated them. At the end of this battle, King Finn honored these Chaykin by ending the Crusades, and forever after, Chaykin were known as the Jewel Folk."

Tanner stopped, looking back across the frozen river. Alex turned and followed his gaze. There, silvered by the moonlight in the far distance, stood the spires of an ancient stone fortress. A castle of immense size. "Rockhaven on the edge of the Blackwood," Tanner said. "Home of the Lion Kings. If not for the kings of that line, the Jewel Folk would have not survived."

Alex said, "That fortress reminds me of the home of the Vlad the Impaler. Dracula, vampire and ruler of Wallachia in the 15th century. Vlad the Dragon of the Order of the Dragon. In Romanian, dracul means devil, which added to the rumor that he followed the Devil. He impaled 300 boys from the markets of Wallachia. When an army invaded Wallachia, they discovered stakes on which twenty thousand men, women, and children had been spitted. There were infants affixed to their mothers on the stakes, birds made their nests in their entrails. Yes, the realm I come from knows evil, too."

Shuddering from the visions he was forced to see, Tanner took to the pathway opening up through the trees. Multicolored fireflies as big as hawks drifted through the air above them. They pulsed, casting shades of green through the dark forest. Tanner said, "Step onto the path to begin the first steps of our journey, Alex. Come. I shall tell you. I assure you, our quest, is one and the same."

Alex stared in wonder at the huge fireflies gracing the woods on either side of the trail. Tanner said, "You are of the Cingane, the Gypsy-born who inhabit this realm of Valasar. Fierce Horse Lords, valuable allies to the Lion Kings over the years. The Three Races, Man, Elf, Dwarf, call the Gypsy-born the Clans. It is quite a heritage you have, Alex. Though in your realm I know you go by the last name of Thorn, your title is Alexander Blackthorn. In Valasar, your ancestor, Arron Blackthorn, was a wizard -warrior, aligned with the Guardians of the One to call the Three Races of the Seven Kingdoms to war. It became known as the Lion War. To read more about him, the book would be a good place to start. *The Lion War*, written by my ancestor, Sanjamon Silvertree six-hundred years ago. Only 12 copies were ever printed in the Elven Kingdom of Mint in the Whispering Timber. The leather-bound books were destroyed by minions of Shadow. The last book stolen by Rifkin the Mink, yet retrieved by Loriel, Lady of the Woods, remained at the Lodge in the Emerald Glens. Six guardians were slain at the Lodge in an attempt to foil the plans of Cain Synn, Elven warlord, fallen from grace. Allied with Shadow Princes, Cain and a company of Stealth traveled to the Lodge to retrieve the book. The six Black Foxes died defending the book, and Cain came to be its keeper."

Alex looked to the trail ahead to see a troop of fairies fluttering off into a garden of roses, trails of scintillating dust drifting from their wings and speckling the roses beneath them with glints of incandescent light. Sprites and woodland imps rode beneath their cousins, mounted on rabbits, weasels, minks, and squirrels.

Tanner continued his tale. "Cain wanted the book to control the Dread. In it are seven secret words written in the Chaykin language, that hold magical leashes on the dragons, leashes that can rule them or slay them. Of course, allies of the Lionlord desire those words to slay the seven dragons of the Dread. Cain wishes to master them to serve him and bring the downfall of the Three Races of Valasar. Your first quest is to retrieve the book."

Chapter Fifty-Six

The Chaykin led the Gypsy boy to a portal there in the woodland. "There are pathways," Tanner said, "in the Otherworld that connect with locations linked to myth. This one opens up in Oxfordshire England, where we need to be at the moment."

The Chaykin passed through the gateway and vanished in the fog beyond. Alex followed his companion through to the other side. They found themselves standing on a hill overlooking a township. Tanner said, "The Year is 1945 in Oxfordshire. We travel to The Eagle and Child Pub, where two friends discuss a book."

Tanner ushered Alex down the hill toward a cobblestone street. Three blocks later, they came to a pub marked by a sign depicting an eagle in flight and carrying a baby in a blue cloth in his beak.

Alex and Tanner stepped into the smoky confines of the pub. An oak floor stretched before them. A bar stood on one side of the room. The hour was late, and all but two of the local patrons had gone home to warm beds for the night. A bartender sat dozing on a stool behind the bar. Blue, sweet-smelling pipe smoke drifted through the air. Two men sat in a booth toking on pipes. One was tall and lean, with silver hair. He was reading from a pile of papers stacked before him on the table between them.

The other man was rather big, buff, and stocky, with a receding hairline and thick jowls, and he listened intently to his silver-haired companion reading. Neither man was aware of Tanner and Alex as they sat in a booth ten feet away.

"Koalbiters," Tanner said, "Norse story tellers who sat so close to the fire they bit coals. What started as a group of writers getting together for an evening of talk turned into the Inklings. They met in the Eagle and Child AKA Bird and Baby. This night, Professor John Ronald Ruel Tolkien shares his work with Clive Staples Lewis. Both will eventually become well-known authors, with Ronald's *Lord of the Rings* and Clive's *Chronicles of Narnia*. Little do both men know that their stories will become popular among the children of Great Britain, read by thousands of parents tucking their lads and lasses in for the night. Thousands of children will drift off to sleep with their stories whirling around in their minds.

"Jack, as he is known by John Ronald is the big bear of a man with the thinning dark hair. Tollers, as he is known by Jack, is the silver-haired fellow, too tall for the booth he sits in. The two men, yet to be Legendary Giants in the field of literature, are at this time simply good friends. Both men draw inspiration from the *Ancrene Wisse*. The Norse myth of *Beowulf*, from the Scandinavia *Book of the Heroes*. *Sir Gawain and the Green Knight*. The Old Norse, involving Sigurd and the dragon Fafnir. Andrew Lang's *Red Fairy Book*. The Finnish *Land of Heroes*.

"In these early years, Tolkien amused his sons by telling them fairy stories. Inventing fairy stories for children was a Victorian past time. A banker, Kenneth Grahme, told his son animal stories, which later became *The Wind in the Willows*. Scottish playwright, James Barrie amused his children by telling them tales about *Peter Pan and Never, Never land*. An Oxford don named Charles Dodgson entertained the three children of a married friend with stories. One of these stories became *Alice in Wonderland.*

Alex looked over at the two men, seated close to the pub's wood stove. Both had pints of beer before them. Jack's glass was empty. John Ronald's was half-full. Both men were dressed in rumpled vests over white shirts, rolled up at the sleeves, neither man having time to change clothing from a day of teaching at Oxford college.

"Tollers," Jack said, grinning through a wreath of pipe smoke, "during the last reading, you had brought the four hobbits to Bree, where they met another wild-looking hobbit named Trotter. I truly want to know more about this new character. Does he save the Ring Bearer? Does he end up as a guide? Who and what significance does this fifth hobbit have do with the tale?"

John Ronald offered his companion a boyish smirk. "Jack," he said, "that question was answered in the wee hours yester morn." He shuffled his papers. "Here it is," he said, his eyes brightening as he read the words scribbled there in the early morning hours in the comforts of his den.

Jack said, "Does Trotter help or harm the hobbits? Is he to become a hero or a villain, leading them off into the wilds where he betrays them? Don't keep me in suspense, dear Tollers!"

John Ronald drew out a pencil and wrote feverishly for the next few minutes. Jack, used to his friend's quirky ways, sat patiently. He puffed on his pipe. When John Ronald looked up from his writing, he said, "This queer little fellow who travels alone in the wilds and befriends the four hobbits in Bree, is not a hobbit at all!"

Picking up his pipe, he gestured with it, making a sweep through Jack's roiling pipe smoke lingering in the air between them. "His real name is Strider, and he has a much grander role to play in the story. Disguised as a lone wanderer, he is walking royalty. He eventually becomes King of Gondor."

Looking surprised, Jack said, "Now that one I did not see coming, Tollers! Nice twist. Nice plot. An extremely interesting character. But where did this idea come from? This Trotter who becomes Strider?"

Shaking his head, John Ronald replied, "A doorway was opened for me during the first few lines of the poem. It was, well, for better lack of words, magical, Jack. An Elven Lord from Loth Lorien opened a door, invited me to take a peek beyond it, and offered me a new plot line for the story. This Elven Lord gave me a name for this Strider the Ranger from the wilds. Aragorn son of Arathorn. He is of the Dunedin, a race of Man descended from the Númenóreans who survived the sinking of their island kingdom and came to Middle-earth, led by Elendil and his sons, Isildur and Anárion.

"The Men of the West were descended from the Elf-friends, the Men of the First Age who sided with the Noldorin Elves. They created fortress-cities on the western coasts of Middle-earth. Sauron, a dark wizard of great power, raised mighty armies to challenge the Dúnedain. With the aid of Gil-galad and the Elves, Sauron was defeated. He vanished into the East for many centuries. But he began to gather strength, and allied with the chief of the Nine Ringwraiths, the Witch-king of Angmar, he succeeded in destroying Arthedain, the last of the Northern kingdoms. After its fall, the Dúnedain became the Rangers of the North."

Jack sucked on his pipe, and after a long exhale of smoke, he said, "Quite a history for this Lone Wanderer of the Wilds, Tollers."

John Ronald said, "A history that was revealed to me by an Elf Lord opening a doorway inside my head. I don't know how else to describe it. We'd like to think that we create these tales we write, but I think they were written long ago, and somehow are revealed to us at just the right time, Jack."

Jack *hmmmed* a bit, his pipe stem clenched between his teeth. When he plucked it from his mouth, he gestured at the wood stove, saying, "I would call these inspirations, *Flames of the Koalbiters*. They seem to be hidden inside our imaginations like flames stirred to life by some strange wind, and these flames burn brightly for a time while we see into them with an inner eye that sees to the edge of hidden realms. And yet, Narnia and Middle-earth have come to life by the workings of our pen and ink upon paper. And who knows the impact those flames may yet have?"

Alex took one last look at Tollers and Jack in deep discussion. Neither man even glanced at him as he made his way to the door. Once outside the Eagle and Child, Tanner said, "I am a Legend Weaver. I bring images to life before an audience's eyes. I know what secrets the Flames of the Koalbiters hold for those who have the inner eye to see them. I know what fires have inspired many other writers of Fantasy to create their own tales that spiral round and round like a Celtic hoop.

"Anne McCaffrey and her Dragons of Pern.

"Katherine Kerr and her Wild Folk and Lords of Wyrd.

"Terry Brooks and his Shanara heritage.

"David Gemmel and his Drenai saga.

"Paul Edwin Zimmer and his Gathering of Heroes.

"Dennis McKiernan and his Warrows.

"David Eddings and his Belgariad.

"Patricia McKillip and her Beasts of Eld.

"Ursula K. Le Guin and her Wizard of Earth-sea.

"Raymond Feist and his Riftwar Cycle.

"All of these writers have had doorways opened in their minds, secret passages from whence came intriguing tales. And through the images planted in their heads, they draw millions in with the ability to paint these images in the minds of their readers. It is really a fascinating concept."

Alex said, "Legend Weaver, huh? Can you teach me the skill?"

Tanner met his earnest gaze. "It is a gift, Alex. Either you have it or not. I can nurture the talent and skill, but it is you who must determine if you have the same gift."

About the Author

Tom Frye has worked for the past 45 years as an advocate for troubled youth. He began his career in high school, serving as a street contact for a runaway shelter. When residents at a detention center, asked for sequels to his stories, Tom knew he had discovered a way to connect with them. He has served as a mediator for his own truancy program, providing escorts to schools for alternative kids. He once produced a substance abuse challenge course that impacted 15,000 at-risk kids. He believes that his greatest accomplishment can be summed up by one troubled boy who wrote to him while confined: "Discovered your book today. It was like reading a letter you wrote directly to me. Thanks for giving me hope."

Check out his website:
www.tomfrye.org
Or send him an email and tell him what you think of the book:
authorfrye@gmail.com

The order of the Havelock Emerald series:

The Havelock Emerald:

1.) Broken Red Road
2.) War Dogs at Wounded Arrow
3.) There be Dragons
4.) Thorns of the Black Rose
5.) Jewels of Kandahar
6.) Sons of Winter
7.) Fallen Heroes